COCAINE EYES

Michael Keenaghan is the author of two previous books,
London is Dead and *Smiler with Knife.*
He lives in London.

Also by this author

London is Dead

Smiler with Knife

COCAINE EYES

MICHAEL KEENAGHAN

Nocturnal

First published 2025

Nocturnal Books
London

A CIP catalogue of this book is
available from the British Library

ISBN: 9798317136260

Cover stars:
A side: London Fields
B side: Dalston

He unholstered his .45 revolver
and aimed it at the world

The Big Nowhere, James Ellroy

Ticket to ride
White line highway…

White Lines (Don't Do It), Melle Mel

CONTENTS

BLACK AND BLUE

We've been called to Archway's Elthorne Estate on an anti-social behaviour call and four of them are hanging by the flats. Clever cunts. One especially, a robbing little scrote called Shaquille Jackson.

We're out of the carrier, arms crossed and having a word, and it's all the usual bravado. Backchat and insults. Some you can laugh off, some you can't.

Shaq issues a quip and his crew whoop with laughter.

I walk towards him. 'Come on then, big man,' I say. 'Repeat what you just said.'

The atmosphere has taken a turn, his mates silent now awaiting his response as he stands feigning unconcern. He's all out of words for a change, wearing a smirk I'd give money to wipe off with a single punch.

I lean in, joke over now. 'Are you fucking deaf or just frightened of me?'

He glances to his crew for support then summons the front to meet my eye.

'I said…' He leaves a pause. 'Go suck your mum.'

His crowd are jumping and laughing.

'That's it, you're nicked.'

I cuff and march him to the carrier, his boys now giving it large about harassment, he didn't do nothing, go catch some real criminals, the usual broken record.

'Get off me man,' he says. 'What are you arresting me for?'

'A public order offence. Section 5.'

'What's that?'

'Being a mouthy little prick.'

I lock him in the cage and climb in next to PC Lee Ballman who's at the wheel.

'Tell me we're bringing him back to the nick, just tell me that,' says Ballsy, hoping for an easy life.

'Afraid not B. You heard desk sergeant Conroy last time we brought Jackson in and he painted the cell wall courtesy of his bodily functions: Don't bring this animal back to my nick again, he said.'

'Conroy's off tonight. He did an early turn. It's old Greavsey at the helm.'

'Whatever, a night in a warm cell with a fried breakfast in the morning is too good for him. No scrote calls my mother a cunt without a slap on the wrist at least.'

'So how hard a slap is it going to be then?'

'Take a guess.'

'Fuck off.'

'Go on, use your imagination.'

'Dump him off on the Seven Acres Estate so he can play hide and seek with his enemies?'

'Did that last time.'

'The woods of Hampstead Heath so he can get bummed?'

'Did that the time before.'

'Okay, I'm all out of ideas.'

'We're bringing him for a swim.'

'No way, not that old one.'

'Afraid so mate, it has to be done.'

We journey towards Camden. Balls is whistling at the wheel as I check out our prisoner's phone. Photos and video footage. There's lots of him and his boys pulling gang signs, another of him smiling with his arm round his Mum, then I stumble on some footage of him hanging out the back of some white slag.

'Look at this dirty fucker,' I say, showing it over. 'Filming himself in the mirror on the job? How old is the cunt, seventeen? Should be ashamed of himself.'

Balls takes a look. 'Hang on, that bit of skirt? I'd knob that.'

'She's a fat slag.'

'Have you seen the size of those baps? They're bouncing for England.'

'That's you all over. You'd stick it in any old pig. And besides, the tart's jailbait. I'd put money on it. She's probably just stripped off her school uniform. Dip your wick in that and you'd be sharing a cell with Gary Glitter.'

There's a screech and Balls turns back to the road. He slams the brakes, narrowly demolishing a VW Beetle.

I lower the window, shouting at the hipster prick behind the wheel. 'Are you fucking thick?'

He points to the red light we've just gone through, but I stare him down anyway. We move on and I laugh.

'Best keep your eyes off the tits and on the road, Ballsy mate.'

'Good idea.'

We turn off Camden Road and venture down St Pancras Way to where it's grotty and ghostly, all blackened Dickensian walls, a slice of Old London, back to the days when you earned your crust by the sweat of your brow or you got sent to the workhouse for a spell of living hell. The good old days. We pull over.

'Right,' I say, rubbing my hands together. 'Funtime.'

'Oh well, here we go,' Ballsy says, shaking his head.

We get out and head round to the back of the van. I open the cage door and pull our friend Shaq out of the pen.

'Are you thirsty?' I ask, marching him towards the bridge. 'Because where you're going you won't be.'

'What are you talking about, you on fucking drugs? And where are you taking me?'

'For a swim, mate.'

We turn down into the steps and catching sight of the murky waters of the Regents Canal he starts to panic. 'No fucking way,' he says. 'You two are jokers.'

'You're not wrong there.'

He starts struggling so Ballsy gets a hold of his feet and we carry him the rest of the way. He's shrieking in panic and I flick my knuckles into his face, tell him to shut the fuck up or he'll be taking a dive with the cuffs on.

We dump him down on the towpath and unlock his paws.

'What did you say about my mother again, Jacko?' I enquire.

'Look bro, I'm sorry. Seriously. Whatever I said I didn't mean it okay.'

'Well you know what my motto is. Sticks and stones may break my bones, but actions speak louder than words. Ever heard that one?'

I grab his arms while Balls gets his legs. We lift him up.

'No way, you two are fucking nuts! You are not going to do this!'

'We all have to pay for our sins Shaq. And what goes up must come down.'

We swing him back and forth. 'Okay partner, ready? One, two, three, and away he goes.'

He lands with an almighty splash in the middle of the brackish water, in there with the floating debris, supermarket trolleys and diverse pondlife.

We check left and right. No prying eyes. And just as well because such methods of crime-fighting are unconventional and potentially controversial to say the least.

'Okay, our cue to get out of here.'

We run up laughing to the van, the sound of splashing and shouting from down below only fuelling our merriment. We climb in and hit the road.

'Swimming with the fishes?' I say. 'People pay good money for that. They travel halfway across the globe to witness the world's natural aquatic wonders, yet don't see a smidgeon of what Mr Jackson must have witnessed down there.'

'Only a few months back they pulled one of his lot from that stretch,' Balls says. 'The man had been underwater for a week. You remember that?'

'Smack dealer from Somers Town, fresh out of Pentonville?'

'That's the one. He had a run-in with some rivals and they chopped him up and chucked his remains in the drink. I know one of the Camden plod who retrieved his head.'

'His head? I wouldn't be surprised if it was fucking hollow. Both him and the ones who put him in. These so-called gangsters don't even cover their tracks these days. Sherlock Holmes would be turning in his grave. He'd be bored stiff. Talent wasted. Where's all the clever criminals gone?'

'True enough. They were rounded up within about five minutes. Apparently they did a clean-up on the flat where they chainsawed him but it was just a mop and bucket job. Forensics shone their magic light and saw the blood on the ceiling. They never found one of his arms, they reckon. Nor a hand I think. Nor his testicles for that matter.'

'We should drive back to check on young Shaq. He's probably got them wrapped round his neck.'

Reaching Holloway Road I'm supping on a protein shake and Ballsy is considering a greasy doner with extra onions and lashings of chilli sauce.

'I'm not having you stinking out the van for the foreseeable, no fucking way,' I tell him. 'Grab yourself a sandwich.'

'Never. I know a late night Indian that does a mean vindaloo, even better.'

'Now you're dreaming.'

An emergency call comes in. Rapist caught in the act. Bemerton Estate N1. Given chase but lost around the flats. IC2, blue top, black joggers.

'That's us then. Playtime over.'

We hit the blues and twos towards King's Cross and it's back to professional coppering mode. Eager beavers fighting the ever-present scourge of crime in the big bad concrete jungle. After all, some cunt has to do it.

We fly down the length of Caledonian Road and pull into the estate. Climbing out I say to myself, I hate this fucking place. I'm hardly an enthusiast of any of Islington's numerous housing monstrosities, but this one truly takes the Michael. It's a dump and a half and should have been resigned to the skip years ago. First time I stepped foot into this tip I slid in a colossal pile of dog shit then landed down into it on my arse. I had to return to the nick to change my kecks, and I got the nickname Dogshit Bob for a while until further scandalous episodes incurred sobriquets less embarrassing, thank fuck.

We have a word with the skipper to a backdrop of plod running round clueless. Updated, Ballsy and I split up to flush the suspect out. I head straight for the junkie hideouts. In the bin room of one of the blocks my torch lights up needles and rancid pools of piss but there's no sight of him. Then I'm heading for shooting gallery number two when I actually spot the fucker lurking behind a bush.

'Stay there, don't move!'

I chase him across the estate, radioing for back-up as I go. He turns a corner and vaults a back-garden fence. I'm straight over no problem, but three gardens in he's struggling on a tricky one. I catch up, whip my steel baton onto his spine and he's down, groaning, wishing he'd stayed at home and put his feet up tonight. I'm kicking and lashing at him because if there's one type of suspect I hate it's a fucker who thinks he can outrun me.

Balls catches up and pulls me away. 'Enough, let's take him in alive for God's sake.'

'He didn't stop running when I told him to,' I say, stepping back out of breath. 'The man's a cunt.'

I hear the cavalry on their way now, scrambling over fences, and about time too. We cuff and stand the suspect up. I notice he's spitting out teeth where my steel toe-cap boot must've caught him in the chops.

'Hope that hurts,' I say. 'And get a load of this too.' I blast some PAVA spray into his face for good measure.

'Shit Bob, you could've warned me,' Balls says, face creased as he turns aside.

'Next time when you're told to stop,' I tell the runner, 'you do as I say, you piece of shit.'

He's doubled over, eyes watering, struggling to breathe, so probably couldn't reply if he wanted to.

It turns out a dose of rough treatment couldn't have happened to a nicer scumbag. I learn I've just caught a wanted serial sex attacker from South London, a big catch who's been plying his trade with impunity for a humiliatingly long time. Back at the nick I'm greeted like a hero, a cheer going up as I walk in.

Shift over and accolades much appreciated, I drive home to High Barnet with a sense of satisfaction. You get good and bad days on the job, but today has been one of the best. A day where you can say: I achieved something out there, I made a difference. If I hadn't spotted the bloke he'd likely still be on the loose to commit his depraved deeds another time. Like anyone, I wanted rapists not only off the streets but flung from the face of the earth. If I had any power in this world he wouldn't be serving half a sentence in a cushy cell watching TV or playing an Xbox, that's for sure.

I was glad to be back on the streets, back on the frontline kicking arse, but for a while I hadn't been sure. A year ago I'd decided to branch out, try something different. I got transferred to Diplomatic Protection. It was a bad idea. Not exciting enough. Working pleb duty outside some bigwig's front door strapping a Hecker & Koch MP5 rifle might look impressive in photos when you're trying to pull some bird, but the standing around all day did my head in. The opportunity to play Action Man and blast some terrorists into the next life would've livened things up no end, but sadly the prospect never arose. I was turning to fat and it took several months gym training to get myself back into shape. I hung up the old Rambo rifle and returned to the streets. Give me the scum of Finsbury Park or the Cally Road any day.

I get home, hang my jacket on the wall and make for the kitchen. I'm looking forward to a quick snack before I hit the sheets when Sarah jumps out from nowhere like a banshee trying to claw my face off.

'You bastard!' she says.

Sarah is a nurse and we've gone out for two years, lived together for one. Things have been rocky but late-night ambush attacks, even for Sarah, is a new one. I'm struggling to throw her off and in the frenzy we land in a heap on the kitchen floor.

'Have you gone fucking loopy?' I shout.

We both get up.

'Who is Alice?' she demands. 'Come on, who is the bitch?'

She goes for me again but I put my hands out. 'Try that once more and I won't hold back this time, I swear it.'

'You never do hold back, that's your problem.'

She goes to the sink, drinking water straight from the tap. Her hair is all messed up and she looks crazy.

'You're pissed,' I say, seeing the two empty wine bottles on the counter. 'No wonder you're imagining things.'

'Bullshit,' she says, slamming a phone into my hand. My other phone, the one I'd forgotten to bring with me today. 'Go on, check the new messages.'

Embarrassingly I do.

Missing you baby, need you right now…

'You've been rumbled, Bob. There's 157 messages from the bitch.'

'Sarah, listen, it means nothing…'

'Don't even bother. I'm sick of your lies. I want you out of here. Tomorrow.'

'Hi there, soldier,' says probationer PC Alice Jones as I arrive at the nick the next day. 'You're quite the hero, I hear.'

I smile and walk on, but she follows me into the changing room. 'Not very talkative today, are you?' she says, smooching up to me.

Alice is a pretty mixed-race girl that I should have thought twice about getting intimately involved with. She's too clingy for a start. Not my style.

'Alice, listen,' I tell her. 'We need to call it a day. Nothing personal but I'm having a bit of a domestic problem at the moment.'

'Domestic problem? You mean the cow indoors has found out you're having an affair and doesn't like it?'

'That's my long-term girlfriend you're talking about there. And let's face it, a few fumbled shags in the back of a car is hardly a full-blown affair is it?'

'So I'm just a piece of meat to you, something you think you can just pick up and throw away?'

'Of course not, but it was just a bit of fun, nothing more. And

I'm sure the feeling is mutual.'

'You arrogant sexist bastard.'

'Come on Alice, don't be like that,' I say, but she swipes my hand away.

'Don't touch me.'

She storms off and I call out to her, but her answer is unequivocal.

'PISS OFF!' she shouts.

I shake my head and continue putting on my uniform. I'm almost dressed when Inspector 'Sourpuss' Saunders sticks his mug around the door.

'McCaffrey, my office now.'

Great. All I need.

'Right,' he says. 'Firstly, good work with that arrest. Even if the suspect looked like he'd been beaten to an inch of his life.'

'He resisted arrest, sir. Violently. It was like trying to control a wild animal. I had no choice but to use the necessary force.'

'We'll skip on that. More importantly, you arrested and de-arrested a youth off the Elthorne last night. Shaquille Jackson, 11.30pm or thereabouts, correct?'

'Yes, there was an ASB call and I nicked him on suspicion of possession after he threw something from his pocket. We were bringing him in for a search. But of course when the emergency call came in.'

'Where did you de-arrest him?'

'Just off Camden Road guv. No choice. More important work to attend to.'

'So you didn't dump him off at St Pancras Way?'

'That location was nearby, yes. We were cutting through.'

'Jackson was at the front desk this morning making a hullabaloo. Claiming you and PC Ballman flung him into the canal.'

'You what?' I laugh. 'Tall stories from the likes of Jackson wouldn't be anything new now, would it? Have you seen the boy's rap sheet? He's not an easy customer.'

Sourpuss remains unimpressed. 'Jackson is a member of the Archway crew who are currently at war with the York Road Soldiers whose turf covers St Pancras Way, am I not wrong?'

'Not sure, guv. It's complicated and ever-changing. I'd have to check with the gang command.'

'Don't give me that bollocks. He said he had to walk home for miles drenched to the skin and on the way he bumped into a ten-strong crew of York Road who chased him with machetes. He said he's lucky to be alive and it's no thanks to you.'

'Did he make a formal complaint?'

'Lucky for you, no. Imagine if the press got hold of this, we'd be up shit creek.'

'Sir, I dropped him from the van because there was a more pressing job to attend to. Had I known it was a risk to his health and wellbeing I would have driven him all the way home. Instead I raced to an emergency and nicked the capital's most wanted rapist.'

He sits back fiddling with his pen. 'I'll be checking the CCTV you know.'

'Do that. In fact I insist you do so I'll be cleared of all error.'

I hold his stare until he turns away.

'By the way, he says, fiddling with some papers. 'Streatham CID have told me to pass on their thanks.'

'Thanks guv, I appreciate that.'

'Okay McCaffrey, back to work.'

I walk out, meeting Ballsy along the corridor.

'Did you just get a bollocking about Jackson?' he asks.

'Yes I did. Twat almost got himself carved up, didn't he. I take it you've seen Saunders already. Did you say we dropped him off when we got the call?'

'Course. Fucked him off then raced to catch the Streatham Rapist on tour.'

'Good man. He was making threats about CCTV, but I know for a fact they've been shut off down there for months. Council cuts. Old Sourpuss can seek but he won't find.'

Just then Alice walks by blanking me and Ballsy senses the tension.

'Everything alright with you two?' he asks.

'No more shafting in the broom cupboard I'm afraid. It's done, finito. She'll get over it.'

'You ended it?'

'I had to. Sarah found my spare phone yesterday. I'm in the shithouse big time. It might even be over. But you know me, I'll win her round. I haven't taken two years punishment for nothing.'

'You should be putting a ring on her finger by now.'

'I will. I reckon I need to. Something to rein me in,' I say, eyeing the passing legs of the new civvy girl from resources.

'The only way you'll get reined in is if Sarah does a John Wayne Bobbitt and snips your member.'

'Knowing her mate, it well might happen.'

'Stay where you are, don't move.'

We're out of the vehicle and heading for two youths sitting on a wall, one having just chucked something behind him. I shine my torch down onto a sizeable bag of weed.

'My my,' I say, holding the offending article in the air.

'That shit ain't mine, no way. What you insinuating, man?'

Balls tells him to shut up and searches him for sharps and anything else that shouldn't be there, while I poke his mate.

'You, it's you're lucky night. Fuck off.'

He walks and we're left with a certain Samuel Owusu who has

several convictions under his belt for robbery and dealing.

'Why are you picking on me, bro?' he says, playing victim. 'I'm just sitting here chilling.'

Balls cuffs his hands behind his back.

'What are you trussing me up for?' he continues. 'Do I look like I'm trying to escape?'

'We can do what we like,' Ballsy reminds him. 'Our gang's bigger than your gang remember, an important fact to bear in mind.'

'This is bullshit.'

'You're a convicted criminal so button it, sunshine.'

Then he turns his attention on me, mouthing in my face calling me all the usual names.

I look up and down the street. We're in one of Islington's less salubrious districts, a boarded pub on the corner, a line of shuttered dead shops spattered in graffiti, a council towerblock looming over. Drizzle is falling, turning to rain, the bloke squaring up to me saying I might feel like a big shot in uniform but man to man without the cuffs he'd punch my lights out.

'You want to fight?' I say, taking him up on the challenge. 'No problem.'

I march him to the alley behind the shops.

Balls is speaking in my ear. 'Come on Bob, let's just haul him in and get out of the rain.'

'Fuck the rain,' I say. 'Get the cuffs off him.' I throw my utility rig and stab vest aside. 'Come on then. Queensberry rules you cunt.'

He's looking unsure now, not so brash, so I crack him in the mouth to tell him the news. He's stunned for a second, then he gets with the programme and piles in with a good little combo. But not good enough. I bang him a beauty straight on the hooter. He staggers, blood appearing now, and I'm getting cocky, dancing about taking the piss, calling the bloke a mummy's boy when in he comes, one-two and BAM with a brain shaker that leaves me starry-eyed. Not fucking bad. I shrug him off and we're prowling in a circle.

Balls is keeping close, playing referee, things nice and steady, jabs going back and forth until WALLOP, I hook him in the eye, a blow that should've floored him, but he's got a good chin and back he comes, BASH, straight to my temple and I'm wobbling. I realise I've got to up the ante now. He's bobbing and weaving but dropping his guard so I go for the big KO. It doesn't go to plan. He swerves, I punch air and he charges for me. Entangling we hit the deck, rolling in the shit until Ballsy drags him aside and says: Enough, raising his stick.

I lie there on the ground laughing in the rain, Ballsy lighting a smoke while Sammy boy sits knackered by some bins wiping his bloody nose.

'You two are crazy,' he says. 'The craziest feds I ever met.'

I get up, walk over and offer him a hand.

'Not bad,' I say. 'But there's no way you kicked my arse.'

'Yeah, but you fucked up my face.'

Balls and I bid him a cheerio and head back to the carrier. Then Sammy, feeling lucky, follows behind.

'Guys, listen. You two seem like decent kind of cops. So any chance of, you know, returning my weed?'

I give Ballsy a wink and stop to stroke my chin. It's consideration time. 'Well, we definitely are decent coppers. So what do you reckon partner?'

Balls weighs the bag in his hand. 'You're right there. I mean, why process it down the nick when we could just…' and he throws it to me.

'Toss it down the drain,' I say, proceeding to do just that.

'Rah!' the scrote says.

'Listen fella, count yourself lucky we're letting you go. We've got an hour left of our tour and quite frankly we can't be arsed.'

He walks away in a sulk and we get into the van. Destination the BP garage for a coffee and a clean-up. I note my injuries. I've got an aching jaw, a sore gut and some swelling above my eye.

'Feel better now?' Ballsy asks.

'Much better.'

I finish and flop back on the sheets, flat out of horsepower. I need a good dose of shut-eye now, but Sarah is leaning up and nattering away.

'So you really mean what you said? I still can't believe it. I've got to announce it. But maybe I should wait until you get the ring… Bob, are you awake?'

'Yeah babe, I'm just a little tired…'

'Things will be perfect for us. We should have made this commitment ages ago. Let's have a full proper wedding like my sister had.'

It had been a hard week. Then earlier today we got a call to some flats in Finsbury Park. A woman being beaten by her husband. We were walking in towards the block when a massive explosion occurred only a few feet behind us. We dived for cover. Turning to view the scene, a refrigerator lay smashed on the ground. It had been dropped from the roof four floors above. Police soon swarmed the place but nobody was nabbed.

We should have been cautious. Six months ago a copper had ammonia thrown down on him from those same flats and suffered burns. As for the fridge, we could have been killed without a doubt.

I mentioned none of this to Sarah. I kept it to myself. What happens at work stays at work. But knowing that certain quarters of the public hate you to the point of wanting you dead was a mindfuck. At Hendon we'd been taught about PC Blakelock at the Broadwater Farm riots, shown pictures of his jacket from that night ragged with stab marks, and told how he was ambushed by a fifty-strong mob who rained down their blades and hatchets in a frenzy. We'd been taught about community copper PC Dunne in Clapham who'd been visiting a local resident when he came into the sight of a vicious career criminal who shot him dead where he stood and walked away laughing. We'd been told about PC King in Walthamstow who had confronted a burglar unloading stolen goods from his car. The perp was fresh out of prison for a set of violent robberies and rabidly hated the police. He stabbed King repeatedly, killing him, and went on to slash the throats of a further two coppers that night. Wet behind the ears, we'd been taught about these hateful murders and more, but it doesn't affect you until you're out there and it's your turn.

I wasn't being paid enough for this kind of shit, but I told Sarah nothing. Instead I turned up with flowers, got down on my knees and proposed there and then. After the phone incident we'd hardly spoken. But I couldn't handle that anymore, I wanted an easy life.

We have the weekend off. We go shopping for a ring then come evening I take her for a romantic meal in Potter's Bar. I'm spending money I don't have, but that's a problem for some other time. On Sunday we drive over to Woodford Green to tell her parents the news and I end up in the pub with her ex-copper old man and firefighter brother Jeff. As we sit chatting about mortgages and good catchment areas for schools, I feel I'm settling down already.

I tear off the message taped to my locker – DIE SCUM – and get changed into my civvies. I've had to block Alice from my phone so now she's gone old school. How long is she going to play these games? Outside in the car park I reach my car and another message has been left under the wiper. I unfold the page.

YOU BETTER SPEAK TO ME BASTARD I'M PREGNANT.

An hour later we're parked in a quiet car park behind a snooker hall.

'How do you know it's mine?'

'What do you think I am, some kind of slag? Of course it's yours.'

'You told me you were on the pill.'

'Well maybe I forgot to take it.'

I exhale and rub my temples. 'This couldn't have come at a worse time. I've just bloody got engaged.'

'Engaged? What about me?'

I turn to her. 'What's that supposed to mean?'

'It means, what about our baby?'

'Our baby, I'm afraid, will have to be terminated. I mean, surely you're not going to have it?'

'I've got a life, your child, growing inside me. How can you say such things?'

'Look, I don't want to break the illusion, but we had a few quick shags. Just a bit of fun. You're talking as if we're in a relationship or something. Me and you are nothing.'

She bursts into tears and suddenly I feel like an insensitive prick.

'Come on, I'm sorry. I didn't mean that.'

She leans over and I hug her. Staring ahead I feel the weight of the world on me. What a mess.

'You're right,' she finally says, wiping her eyes. 'Maybe an abortion is the best thing. I hardly want to give up my career to have a child, do I?' Then she's looking in my eyes and letting down the seat. 'So lie back.'

'Whoa, Alice, come on…'

'One last time, that's all I ask.'

She undoes her blouse showing a sexy white bra with lots of

cleavage. She removes her underwear and begins ripping at my belt.

'And then what happened?' Ballsy asks as we negotiate Highbury Corner, turning onto Upper Street.

'Well, I'm sure you can guess.'

'Not again?' he laughs.

'I couldn't help it. She was shoving her knockers in my face. It's human nature, what would you have done?'

After a bit he says, 'You know what I reckon? She's full of shit. She's not preggers at all, just wants you all to herself.'

'Alice can't be that mad.'

'Unfortunately she is. Those messages you were getting were pure psycho. Not just that, I've heard all sorts lately.'

'It's hearsay.'

'Maybe, but maybe not.'

'Well go on then, spill the beans.'

'Apparently she once attacked a boyfriend with a scissors, really went to work on him, left him in a bloody mess, but it was fobbed off as an accident. Talk to Lezzie Lauren from upstairs. She knows her from way back. Reckons she's slept with her and knows a few other women who have too.'

'Alice swings both ways?'

'That's the story. And she's handy with a pair of scissors.'

'Nah, Lauren reckons everyone's gay. All men, all women, we're all secret benders, we just don't know it yet. I wouldn't believe a word she says. As for the attack, it sounds like a fairy story.'

'Lauren knows her from way back. They went to school in Camden together. She reckons Alice is unstable. She set fire to a teacher's car once after being given detention. Burnt it down to a cinder. Never caught. She doesn't play by halves. Talk to Lauren, I'm telling you.'

'Jesus, I don't think I'll bother. Me and Alice are done, I want nothing more to do with her.'

A call comes in. A burglary in process on Citizen Road N7. We radio in to take the job, then with disco lights blazing we take a U-turn and head towards the Arsenal.

The front window has been forced, flat empty, burglars gone. A quick check reveals the address is occupied by a known drug dealer. Whatever the burglars came for has most likely been located and swiped, but you never know. We snap on gloves and give the place a search. Ballsy checks the bedroom while I turn over the living room. I find nothing. Then under the kitchen sink I pull away a false panel to find a bundle wrapped in cloth. Inside is a handgun and a bag stuffed full of cash. My pulse is racing. The firearm is getting logged in no problem, but the cash?

'Ballsy,' I call. 'I think you better come here now.'

The DCI's leaving do is in full swing, the drink flowing, DJ banging out the tunes and everyone making prats of themselves on the floor, including me, the crowd cheering me on as I incorporate Wacko Jacko's moonwalk into a body-popping extravaganza.

'This will be going viral tomorrow Bob,' laughs Mike 'Ken' Dodd, showing the phone footage to Nathalie, a young probationer, as I cool off at the bar.

'Those were some sexy moves Bob,' she says, leaning close and smelling good. 'I like a man with confidence.'

At work Nathalie and I have never looked at each other twice, but it's funny what alcohol and a few lines of sniff can do. She's got her hair down tonight and must be throwing off some serious pheromones because it's causing a stir in my trouser department.

'Maybe you and me should have a dance then,' I say as the sax intro to 'Careless Whisper' sounds out.

Just then someone taps my shoulder and I turn to see Alice.

'Hi Bob,' she smiles.

She looks stunning, bright crimson lipstick matching a tight red dress. Nathalie is forgotten and fifteen minutes later Alice and I are out in the bushes and I'm banging into her.

Job done I lean by a tree getting my bearings back, Alice fixing her dress and lighting a cigarette.

'We've got to stop meeting like this,' I say, taking a swig from the bottle of Becks I brought out with me.

'I don't mind. In fact I quite like it,' she says, blowing smoke in my face.

'Easy,' I laugh, swiping the air.

'By the way,' she says. 'I've got a date booked for the abortion.'

'Oh right. Good. When is that then?'

'In your dreams,' she says.

I sober up instantly.

'I thought as much. It was just another of your little mind games, wasn't it?'

'How's the fiancée,' she says. 'Still all pretty and blonde?'

'What's it got to do with you?'

She turns aside, smoking in profile, figures through the clubhouse window dancing to 'Walking on Sunshine'.

'You're going to pay, you bastard,' she says under her breath.

I step forward. 'What did you just say?'

She gives me an arrogant smile and I grab her, shake her by the shoulders. 'Now you listen here…'

'Don't you ever,' she says, pushing me away.

She picks up her phone and drink, and I watch her stroll back to the club.

*

Ballsy is at the wheel talking football. He's Spurs and I'm a Gooner so there's usually lots of banter, but right now my mind is elsewhere. That episode in the bushes was a mistake I'm not going to make again. From now on Alice is persona non grata. She's dead to me. Ballsy gives me a nudge and I'm back on the road.

'Jesus, Bob, you were away with the fairies there.'

Along the street I see two loitering youths giving me eyes. One is Shaquille Jackson.

'Pull over, now,' I say.

I charge out and head straight for him, his sideman departing when he sees I'm not fucking about. I punch Jackson in the face then drag him behind a wall so we can share a little private time.

'Think you can fuck with me, do you?'

Balls is urging me to calm down but I'm not interested.

I've wanted this bastard ever since he grassed me. Running into the nick's front desk shouting the odds. I've got one hand choking him, the other rifling through his pockets. I find a lock knife, bag of weed, some rocks and a roll of notes. I throw the lot in his face.

'Look at you, you're a fucking little criminal and you're going crying to the nick telling tales on me, you scummy cunt.'

I flick out my steel baton, smash him twice across the knees and he drops screaming to the floor.

I kick him in the chest and he curls up in pain.

'Fuck with me again and I'll put you in intensive care, I swear to God.'

At work Alice and I ignore each other. The silly notes have ceased and it seems the situation is thankfully in the past. Just the way I like it. Nobody trying to add a severe headache on top of my already mounting hassles.

Then one day I get home and call out for Sarah but hear

nothing. I walk into the living room, shocked to see half the furniture has disappeared. I hear a sound and her brother Jeff appears behind me. The bloke's all pumped up, a firefighting juicehead, no pushover.

'You cheating bastard,' he says, his blow sending me backwards.

I lunge back at him and we're wrestling to and fro, creating a stir until Sarah appears.

'Enough, stop it. The two of you.'

We straighten up and I notice her eyes are red with tears.

'She sent me video footage, Bob,' she says, holding up her phone. It plays on the screen and I see and hear me and Alice in action. 'The night of your works party, you and her. How could you do this to me?'

Her brother walks away in disgust, says he'll be out in the van.

I search for words but can't find any.

Alice ignores my calls. The next day I search the nick for her, only to be told she doesn't work there anymore. She got a transfer to Croydon, the other side of London. Hadn't I heard? She collected her things this morning.

I go to the changing room and on my locker someone has scrawled in felt pen: WOG.

I throw down my bag. That's not Alice, it's one of the other muppets trying to wind me up. Yes, I'm a black policeman and it's hard enough the stick I get on the streets from my own race without my colleagues trying to piss me off.

I go up to search for Big Matt or Barney, arseholes the pair of them. Nobody else would write something like that. I don't find them. Then I'm told that Matt is on sick leave and Barney is kayaking in Croatia.

I walk back to the changing room. I scrub off the graffiti, then take out my phone. This time she picks up.

'You're one mind-game playing twisted bitch, do you know that?'

If you say so,' she laughs. 'But you're all on your own now lover boy, so what do I care?'

I punch my locker and sit with my head in my hands. But not for long. Soon I'm up on my feet, dressed in my uniform and ready for patrol.

Ballsy rushes in late.

'Look at you,' he says. 'You look ready to take on the world.'

'That's right,' I tell him. 'Business as usual.'

BORROWED TIME

I walked in and pulled a stool next to Tony who was sitting at the bar. I took the pint he had waiting for me and downed half of it in one. I was sweating like a pig.

'Alright Joe?' he said. 'What's the news?'

I turned to him. He was dressed in his usual jacket and cravat, a picture of respectability rather than the two-bob chancer he actually was.

'He's back, Tone. He's back from Spain.'

'Who?' he said, concerned now.

'Kenny fucking Knight.'

'No way,' he scoffed. 'Knight would never come back to England. The bloke's wanted. They'd arrest him in a heartbeat.'

I shook my head. 'That's all been sorted now.'

'What are you on about? They'd chuck him inside for a ten stretch.'

'Not any more they won't. The police have dropped the whole case. He's a free man and he's back.'

I showed him the text.

Looking forward to meeting you gents for a drink. Business to discuss. Call you later.

'What the fuck?' Tony said. Then he lost his cool, shrieking:

'What are we going to do?'

'Keep it down,' I hissed, looking left and right.

Suddenly my phone pinged and I almost jumped. To say I was any less stressed than Tony would be a lie. It was another message: *Tonight 9pm. The Admiral Vernon, Dagenham. See you there.*

'Jesus Christ,' Tony said, wiping the sweat from his face. 'We'll have to disappear, get packing, leave right now...'

'Stop it,' I told him. 'You're not being realistic. We can't just up and go, what about our wives and kids? For all I know he could be watching us or them as we speak. We'll have to face the music.'

'I don't know if I can handle that, Joe.'

'We'll handle it. We'll just have to get our story straight.'

Our story was true, but not entirely. Knight had masterminded a jewellery heist that we helped him pull off. Afterwards the loot was stored in the garage of a trusted friend called Willie Crossman. Within three days Crossman had disappeared along with most of the stash, never to be seen again. By this time, Knight was nicked and went on to serve his stretch without naming names. A small bag of gems Crossman had overlooked still fetched us a pretty penny, but we kept that one quiet. Knight, however, clever bastard that he was, always sensed something wasn't kosher. Especially with word of Tony running round on the outside wearing cravats and driving a Merc.

I slammed my fist down on the bar. 'What did I tell you about flaunting it Tone, what did I say?'

'Are you trying to blame it all on me?'

'I fucking told you.'

'Just give it a rest you prick.'

I jumped off my stool, my patience all but spent now. 'Yeah, come on then, you want to fucking start?'

'Right, that's it lads,' said Big Den the landlord, coming over.

'Now keep it down or take it elsewhere.'

We sat staring into our pints, Tony shaking his head like he was going to burst into tears.

The thing is, for me it would've been better if Crossman really had taken the lot. Jewels included. I didn't even profit from the job. I threw my share into investments that went tits up. The first was the building of a massive house with stables in Wickford. I chucked money into the scheme but within months the other investors pulled out and all was lost. Then there was another gaff out by Waltham Abbey; it got to the half built stage until it turned out there'd been no fucking planning application and it had to be torn the fuck down. More money lost. Neither jobs were exactly legit, but I knew that. I didn't expect to walk away potless though. I told myself I was simply unlucky, but on top there was a bigger nagging doubt. I was worried I'd lost my touch, that people were taking me for a fool.

Tony was more astute with his finances, but six years on even he was feeling the squeeze. Or so he liked to say.

'You better bring Knight some dough,' I told him. 'A grand or something to keep him sweet. Until we can think of a solution.'

'A grand, tonight?' He turned to me. 'Okay, I'll go and print some up, should I?'

'You do that. And meantime you can get me another drink because I'm fucking skint.'

When I got home Linda was pottering about in the kitchen, wiping down the worktop. She looked at me and turned away like I was a bad aroma.

'Lind, I need to borrow twenty quid. I've got to meet a bloke tonight about some work.'

'Ask some other mug,' she said. 'I'm sick of financing your drinking habit.'

'Please, I can't pass on this. He might give me a start.'

She shook her head then went to get her purse.

'Thanks,' I said, taking the note. 'I'll pay it back.'

'Don't bother,' she said and thrust the electricity bill in my face. 'Pay this instead. We've got fourteen days before they cut us off.'

I went upstairs for a shower but the door was locked. Must be Danny. Jesus, the lad spent half his life in that bathroom. I knocked, asking how long he'd be and he told me to fuck off.

'What did you just say? Is that any way to talk to your father?'

'I'll talk to you how I like, now piss off, I'm busy.'

'Leave him alone,' Linda said, coming up the stairs. 'He's upset. He's had a row with his boyfriend.'

'Boyfriend...? Linda, look, we need to talk about this. The lad has just turned seventeen. He's confused…'

'You're the one who's confused. Our son is gay and I'm proud of him. He sat us both down and came out to us. That took a lot of guts. You should respect him for that. Instead you're acting like some old-fashioned bigot and it's not helping matters. No wonder he's in a mood with you.'

'Look, the night he came out as you say, he was pissed. He had a few drinks too many, then he came home talking a load of gibberish. He's a confused teenager, hormones all over the place. You're encouraging something you shouldn't be.'

'Get real Joe. He confided in me years ago. I've known since he was a boy, and if you'd only be honest so have you.'

I stood there open-mouthed. A bullet in the brain like this was the last thing I needed. Then my phone rang. I went in to the bedroom and closed the door.

'The fucker just texted me,' Tony said in a panic. 'He's coming over all sarcastic. I swear to God I'm almost having an aneurism here.'

'You're not, so pull yourself together.' I took a deep breath to gather my thoughts, then said, 'Tone, listen. Message Kenny back. Tell him you're looking forward to seeing him. Say that now he's no longer on the run we can get together to track down Crossman and our cash. Let's play it like that. We can do this.'

Tony was still nagging in my ear. 'Just man up for Christ's sake,' I said and hung up.

Linda opened the door and stuck her head round. 'Bathroom is free.'

'Thanks,' I said.

I walked out and Danny barged past me in a towel. He went into his bedroom and slammed the door behind him.

I shook my head. It seemed only a couple of years ago that I was down the park pushing him on a swing. Bringing him up West Ham. Teaching him boxing moves in the garden. An innocent little boy. Life was moving too fast.

I entered the bathroom and showered for ages. Then I had a shave. Wiping the condensation off the mirror, I saw two worried eyes burning back at me. My face looked bloodless, a whiter shade of pale. What if Knight had dark plans for me? What if he'd already decided I wasn't coming home tonight?

I'd never killed a man in my life, nor had Tony, but Knight had. Once he told us how he'd taken an axe to a bloke out in Fuengirola. Some North Londoner who'd ripped him off. He hacked him up then paid a pig farmer up in the hills to take care of the disposal. At the time I'd laughed; after a bit of sniff people say all sorts. Then one night I witnessed his handiwork for myself. We were in a pub in Chadwell Heath discussing an upcoming job. Knight said cheerio and Tony and I stayed for one more. Five minutes later back he comes all dishevelled. 'I've just done a bloke in the car park, you better help.'

A homeless druggie-type lay on the tarmac next to his car, dead. Knight said he was about to get into his motor when the man approached asking him for money. Words were exchanged and they had a row. Kenny stabbed him in the heart.

'Let's put him in your boot,' he said.

'What's wrong with yours?' I asked.

'Mine's full and you owe me a favour. You'll be a rich man after this next job.'

The following day in a lock-up down Barking Knight showed us the best way to concrete a man. Then in the darkness me and Tony dropped the body from a small boat into the Thames at Purfleet.

I got dressed. Loud dance beats were pumping from Danny's room. I was about to knock on his door and tell him to reduce the volume or we'd have the neighbours banging, but I stopped when I heard voices. He had friends in there.

I went downstairs.

'Look at you, all ready to hit the town,' Linda said. 'It's good for some, isn't it?'

'Yeah right, a big night out with twenty quid in my pocket?'

'If you want more you can whistle for it,' she said, throwing clothes into the washing machine.

I hesitated. I didn't need all this now. I wanted to give my wife a hug; who knows what could happen tonight.

I took her hands, looked into her eyes. 'Linda, I...'

'What is it?' she said, suddenly worried.

I exhaled. 'It's nothing. I just…' I couldn't complete the sentence. Truth was I didn't know what to say.

'Are you in trouble?' she said. 'You better tell me Joe.' Then her expression turned sceptical. 'Look, if you're trying to cadge more beer money...'

Just then Danny and his two mates came trooping down the stairs. His friends looked well suspect and the expression on my face wasn't happy. Then I saw Danny's get-up and was hit with a brick.

'We're off clubbing, Mum,' he said.

Linda approached him in the hall, smiling and fussing at him. 'Let me see you then,' she said. 'You look beautiful - all three of you.' Danny's face was covered in make-up and he was wearing a short skirt.

'No way,' I said.

All turned and there was silence.

'No son of mine's going out dressed like that,' I said.

Danny turned to his friends and tutted, eyes rolling to the heavens. 'I told you my dad was a homophobe. Let's get out of here.'

'Ignore him,' Linda said and turned to me pointing her finger. 'Now you shut your gob.'

She returned to the boys as they left the house, praising and telling them to make sure to have a good time.

'I'll be staying around Sebastian's,' Danny said, glancing at me with distaste. 'There's no way I'm coming back home to him tonight.'

'You do that, but make sure to message me.'

'Will do Mum,' he said, kissing her on the cheek. Again he caught my eye. 'Homophobic pig,' he muttered and turned on his high heels down the garden path.

I was speechless. I felt myself somehow caving in. I sat down on the stairs, knocked for six.

Linda closed the front door behind her. Her smile faded.

'Don't you ever speak to Daniel like that again, are you listening to me? Embarrassing him in front of his friends. I don't know about you but I actually love and care for our son.'

'Okay, he thinks he's gay,' I conceded. 'But why does he have to be the one wearing the skirt?'

'He's going clubbing. People get dressed up. It's called going out and having fun. Things have changed since our day, people aren't so uptight anymore.'

'It's rough round this way,' I told her. 'You've got to watch yourself out there. What if someone kicks the shit out of him? I don't want that to happen. He's my son too you know.'

'Act like his father then and give him some support. Would you rather he be gay in secret? He came out to us because he trusted us and you're throwing that trust back in his face.'

I stared at the floor. 'I don't care what he is, but if anyone touches my boy out there they're dead meat.'

'Well luckily he can look after himself. You taught him how to box for long enough. I never told you this but back at school he saw off several bullies.'

I looked at her. 'Did he?'

'Yes he did. And I suppose that's thanks to you.' She softened her tone. 'Come here,' she said. 'Get up and give me a hug.' I stood up and we held each other.

'I can see things from your view Joe, and I know it's not easy. You're of a time and place and so am I, I suppose, but you have to move with the times. Let's not turn against our own, okay?'

Daniel was all we had, our only kid and Linda had almost died giving birth to him.

'You're right Lind,' I said. 'I was too harsh. I shouldn't have shot my mouth off. I'll make it up to him.'

'There you go. Now you're talking.' She gave me a peck on the cheek. 'Now go on Joe. Go off and have yourself a pint.'

I stood there nodding as she returned to the kitchen, the thought of Kenny Knight flooding back with a vengeance, almost sinking me to the floor. For a moment I remembered what Tony had said about packing up and running away. I pictured myself and Linda frantically filling suitcases and searching out Danny. My brother John had moved to a big place out in Cornwall. He even had a guest cottage on his land. We didn't exactly get on but life or death he'd put me up no problem. Maybe even lend me some dough to get out of the country. The bastard even had a bolthole in Portugal. There were options.

'Well go on then Joe,' Linda called. 'Are you still there? Go and have yourself a drink but don't be late.'

'Yeah, I'm just going,' I said, tapping my pockets for my keys and phone.

Of course there weren't options. John would never let me stay in Cornwall. Nor would he let me stay in his bolthole or even lend me a penny. The last time I saw the bloke was at the end of our sister's wedding party five years back when he was kicking fuck out of me on the floor. Several stragglers had to hold him back when he smashed a bottle and was struggling to shove it in my face. Psycho John they used to call him. I remembered his last words: 'If I ever see your thieving arse again I'll have your head on a fucking pole'.

I said goodbye to Linda and headed off to the meet.

'Long time no action chaps,' Knight said in the pub as we shook hands at the bar. He introduced us to the man accompanying him, a broad-necked Ukrainian who was built like a brick shithouse. 'This is Vic. Cross the cunt and he'll have you for breakfast.'

'And dinner,' Vic added without a smile, then the both of them laughed.

We took our drinks and sat in at a table. Knight looked well. Black cashmere overcoat, slicked-back hair; he hadn't aged a day. We offered him congrats on his freedom from the police, but he waved it off.

'Celebrations all in good time,' he said. Then he folded his arms and looked me in the eye: 'First things first.'

An awkward silence followed before Tony quickly pulled out an envelope and handed it over. Knight gave the cash a once-over and with a curt nod he pocketed it.

'So Joe,' he said, turning to me. 'How's life been treating you?'

'Not bad. Not bad at all.'

'How's the wife?'

'Good,' I told him.

'Son?'

'Same,' I nodded. 'All good, all doing well.'

'Is your son at college now?'

'Yeah, he's doing his A levels.'

Knight turned to Vic and a knowing glint passed between them. 'So what kind of A levels are these then?' he asked.

I took a swig of my drink, returning my glass to the table with an unsubtle thud. 'Fuck knows. I just want him to pass and do well so he doesn't have to live the life I've lived, you know what I mean?'

'That's fair enough,' Knight said. 'So how's the day job, you still driving the tipper lorries?'

'That's over. I lost my licence. I got pulled over one morning and breathalysed, didn't I? Not on the job though, just on my way to work in the car.'

He gave a slight laugh, looking from one of us to the other. Tony, I noticed, had lost his composure, wearing a nervous smile that I wanted to scrape from his face. Give someone like Knight an inch and he'll take a hundred miles.

'Still quite the pair of comedians, aren't you?'

He focused on Tony now. 'So mate, what's your story?'

'It's all good,' he said with minimal eye contact. 'Well, not too bad anyway. You know how it is Ken, doing this, doing that, all the usual.'

Knight stared at him for what felt like an age.

'That's not what I heard,' he said.

'No?'

'No Tone.'

Tony was speechless; he didn't know where to look. He stood

up. 'Sorry, I need to use the men's.'

'Sit down,' Knight told him, and he promptly obeyed.

Knight leaned forward, addressing the both of us. 'I'd say it's time we stopped the bullshit and started talking business, don't you?'

For the next hour I ran through the story repeatedly, every detail. How when I'd heard Knight was arrested I attempted to move the loot to a safer spot, only to discover it had vanished along with Willie Crossman. As I spoke I could see Knight observing the two of us with a subtle but growing disgust. By the time I finished my explanation, his attention was focusing on Tony, eyes going up and down on his face. Tony stared at the table, his breathing audible now.

Knight swallowed a mouthful of whisky then placed down his glass.

'Let's go for a ride,' he said.

We headed out. Knight got in the back of the Audi with Tony, so I was left to sit up front with Vic who was driving. We travelled in silence, the London-Essex borderlands flashing by in an ominous blur until I lost all sense of direction. My mind was going loopy, while behind me Knight sat penetrating Tony with a callous smirk.

'Okay, I can't take much more of this,' Tony relented, almost shouting. 'What do you want Kenny, where are you taking us?'

Knight laughed. 'At last we're on the same page.'

We pulled in on a patch of wasteland within sight of the Dartford Crossover, its chain of lights twinkling over the black waters of the Thames. Vic killed the engine and Knight grabbed Tony by the throat, holding a knife to his cheek.

'The truth, you cunt. That's all I ask for.'

Tony was snotting away, failing to tell him what he wanted, so Knight grabbed one of his hands and pulled it towards Vic. He ordered him to break his thumb.

'One last chance Tone. Did you pinch my fucking loot?'

Tony's tearful denials brought no joy and I winced at his screams as Vic slowly pulled back his thumb. Amidst the deafening shrieks a distinctive crack sounded and Vic's eyes lit up with a sadistic joy. He released his hand and Tony whimpered in the corner, a broken man.

'Living it up on my cash for years, now look at you,' Knight said. 'You're a fucking disgrace.'

He turned to me. 'At least you Joe, you've never had a pot to piss in. I heard you were still on the lorries until a year ago. Not this cunt. He's been swanning round in fancy threads and driving a posh motor ever since. He's a cunt, ain't that right Tone?' He grabbed his sore hand and Tony howled in pain.

'Now I'll tell you what really happened – and I hope you're listening Joe, because he got one over on you too. Tony cleared the garage out himself and then put old Crossman in the drink. Concreted and drowned the fucker. Just like that tramp we did that time. Tony here was the one with the keys to the garage, remember? How you never suspected him I'll never know.'

He told Vic to drive. Dutifully Vic turned on the engine. 'You know where,' Knight said.

We travelled north along the M25, finally taking a turn for Epping Forest. Along the way Tony was begging for me to speak up for him. 'Tell him Joe, please, say something...' But not once did I break my silence. Tony was a mate, but it was either him take the fall or the pair of us.

As the car approached the woods he began spilling the beans. 'We only took what was left... the stuff Crossman hadn't noticed... but it was hardly anything. He'd all but cleared the place... Tell him Joe, tell him!'

Knight was suddenly interested. 'Elaborate on that.'

Words gushed as Tony recounted what actually happened.

'Okay,' Knight said after hearing his tale, and turned to me.

'The ball is in your court, Joe. Is Tony telling me the truth?'

My heart was banging like a jackhammer, but calmly I turned around, shaking my head sadly with a glance at Tony.

'I don't know whether to feel angry or sorry for the cunt. But one thing I do know, he's talking bollocks.'

Tony leapt forward screaming that he was going to kill me, until Knight pulled him back and again twisted his broken thumb. 'Now sit down and shut it.'

We parked in on a remote wooded lane. Knight and Vic both put on leather gloves and got out of the car. Vic threw Knight a sawn-off shotgun that he caught with one hand and we trekked through the woods. A full moon shone down through the trees, lighting the way. We finally stopped by an oak where from one of its strong branches hung a noose.

'Here we are,' said Knight. 'Suicide Spinney.'

Vic rummaged in a bush and pulled out a bar stool, placing it beneath the rope. Knight levelled the long shooter at Tony.

'Right, get the fuck up there.'

Tony was in tears, pleading on his knees until Knight warned him it was him or his missus. 'And with her I won't be so nice. Nor will Vic, will you mate?'

Vic grabbed his own crotch, smile revealing a single gold tooth. 'I like it rough,' he said.

Watching Tony tearfully climb up onto the stool was a sorry sight. He stood there, literally a condemned man.

'Well go on then, the rope's not been put there for nothing you know.'

'Please…' Tony said.

In response Knight cocked the shotgun, its loud double click clearing the trees of several crows.

'Put that rope around your neck, you fucking traitor. Look at all the things I did for you through the years. All the jobs I took you on. I provided for you, put food on your family's table and look at how you treated me. Like a fucking mug.'

Tony placed the noose around his neck and I turned away as Vic kicked the stool from beneath his feet.

When I turned back, his body was hanging there wildly convulsing. I felt sick.

'Look, check his face,' Knight said, the two of them loving it.

'His right leg, you see that?' Vic added.

'He's pissing himself the cunt,' Knight laughed.

It seemed an age before Tony's body stopped twitching.

'Show over boys,' said Knight, and whistling with the shotgun over his shoulder we trekked back through the fallen leaves to the motor.

We climbed in and set off. I stared out the window as the night scenes passed by, mindful of my state of shock, yet not wanting to jinx the feeling of gladness that I hadn't suffered the same fate.

'Well then,' Knight said, several minutes later. 'That's old Tony for you. Once a cunt always a cunt. What now?' He turned to me. 'You fancy a late drink?'

I'd rather have gone home, climbed into bed and stayed there safe beneath the sheets, but I didn't want to upset the bloke.

'Yeah, why not?' I said.

We headed for somewhere near Brentwood and arrived at a lone detached house with a big half-finished extension. Apparently it was a site Vic was overseeing. He had the key, the homeowners away on holiday.

'Look at this place,' Knight said as we walked up the gravel drive. 'Almost three mil this gaff. Swimming pool and gym in the basement, the works. It's alright for some, ain't it?'

Heading inside we entered a lounge complete with bar, snooker table and monster-sized TV screen. Knight adjusted the various lights including a mirror ball that spun overhead.

'What do you reckon?' he said as he walked behind the bar.

'Not fucking bad,' I said, catching the ice-cold bottle of Becks he threw me. I was more at ease now, willing to go with the flow.

'It's owned by a football executive. Spurs unfortunately. We should smash the place up,' he laughed, preparing himself a cocktail.

Vic got a music channel going on the TV and before long we were playing snooker and snorting up lines of coke from the side of the table. Considering my reprieve, a party didn't seem inappropriate. I was lucky to be alive.

I let Knight win the first few games and laughed inwardly when afterwards he shook my hand and said, 'Sorry Joe, but that's the thing, no cunt can win me at this game.'

Underworld's 'Born Slippy' came on and Knight turned up the volume. 'Banging tune. Even Vic likes this one.'

Vic started thrusting his hips to the repetitive beat, pool cue extended from his crotch like an alien's knob.

We laughed and Knight said, 'Believe me Joe, I've been there, I've seen Vic in action in the bedroom and it ain't pretty. We picked up these tarts from Basildon the other night, brought them back here and shagged the arse off the pair of them. Check this footage.' He got scrolling on his phone. 'I walked in and Vic was hanging out the back of this blonde bird while not only conversing on his phone but stuffing his face with a fucking ham sandwich.'

'It wasn't a ham sandwich, it was a leg of chicken,' Vic said. 'I need protein while on the job.'

'I know you do, you mad cunt.' He kept scrolling. 'I can't find the footage.'

'That's because I wiped it,' Vic said.

'No way.' Knight threw down his phone. 'Talk about a miserable cunt. What did you go and wipe it for?'

'I like privacy when I perform,' he said. 'I'm a shy guy.'

'Shy? You weren't shy last night when you were riding that big

Brazilian bitch. You two were going at it so hard I thought you'd put the bed through the fucking floor.'

'I think of sex as exercise,' he said, leaning down to take a shot. 'And I like to exercise with vigour.'

'He likes to do everything with vigour Vic does, I know that much. Here, Joe, do you know Mad Shaun?'

'Shaun from Ilford, did the Chelmsford job with us?'

'That's the bloke.'

'I haven't seen him in a while. Nobody has, come to think of it. Is he inside?'

'Ask this cunt,' Knight laughed, nodding to Vic. 'He did him with vigour. Go on Vic mate, spill the beans, tell Joe how you did him.'

'No dice.' Vic shook his head. 'I'm a humble man. A man of few words.'

'Actions speak louder, don't they mate, especially when you shove a man into an industrial sized cement mixer.'

'It was fun,' Vic shrugged.

'Great fun, yeah. Jesus, that's what I like about you Vic, you're a genuine nutjob. A good man to have on the team.'

Just then I remembered what I'd heard about Ilford Shaun. How he'd ripped off a South London drug firm and escaped with his riches to Thailand or Cambodia. Somewhere out that way.

'Didn't Shaun rip off some Carshalton mob then fly out east?' I asked. 'I could've sworn I heard that.'

'He went out east alright. As far as a fucking landfill near Southend. You can thank Vic for that.'

I looked over at Vic who was still taking shots, giving little away.

'Shaun ripped off the Carshalton crowd though, didn't he?'

'Too many questions now Joe,' Knight said, shaking his head. Then he exchanged a look at Vic. 'Fuck it. Makes no difference now so I might as well fill you in. The money went from the Carshalton mob to Shaun and then straight in my pocket. And that's how I paid off the coppers to get off the run. There are several senior staff at Scotland Yard basking in a lot of my dough right now. Freedom don't come cheap these days.'

'You jammy git,' I said. 'So that's how you got off the rap?'

His face dropped for a moment and I wondered if I was getting too relaxed, too informal with him. Not showing enough respect.

He gave my shoulder a reassuring shake. 'Don't worry Joe. What's a bit of info between old friends? Yeah, I paid the cunts off, bought myself some liberty with cold hard currency. I mean, it's not like you're going to go running to the authorities telling tales now, is it?'

'Of course not,' I said, a little unnerved now. 'You know me Kenny, I've never grassed to the fuckers in my life.'

'Yeah, course,' he winked. 'Squeaky clean, that's you Joe.'

'No, seriously,' I said, emphasising my point for fear of any doubts. 'Remember that three bit I did inside that time? If I'd grassed up Nutty Mason's lot for that Hornchurch robbery they pulled off I wouldn't have served a day. The coppers made that clear. I don't even like Mason and I know you don't either, but grass to the police? Never.'

'I don't need convincing,' he said. 'You've got qualities, I know that. And you know something else, those qualities can be put to good use when you come back working for me.'

He smiled awaiting my reaction.

'Are you serious, you'd take me on again?'

'Why wouldn't I?'

'I don't know, it's just...'

'It's just nothing. So how about it, getting some big money into your pocket for a change? Get out of the scruffy council house, get a nice motor, some decent holidays under your belt, treat the wife and boy, what do you reckon?'

'Fucking hell Kenny,' I said, gobsmacked. 'I appreciate this, I really do.'

'No problem. Listen, it's early days but there's a big Newham Council contract coming up and I'm going to be bang on that. How about I get you signed up to a legit position, steady wage, keep the taxman off your back while the real money flows in on the side? I'm talking big finance here. A massive fiddle I'm getting on the go. Waste, Joe, there's big money in waste, you know that yourself. With all the building work going on in Newham we're talking millions of tonnes of the stuff needing to be cleared. How does this sound: Joe Shelton,' he said, sweeping his hand through the air. 'Bossman of a new waste depot in Thurrock?'

My eyes were wide in astonishment. 'Me?'

'Lots of things have been happening. I might've been away but I've been turning some wheels, getting shit done. All I can say at this point is if you'll accept the position your official salary will be 60K a year. Which pales to insignificance compared to what will actually be flowing into your pocket.' He nodded to Vic. 'Vic's going to be your sideman, ain't that right, Vic mate? He'll be taking a more hands-on role while you play frontman. Me, I'll be pulling magic tricks but strictly in the background. What do you say?'

'I don't know what to say apart from yes and fucking thanks Kenny. I'll do it.'

'Good man. That's settled then. You know waste management inside out. For years you were shifting enough of the shit. Now it's time to play a more mature role, get yourself in a nice warm office and let the younger and less wise do the donkey work. What I'm saying is, you and me are going to be rich men. Look around you at this house. The exec who lives here has done nothing more in life than push a fucking pen, while the likes of me and you have been out there grafting, putting our arses on the line for years. The time has come for a payoff. I don't know about you but I've been waiting long enough.'

'I agree,' I nodded. 'I've been waiting all my fucking life.'

'Are you willing to work then, put in the hours like a good honest citizen?'

'I'm willing to do whatever you tell me to do.'

'That's what I like to hear.' He put his arm around me and gave me a shake. 'You're a good man Joe, I've always known it.' And with that he stood up. 'Now get your arse over to the snooker table and I'll thrash you again.'

The outcome of meeting Kenny Knight was looking to be more fruitful than I ever imagined. I'd finally come into some luck. I swore to myself that from this moment onwards I'd never waste another day. I'd earn money and make my family happy. So what if my son was bent? It's a fact of life, some people just are. You get on, you live with it. I wouldn't have anyone taking the piss though. I'd make that known loud and clear, even to Knight if I had to.

We got cracking on the snooker table, and with more beers and powder in me I was singing along to Oasis's 'Live Forever', the three of us getting along like old pals, even Vic loosening up.

'Vic knows all about Oasis. He did some minding when they were touring Europe once.'

'They're a bunch of pissheads,' he said. 'Did nothing but row with each other.'

'No shit,' Knight laughed. 'You learn something every day with Vic I tell you.'

It was almost dawn and Kenny and I were outside having a smoke. The garden was a mess, tarpaulin and building gear strewn across the lawn. We both had a glass of whisky in hand when finally the charlie started talking.

I turned to him. 'How come you never suspected it was me?'

Knight took his time, contemplating my question.

'Tony had no guts, but he was canny enough. You've got guts, but you're not.'

'Thanks a lot,' I laughed.

'But of course if you were,' he added, 'you'd already be where Tony is now.'

I turned to check if he was smiling. He wasn't.

'Yeah, I suppose I would,' I said, knocking back my scotch.

We stared out into the blue twilight, the early birds singing.

'There's still something though,' he said. 'A little detail I want to discuss.'

Just then I noticed Vic coming through the doorway with a smirk on his face.

'Detail?' I asked, watching the Ukrainian walk over and plug in the cement mixer.

'The keys to Crossman's garage,' Knight said. 'Tony never had them in his possession at all. It was you who had them.'

'Me?'

'That's right. You.'

I looked at him, then I turned away.

'That's not true.'

'It is true,' he said.

I started to laugh. The whole idea was insane. Tony was the guilty party. He knew it and I knew it. He'd just hung the bloke from a fucking tree because of it.

'No way Kenny, you're having me on. You know it wasn't me. It was Tony, you know that.'

He took a drink of whisky, pursing his lips as it burned down. Then he turned to me, a strange glint in his eye.

'Not at all. Tony did fuck all, Joe. It was you.'

Suddenly I realised he might be serious. Also I noticed that Vic had disappeared from view. Not a good sign.

'What are you saying Kenny?' I gulped. 'I don't like the sound of this.'

'You did it,' he shrugged. 'So it is what it is.'

'Are you saying you killed Tony tonight when you thought it was me? No way. You're on a wind-up here.'

'I hung that cunt from a tree simply to see your reaction. That's why I brought you out to this gaff too. It's also why I filled your head with shit earlier about taking you on again, something you know well I wouldn't do.'

Again he took a sip of whisky.

'Look Kenny, we've both had a lot of drink and gear tonight. Just tell me you're having me on, please.'

He turned to me and crossed himself. 'I don't lie Joe. God's honest truth.'

I studied his face up and down.

Just then I heard a noise from behind as a shovel came down on my head.

OPERATION HEADFUCK

Jacks glanced up from his overpriced beer. Places like this tested his patience, they really did. Brixton was all trendies now, arts and media workers, ponces the lot of them. But Jacks remembered the days when on this manor you had to watch yourself; a gangbanger's paradise, moody as fuck. Not to say there still wasn't plenty of them about, but not in this dive. He took out his phone and once more texted her. No response. What a mug he was, last night listening to some posh bird warbling in his ear about meeting up. What was her parting shot again? Be there, big boy. Taking the fucking piss. But of course all along he'd known it – only turned up just in case. But fuck it anyway. Served him right for going on the lash in Stoke Newington. Another gentrified shithole. Nothing but Guardian-reading cunts. He had a choice: either sit here getting more depressed by the minute or move on somewhere better. But where? Stuck in South fucking London.

Fuck this. He headed to the bogs, chopped out some charlie right there on the sink top not giving a shit. Life was getting monotonous. Sometimes he wished he was back in Afghanistan. Those were the days alright, even if it had left him with a steel bolt in his back, shrapnel still in his legs, not to mention marks and gashes all over him. Never mind though, war wounds to impress the ladies. But on a bad day the psychological thing could be a bit much. Dwelling on the bad aspects. And coming down from the old marching powder didn't always help, never helped, but fucking hell you've got to live.

He remembered the attack in Marjah. A missile blowing them off their feet. Then the gunfire began, bullets thudding the earth around them. Jacks lay low firing his rifle and when the dust cleared he saw his mate slumped nearby, injured but alive. He pulled him to safety, dragged him by the scruff of the neck, not realising the bloke's legs were gone, arms hanging off in tatters, nothing but a stump. He had to leave him when another rocket came in, but he'd never forget his eyes, never.

Things weren't all fun and laughter, far from it, but the camaraderie, that closeness, you miss it. You want it back. Not to mention the action and excitement. Return to civvy street after a tour in a war zone and it's like watching life in slow motion.

Jacks strolled to the urinal for a piss. Another bloke was there too. Highlights and a trendy little T-shirt like some kind of bumboy hairdresser. Probably spot on there. The man turned, gave him a smile then lowered his eyes to check his wares. Now hang on a minute, I'm seeing things. Bewildered, Jacks zipped up and returned to the sinks. Had he just imagined that? The man was pissing away like nothing had happened. He watched him finish up and come over to wash his hands. Jacks must've been fucking hallucinating. He'd been caning it for quite a while and the doctor had warned him not to mess about on top of the stress tablets. But no, you don't imagine shit like that. And not in a place like this. Fucking full of them.

Jacks charged at him, sent him crashing into one of the cubicles. The bloke was down by the bog clutching his shoulder. 'What have I done?' Jacks kicked him in the face, broke his nose just like that. Then he followed through putting the boot in. Fucking nancy cunt. Thing was, the bloke was probably loving it – ooh, the aggression, the danger, the violence. But these pricks knew nothing about violence. Nothing about pain. Jacks recalled the time their vehicle was blown in the air by a roadside IED. Two of his mates were torn apart, killed outright, another left crippled for life. Jacks was thrown from the vehicle and with bullets incoming he'd had to stave off a dozen of the cunts alone. If back-up hadn't come quickly he'd have met his maker. Back at camp the mood was sullen. They were losing the fight, bodies piling up and the lads wanted revenge.

One night after downing some bootleg whisky Jacko and a couple of the boys took things into their own hands. They raided the compound of a local insurgent who spent his nights quietly planting explosive devices that would blow the legs from soldiers' bodies. Bursting in they got him down on his knees to watch as they raped his daughter. Then they bludgeoned his son with the butts of their rifles and silenced his screaming wife with a bullet to the brain. On exit they tossed grenades, and blame of the family's demise was laid on the criminal gangs. Insurgent attacks intensified after that, more squaddies paying the price, the situation hopeless, the whole country a stinking hell of mayhem and murder, man's worst instincts. Maybe they'd got carried away, especially with the girl who it turned out was only fourteen, but war is war, you're out there, you're fired up, the strain takes its toll. But what happens in the desert stays in the desert, war a different game with a different set of rules.

The hairdressing ponce was down on the floor with all the piss and shit, Jacks firing in some decent shots. In the morning that'd hurt like a bastard. Such a skinny little cunt as well. Typical white weed. Made you think, if ever there was another major riot in Brixton these pricks would be running to the hills. No way would they fight in no urban nigger war, that's for sure, even if the cunts were ransacking their pads and coming at them with machetes. Jacks recalled the nonstop intensity of his final tour. 24/7 adrenaline. Wide awake and raring to go. Pushing life to its extremes. Real living. Then you come home and everyone is half asleep, staring at their phones, bogged down with trivialities, obsessed with inane shit. No guts, no gusto. Sitting there playing soldier on a computer screen instead of getting out there and stirring up some shit for real. Jacks looked down at the poor specimen of humanity on the deck. It looked like the first kicking he'd ever taken, the weak prick. Jacks had more respect for the blacks on the street. At least they took some risks, had a bit of life to them. After all, it couldn't be all roses out selling crack and heroin to scumbag addicts night and day.

He put in some final kicks, had to halt his vigour before he fucking killed the cunt, closed the cubicle door on him and got the hell out of there – and good job as someone was on their way in. He moved sharpish through the bar and hit the air of the street, working through the revellers to the main drag, noise, laughter, buzzing life everywhere, and there was a commotion near the station, police lights and an ambulance, a crowd of onlookers, Jacks squeezing through, some black kid being lifted onto a stretcher, someone saying it was a knife fight, Brixton v Peckham, or New Cross, or Croydon, same old shit you hear about every day, stabbings, shootings, kids playing with tools they don't even know how to use, and Jacks headed down the steps into the tube but the station was shut now, coppers clearing the place, a crime scene because of the stabbing, Jacks walking on to the next stop, glad to be out in the night working off the tension, some cunt trying to beg money off him near the Academy, Jacks belting him in the face and the bloke flying out of view, comedy stuff, and he marched on to Stockwell tube, down the escalators, a train tearing through the tunnel, false lighting sending flashes before his eyes, good coke but not half fucking strong, and he journeyed the several clammy stops to Oxford Circus and emerged onto the street, fresh air at last and headed straight for Soho, he hadn't ventured round here in years, but there was hardly a sex shop or porno cinema in sight, the whole place spanking new, all cafes and restaurants and posh fuckers everywhere, and he remembered when he was young, how it was all knocking shops and arcades, a gutter world full of seedy sex and rough as fuck, the perfect place to come down and chat up some tarts or bash up some pervs. He stopped in an off licence for a can of Stella and some bloke asked if he wanted drugs, then he watched a little fight flare up outside a club, but he wasn't convinced. It was nothing like the old days. Back then you'd be fucking and fighting in the streets. Now the place was lit up like a Christmas tree and so many coppers about you probably couldn't take a piss without getting arrested.

Fuck it. He jumped in the back of a cab and said Seven Sisters; he knew a little place up there, always a friendly welcome and a decent pick of women, guaranteed to end his night on a high. He sat back, gliding north through Camden Town, Holloway, Finsbury Park, good old gritty London. He passed the old Rainbow Theatre, now some kind of church, the George Robey pub still standing after all these years, a rotting derelict shell held up with scaffolding, then on past the station and the darkness of Finsbury Park itself where he'd bashed up a few queers in his day, used to hide in the bushes with some mates he had down here, grab some cunt and beat the bastard black and blue. Happy memories. Manor House flashing by and on into N15, the same old reliable shithole it ever was, boarded up shops and tower blocks in the sky, desolate side streets, hooded ghosts hovering in the shadows, slit your throat for a fiver. But tonight Tottenham was the place to be.

He was sniffing up coke from his fist and looking forward to getting his end away when the scenes from his window became unfamiliar. Houses were boarded and buildings crumbling. Scavenged cars sat on breezeblocks, litter piled high and not a soul to be seen. Things turned industrial. Broken-down warehouses and empty lots, the scene becoming even bleaker as the streets emptied out into a vast rubble-strewn wasteland. A lone signpost flashed by written in Arabic. No way. Jacks was clearly off his face, he needed to get a grip.

He gazed in awe to an apparent fire at the distant horizon.

'Where are we going?' he asked the driver.

'Hell,' the man answered.

Jacks was silent; he was lost for words.

The cabbie turned round and they locked eyes. 'I'm driving you to your death, my friend.'

The foreigner's features seemed eerily familiar. Then Jacks remembered… but no, it couldn't be.

With a start he turned to see the man's son next to him in the back. 'You heard him,' the boy said, sporting an AK. 'We're bringing you to the place you brought us.'

A slow thumping sound issued from behind. Pressed to the back window was a naked girl, face bruised, eyes wide, blood smearing the glass as she pounded her fist.

Jacks gripped his face with both hands. Then he opened his eyes to see the mother glaring at him from the front passenger seat, a scorched black hole where he'd blasted a bullet through her left eye.

'Time to pay for your sins, my friend,' the driver smiled, clocking him in the rearview.

The family began to laugh, their cackling filling the car. Jacks turned to view the apocalyptic scene from his window. There was no surprise now, no shock. In his nightmares he'd long known this day was overdue.

'Nearly there,' the driver announced as the hot flames raged closer.

COCAINE EYES

Standing on Kym's doorstep having delivered my speech, she hands me back the flowers.

'I'm sorry, Michael,' she says. 'I'm glad you're clean now, I really am. But we've talked about this before – it's over. Finished. I'm sorry.'

I hear somebody behind her. A man.

'What's going on?' he says, standing next to her.

'Michael's an old friend,' she says. 'He was just going.'

Putting his arm around her, he closes the door.

A week later, standing on my tenth-floor balcony, I feel a click in my skull and it's as though I've woken out of a bad dream. I walk back inside, the flat a complete mess. I flash back to how I've spent the past seven days and I'm horrified. I tidy the place, shower, put on clean clothes. Then I sit, take deep breaths and tell myself: There is nothing to worry about. So I lapsed, I binged. It was a mistake. I'm clean now.

Up until a few months before, I'd been an investment banker working in the City. Unemployment was hard to take. It wasn't so much the lack of money – I had savings – than the sudden lack of structure to my life. I started drinking more and my coke habit spiralled. I'd been seeing Kym since before being laid off, but then it was all up in the air. I ended up in rehab. But it was the best place for me. It went well. During those weeks away I met some good people and it changed my outlook, made me re-evaluate things.

But later as I rack up a line – just the one – I tell myself: so what, it's a line. One fucking line. I mean, come on, the idea of one hundred percent abstinence just isn't realistic yet. One step at a time. Besides, I've got a lot to think about. Like putting my life back together - and getting back with Kym. This time really giving it a go.

Kym lives in Dalston. I begin frequenting the pub at the corner of her street. It's used by the mostly young professionals who have part-gentrified the area. Kym hasn't returned any of my messages and I tell myself I'm just trying to build up the courage to once again knock on her door, but realistically I'm spying. I watch her return from work. Watch the man follow minutes after. Watch them sometimes return together. I sit drinking, sit watching. Why do I torture myself like this?

One day I walk in and a couple are occupying my usual table by the window. I watch them talk animatedly, and as I stand at the bar drinking pints I'm itching for them to piss off and give me my seat back. I try staring them out, try making them uncomfortable so they'll move seats. The woman looks me up and down, whispers something; the man looks me over and laughs into his hand.

Something snaps. I lunge at them, upturn their table, drinks flying. The woman is screaming as I grapple with the man. Standing up he's a lot bigger than I realised and suddenly he's punching me hard in the face. I fall to the floor and he's shouting at me, but the barman pulls him away. I get up. People are around me now, asking what happened, if I'm alright, but I shrug them off. There's blood pouring from my nose; the man looking embarrassed now, trying to explain what happened, his girlfriend crying in the background. I get out of there. I know I can't come back.

Back at home I feel completely out of it. With a pack of frozen peas against my face, I phone my dealer. The runner arrives, a friendly black kid.

'Rah bro, you okay? What happened to you?'

I make up some bullshit that I'd been jumped – but guess what, I pulled a fucking gun on the bastards. You should have seen their faces. Scattered like mice the lot of them. I'm re-enacting the scene, really getting into it and he probably doesn't believe me, but saying goodbye I don't really care.

I rack up some lines of coke and pull a pack of Stellas from the fridge. I put on an old Oasis album and swagger about the flat singing and drinking like I don't give a fuck. Then I go out to the balcony to cool off. It's dark now, the whole of London spread out before me.

Suddenly I feel insignificant. So alone. I start to panic. Then I do what I always do. I phone for some company. Next thing I'm sitting on the sofa, trousers around my ankles and a blonde head going up and down on my lap. Who the fuck is she? I pull her up, her blonde wig coming off in my hand; short black hair beneath. She's Japanese or something. Looks nothing like Kym at all.

'Get out!' I throw her off me and she falls back on the floor shocked.

I grab her coat and throw it at her, an unexplained panic coursing through me. 'Get the fuck out of here, now!'

By the door she warns me that I won't get away with this, slamming it behind her. I go out to the balcony for some night air, smoking cigarettes, drinking vodka, not even realizing what I've done.

Suddenly the doorbell goes. I freeze. My biggest fear is the police, my coffee table covered in coke.

'Answer the door now!'

Fists are pounding and I'm starting to sweat.

'Open up or we'll kick the fucking door in.'

I open it and I'm met by two men, Eastern European-looking. One punches me in the face and I fly. They charge in, the other dragging me up onto the sofa. 'I think you owe somebody an apology.'

I look over and see the prostitute. They stand back laughing as she grabs me by the hair, punching me in the face. She's shouting at me, calling me a prick, a bastard, a piece of shit, pounding me as I curl tight into a ball.

When she's finished they pull me up. One holds me from behind while the other works me over with his fists. They take this in turns until I'm semi-conscious. Then they round up all my coke and cash off the table and say next time they'll throw me off the fucking balcony.

The next thing I remember is staggering out into the communal hallway in a bloody mess.

I wake up in hospital.

I rent a new place in Stoke Newington, a mile or so from Kym. Moving in I feel invigorated. It's a new start, a new environment to clean up in. I've lost weight and need to build myself up. One day on the high street a girl hands me a leaflet for a local gym. I join up. Every morning I go there and work myself rigid. It's the beginning of something I desperately need, a routine.

I make a gym buddy in Neil. He uses the weight room daily and first showed me the ropes when he saw me struggling. He's a good bloke; well built, but not your typical meathead. He likes to party, enjoys a line here and there, but tells me he keeps it mainly to weekends. I lie and say I'm like that too. I never see him out of the gym, but sometimes we have a coffee afterwards in the gym cafe. He drives a BMW 7, has a black girlfriend and works in music; he runs a PA hire business, keeps his own hours. Neil is happy, seems to have it all worked out, has the balance right. I need to learn from that.

Despite supplements and a high protein diet, weight-gain for me is slow. In the mirror doing weights next to Neil I feel a little pathetic. I need to bulk up, fast.

'There's always things you can take,' he winks. 'If you're desperate like.'

'What, steroids?' I laugh.

'Don't believe the hype. I've used them myself. Like any drug there's dangerous levels and safe. It's all about common sense really. If you want fast results it's a good temporary option. Long term though it's about putting in the work.'

Looking at his physique I envy him, yet I tell him I'll stick to the shakes. Secretly I'm still on the coke every day but trying to keep the mad binges to a minimum. The last thing I need is a newcomer on top of it.

Days later, however, I'm asking about side effects.

'They're over-hyped and over-reported,' he says. 'Some just plain nonsense. What does the media know? All it's interested in is horror stories, blowing things out of proportion. The minute GlaxoSmithKline get the go-ahead to market the stuff for bodybuilding – which eventually they will – it'll suddenly be all harmless... Listen, if you're interested I've got contacts and can sort you out with some quality stuff. If not, don't worry about it.'

I'm done waiting, I want to see some results. Every few days he has a package for me.

In the mirror I'm beginning to like what I see. Neil agrees. 'How the fuck do you think I get to look like this?' he says, strutting out of the shower. In the changing room we talk about sex. He tells me about his girlfriend's insatiable appetite, all the positions they do. Says I should come over some time, bring the missus for a foursome.

One day over a post-workout coffee he confides that until a big contract comes up in the summer things are going to be a little tight for him.

'I've got debts and bills coming out of my ears,' he says. 'Roll on summer, hey?'

I begin loaning him money; eighty here, a hundred there. Each time he acts embarrassed, says he doesn't want to take it, but I tell him it's no problem. I like Neil, he's a decent fella. In fact, he's the only kind of friend I've got. I burned all my bridges in that department long ago, pissed off untold people, my behaviour out of control. But looking back a lot of them weren't real friends anyway. One day I give him £450 quid to pay off some bills. Another time I give him a grand for his car's MOT.

The day arrives when I'm knocking on his flat at 11pm, the sweat pouring off me. Finally he answers, standing there in a leopardskin thong, his girlfriend looking on in the background.

He asks me what the fuck I want.

'I want my gear,' I tell him. 'You haven't been at the gym for over a week and haven't answered my calls. I need my roids.'

'How did you get my address?' he asks.

I tell him I paid off the gym receptionist, which I did.

He disappears inside for a minute, returns and bangs the stuff into my hand. He looks left and right then leans into me.

'Listen here you cokehead cunt. You don't know me, don't know where I live, know nothing about me. You fucking got that?'

Then he slams the door. He's gone.

Neil doesn't return to the gym. Then nor do I. One day picking up the *Hackney Gazette* I see his mugshot looking back at me. DRUG DEALER SHOT DEAD. I stare at it in shock. He'd been pushing coke and heroin, and crossed people who vowed to kill him. He was laying low until one night they kicked his door in, shot him four times in the head.

There had been no friendship there at all. Neil had been taking the piss while I lapped it up like a mug. I hated him for that. You think somebody's your friend and they just use you. Shit on you like that. Just like Kym. You think somebody's the love of your life and they don't seem to care if you're alive or dead.

I'd been messaging her for months without a single reply. I couldn't work it out any more. Why was she doing this to me?

One day, trying to fend off my craving, I tidy the flat. I find the number of a man I met at rehab. He worked in finance, but dropped out to travel. He returned from Goa a heroin addict. Right now I need a friend. I give him a ring and his mother answers. She tells me that he relapsed and died. I sit staring at the wall. Then I phone my dealer.

Since coming off the steroids I feel drained. Walking the dark streets I feel vulnerable. One day I read of some Hackney teens jailed for several dozen vicious muggings. Their targets lone professionals returning from work. They'd batter their victims with chains and bats. A man was blinded. A woman raped. One man suffered brain damage and later committed suicide.

I dream of violence. Burglars enter my flat and I crucify them against my living room wall. I stand throwing acid at them, laughing at their screams as their bodies melt. I dream of running through the streets, a gun in each hand, firing randomly. I dream of avenging all the bad luck I've been bestowed – ex-bosses, work colleagues, old friends – making them pay.

I buy a dartboard. I hang it up in the flat. Instead of using darts I use knives. I never leave the house now without one. I've started screwing more women. Just like Neil. I order prostitutes and have them over the kitchen table.

'Doing well, Mick,' he says, and there he is, observing from the doorway. 'Get in there, my son.'

I turn back to the whore and thrust harder. Then I turn to Neil. This time he has his knob out. He's weighing it in his hand, laughing at me. I pump harder, giving it my all. Then I notice his face is deadly serious. Slowly he reaches into his leather jacket. Pulls out a revolver. Points it at me.

BANG!!!

I scream and push the woman away. I'm shaking in shock.

'What's wrong darling?' she says in a West Indian accent. I notice she's well into middle-age, a lot older than I thought.

'Come on,' she coos, coming off the table, her huge breasts moving beneath her. 'I'll take you in my mouth. You'll like that.'

'Leave,' I tell her. 'Please.'

'But I want to give you pleasure,' she smiles. She reaches for me but I push her hand away.

'Tsss!' she sucks her teeth, then grabs her clothes and gives me the evil eye as she gets dressed.

'I'm sorry,' I tell her. 'I really am. It's not your fault…' I'm pulling notes out of my wallet, telling her she's beautiful, she's lovely…

She holds me as I break down.

'You need to go easy on the coke darling. Trust me on that. You need to get some help.'

The next day, after the worst nightmares of my life, I once again check into rehab.

I spend my days in my room sketching on paper then attending group meetings. Most are like me, professionals who have fallen by the wayside due to spiralling addiction. There's a banker. A civil servant. A musician from a band I've never heard of. He tells me he's sold several million albums and toured the globe. It's his fourth time in the Priory.

Two weeks later I check out. I'm clean at last. I get off the train at Dalston Junction and with the sun shining on the streets, amble back up to Stokey feeling happier than I've felt in years.

I arrive at the flat and sit down in the living room. Everything is exactly as I left it. I look around at the walls, windows, blank TV screen and slowly the euphoria drains. Eventually the emptiness becomes unbearable. The idea of living without drugs scares me to the core.

Three days later I wake from my binge. The flat is a mess, but it doesn't faze me anymore. I read some of the letters that have been building by the door. I've spent all my savings, all my inheritance; I've overdrafted and loaned as far as I can go. I'm broke.

I tear open more mail. I owe the banks, utility companies and my landlord. Several letters are from bailiffs. I'm sweating now. Where is my coke money going to come from? Suddenly I remember I have a stash of cash in the cupboard. I find the bag, three or four grand spilling across the floor. Thank fucking Christ.

It keeps me going for a while, but when it runs out I'm back to square one. I begin shoplifting, breaking into the houses of friends I used to work with, even propositioning men on the street for money.

One night a drunk banker outside a pub in Shoreditch agrees for me to pleasure him in an alley. I insist on the money first, but when I try to grab his wallet it doesn't go to plan. We're struggling, but he's fitter and stronger than I am and before long he's kicking fuck out of me on the cobbled ground.

He gets down, opens my mouth and shoves in a twenty-pound note. 'You want money? Here's some fucking money. Peasant.'

Battered and bruised I spend it in a local crack house.

I really need to get things sorted. Get off the gear and get back with Kym. I've had enough, I need my life back.

One day I decide to return to the pub by Kym's road. The fight happened ages ago and the staff probably won't recognize me. These days I can hardly recognise myself. I'd lost the habit of shaving and looking in the mirror one morning at the face staring back at me I thought I was hallucinating.

I walk in. I get to the counter and the barman recognizes me.

'Out,' he says. 'Out now or I'll call the police.'

I head to an off licence. Then I walk up and down past Kym's house. Finally I think: fuck it, and I sit on the steps by her front door waiting for her to return from work. At one stage the gay couple who live upstairs walk around me to get in. I raise my can of Special Brew, say hello; they politely ignore me.

Finally I see them both coming along the street with shopping bags. They open the gate, see me and stop. The man continues towards me.

'Greg, no,' she says.

I'm standing on the steps, looking down on him. 'This has got nothing to do with you,' I warn. 'I'm here to speak to Kym.'

'You're the bastard who's been sending her threatening messages, aren't you?'

'I've never threatened Kym in my life.'

I call to her, 'Go on, tell him who you really love. You don't love him at all, do you? It's me you really want. Tell him.'

Kym stands there frozen. Greg turns back to me and laughs.

'If I'm correct, you dated Kym for a few weeks at most then that was that. You hardly even know her. You're deluded. A pest. Now if you don't go away I'm going to call the police.'

Kym is standing behind him now.

I walk towards him. He shades Kym from me as I make to walk past. Suddenly I turn and swing for him. He grabs my arm, twists it behind my back and I'm down on my knees. 'Come around here again and I'll break every bone in your body,' he says, twisting harder. 'Have you got that?'

The pain is excruciating. '...Yes.'

'Now piss off.' He pushes me down the path.

By the gate I stop and turn. I'm packing a cleaver in my coat and I consider getting it out and taking a run for him. Then the men upstairs appear at their open window asking Greg if everything's okay. Too many witnesses.

'You're not going to get away with this,' I point at him.

Heading off I'm livid. I buy some brown from a street dealer and sit smoking it by a tree in London Fields. I need to chill the fuck out. Young trendy middle-class types are dotted about on the grass; local estate youths patrolling the sidelines with bull-terriers. The H mellows me so much I fall asleep.

Hours later I wake up. It's dark now; I can hear voices and laughter. A figure is standing over me and I feel warm liquid splashing down over my hair and face. A little further back stands his friend, cheering him on. I can't understand what language they're speaking but as the man finishes and tucks himself in, I hear the word 'pussy'. He gives me a kick, almost falling over from the effort and I notice his mate swigging from a bottle of drink. Both are pissed.

Livid I jump to my feet. I draw my cleaver, chopping out at him. I land him a direct hit in the forehead. In a stupor he staggers back and falls, then his sidekick comes forward trying to kick out at me. I go for him too, catch him with a swipe across the face, then get him in the back as he tries to run away. He's down and groaning, so I return to the pisser. He's floored, hands out and begging, tears mixing with blood. I explode on him, chopping and slashing away until his friend pushes me aside and pulls him up.

They run wailing across the grass, sometimes falling, one helping the other up, and I stand watching them get further away, disappear into the dark. I'm alone now, breathing hard, the whole thing a mad dream. I look at the blade in my hand and the path around me smeared in blood. I put it away. Think of cut-open cows being dragged half-dead across abattoir floors as I make my way to the park gate. Sirens sounding their nightly wail as I walk the fifteen minutes home.

I dream of hell. I am Jesus on the day of his crucifixion. Whips lash my back as I bear my cross through the Hackney streets, the hill of Springfield Park my Calvary. Demons flit in and out of the fiery darkness as crowds heave and buildings burn. I reach the gates of the park, local Hasidic Jews screaming psalms, gang kids waving blades and firing guns. I climb the mount. I am nailed to the wood and risen high on my cross, the rabble frenzied in celebration. I spot the faces of Kym and Greg, then they are lost in the swell. Slowly I pan from the scene. See myself from above revolving on a swastika cross. Hackney raging in a furnace. I long to die, for the pain to end. But it never will. My pain is eternal.

On the cover of the *Hackney Gazette* a mother holds a picture of a smiling young man in a neat suit and tie. PLEASE FIND

THE MONSTER WHO KILLED MY SON. The 21-year-old was murdered by a stranger in London Fields. Also his friend was seriously injured in the unprovoked attack. I scan the article with fascination, half expecting to see my picture somewhere: This is the man we are looking for. But no. This is Hackney, one of the great murder capitals of Great Britain. A part gentrified, part council estate ridden mess that the police have no hold over. I've killed and I'm going to kill again. One more piece of dead meat on the Hackney streets. Who cares. Nobody gives a shit.

I dream of the past. I work, I come home, I'm contented. I have found love. She is beautiful, caring, kind, everything I've ever wished for. In the evening we're drinking wine, cuddling close in front of the television. The door swings open. It's Greg. He's naked. Erect. Kym slips from my arms and slowly approaches him. I try to move, try to shout, but I can't. Kym looks at me then gets to her knees and begins to suck.

I am falling downwards through space. Tossing, turning for hours, sweating, screaming, plunging to hell. I land with a thud. I'm on a butcher's table. My arms and legs have been severed. I can't move. The butcher pulls off his mask. It's Greg. Kym is standing by him. Greg smiles. Then he lifts the cleaver high in the air and brings it down towards my face. I wake up screaming.

My floor is littered with wraps, bottles, newspapers everywhere ... police are urging members of the public in Hackney to beware after a string of violent cashpoint robberies... Broadway Market gun chase horror... boy shot in gang fight... crack addict's year long mugging spree... picnic couple slashed...

pregnant woman stabbed... cyclist battered with iron bar... estate residents living in hell... girl, 13, gang raped in flat... machete mugger on the loose... axe gang in rampage... body parts in bin... man stabbed after leaving pub... man tortured in flat... man shot in the head.

WE WILL FIND YOU, police say in a warning to a killer on the loose in Hackney after a new attack is linked to the same suspect. Det Sgt Carrol said, 'The net is closing in on this man, but for the safety of the public we urge him to do the right thing and hand himself in immediately.'

The victim of the latest attack, a magazine sub editor who lives locally, had visited a cash machine on Kingsland Road at 9pm on Monday night when he was approached by 'a hooded man, white, with a beard and scruffy dark clothing.' A struggle ensued as the victim clung to his bag. 'Then he produced a machete,' the victim told the *Hackney Gazette* from his hospital bed. 'Next thing I was on the floor with my hand severed, literally hanging by the skin.' Surgeons worked through the night to reattach his hand and are hoping the operation will be a success. 'I still may lose my hand, only time will tell,' the victim said.

Police urge the public to be aware: 'One man is dead, another has suffered potentially life-changing injuries and the perpetrator is still on the loose. If you know who this man is, please don't hesitate to contact us.'

Saturday evening. It's all worked out. I stand in front of the mirror. Hood, scarf, jacket padded for bulk. Boot polish smeared over my face. The plan: Kym and Greg head out to socialize - Greg gets it. A botched mugging. I hold the machete, snarling into the glass. Will I be recognized? Maybe I will, maybe I won't. Maybe I don't care anymore.

In the mirror Neil stands behind me. 'You look just like one of those cunts that killed me,' he says, adjusting my clothes.

'I know I do, Neil. I know I do.'

Nightfall. I'm hiding in a front garden across from Kym's flat.

'Okay,' Neil instructs from his vantage point. 'Get ready.'

They step out and head along the street. I follow. They're talking and laughing together and I feel the hate swell. I up my pace. I'm running now.

'You bastard.' I bring the cleaver down. Greg turns then staggers as it catches him deep in the shoulder. Kym screams. My mugging plan forgotten now, I go for him again. Headfirst he runs at me, but I slash at him wildly and he falls back against the wall covered in blood. Kym is shrieking at me but I push her away.

Greg is down. I'm ready to kill him now.

'Please,' he says.

Suddenly Kym flies at me, clawing at my eyes, and I knock her back with force. I feel the rage explode - and something happens. Then she's down on her knees clutching the side of her neck. Her eyes are shocked, blood gushing through her fingers. She crumples downwards next to Greg.

'What have you done?' Greg is screaming. He's struggling to cradle her in his arms, Kym lifeless, head angled, the whole scene drenched in blood. Figures emerge at the sidelines. Voices scream.

I run. I tear through the streets. I don't stop until I reach the flat, and then inside I'm frantically snorting up coke trying to stop the shrieking demons from bursting through my door.

I'm slamming the table in front of me, fists dried with blood.

What have I done? What have I done?

Neil sits opposite, laughing through the chaos.

‘Come on, Mick. You wanted to do her anyway. You hated the bitch.’

‘I didn’t, you bastard. I fucking didn’t!’

I pick up a full bottle of vodka, throw it at him.

It passes right through his body.

‘Oh yes you did, Mick. Oh yes you fucking did.’

I toss back the table. Tear the place apart. The sound of Neil’s laughter echoing in my head.

Next thing I’m in the kitchen. I’m slashing my wrists.

Suddenly all hell breaks through my front door. Police telling me to drop the knife, drop the fucking knife…

‘Don’t come near me!... I’ll kill you!... Kill the lot of you!’

I kill none of them.

But part of me dies that day.

FRIENDS

I sat parked up from the off licence trying to see through the belting rain. Skills and Biggie were due to burst from the shop's door any second, but they were taking their time and if they didn't hurry up I'd be burning rubber without them.

One last job, Skills had told me. He had all the intel and the safe was loaded, a payout I'd be crazy to refuse. Six months ago I'd have needed no persuading, but I had priorities now. A permanent girlfriend, a baby daughter, the first stable set up of my life. Skills and Biggie better not be fucking this up.

Then there they were, running along the street in their balaclavas, followed by four bat-wielding Asian guys. They jumped in to the car shouting at me to 'Go!' and I pulled out, the vehicle under assault, one of the shop guys jumping onto the back, his face pressed to the glass as I sped along the street, the boys panicking until I swerved at the next corner and he was gone.

'What the fuck happened back there?' I shouted when we were back on the North Circular.

Skills was next to me, pulling off his mask and running his hands over his cornrows, Biggie in the back, both of them out of breath.

'We got nothing,' Skills said. 'It was like an ambush. Five or six guys jumped out from nowhere.' Then he took out his Glock handgun, staring at it. 'And I had to use this thing.'

'Tell me it was a warning shot, please.'

He shook his head and I slammed the wheel. 'Jesus!'

'Listen,' Biggie said, leaning forward. 'If Skills hadn't shot the man we'd have never got out of there. And anyway, the guy fucking deserved it. You should've heard him, he was shouting at his sons to kill us.'

'And what if the man's dead? I don't believe this. You're useless, the both of you.'

Biggie kissed his teeth. 'Who are you calling useless, you fucking prick?'

'Shut it fatman, I'm not in the mood.'

'Yeah, you want to pull over and settle this then?'

The cussing continued until Skills said, 'Shut the fuck up, the pair of you! Serious shit has happened tonight. We've got to be united on this.'

For the first time ever, Skills looked nervous. 'We're in trouble,' he continued. 'I think I might've shot him in the neck.'

'No you didn't,' said Biggie. 'It was the arm, the shoulder maybe. Minor shit.'

'I don't think so. The amount of blood, didn't you see it?'

Right then all I could envisage was prison. And no silly few months this time either. Thinking fast I took a turn off the A406, heading for Wembley.

'Where we going?'

'Somewhere I know. We're burning this thing. And Skills, say goodbye to your Glock.'

We torched the car on some wasteland and buried the gun. Then we headed to my Uncle Roy's house. It was a big ask, but who else could I turn to? Luckily he was welcoming. He took our clothes and we showered ourselves down of gun residue.

Roy was an old lag himself, but taking me aside he said he was disappointed in me.

'What happened, Jase? I thought you were finally pulling yourself together?' I shrugged my shoulders, didn't know what to say. Then he gave me some advice. 'If you get away with this, and you'll be lucky if you do, ditch the buddies. Get rid of them. Blokes like that will just drag you down.'

By the door, kitted out in whatever odds and ends he could find, we thanked him.

'Okay, now piss off, get out of here.'

We owed him one.

I woke up the next morning with Mel stroking my chest and saying she'd just got Kellie off to sleep. Her hair was down and she was wearing my favourite bra. But I wasn't in the mood. I jumped up and headed to the living room, opening the laptop to scour the London news. *'A Cricklewood shopkeeper is today recovering in hospital after being shot in an attempted robbery...'* I read on. The police were hunting for the suspects who left the scene in a black Ford Astra etc... but the guy was alive, making a recovery and that's all I wanted to hear.

I looked up and saw Mel in front of me, in tears.

'You don't love me anymore. It's since I had Kellie, isn't it? I'm twice the size and you don't want me...'

I stood up, clicking into gear. 'No way. I've just had a lot on lately, that's all.'

She looked at me and suddenly her face changed. 'You're seeing someone else, aren't you?'

'Okay, you're joking now.'

I came close but she pushed me away. 'Where were you last night till two in the morning then?'

'I told you, I was round Skills's place.'

‘Okay,’ she said, taking out her phone. ‘I’ll call his mum right now, see what she has to say.’

‘Stop.’

‘Ah...’

‘Listen, last night I was...’ I turned away. ‘I was out gambling last night.’

‘Where?’

‘A place down Edgware Road.’

‘This is insane. You promised me.’

I sat down, putting my head in my hands. ‘I lapsed... I’m sorry. I know I shouldn’t have but... I think I might need to get some help again.’

I must have been good because within a minute she had her arm around me.

‘Listen, we can work on this. You can go back to Gamblers Anonymous. You can do it, just like you did before.’

When we were first together I’d explain any sudden drug earnings as gambling wins. After all, the curse was in my family and she knew it. Then during disputes with my suppliers when heavies came knocking, I told her it was to do with gambling debts. It was mad, but how else could I explain the cash and the late nights? Mel’s brother had died of a drug overdose and she’d never have tolerated being with a guy who dealt the stuff, no way. Once Kellie was born I told her I was getting help, knocking it all on the head, and in a way I wasn’t lying. My life was different now. Or at least it had been until last night.

‘I’m glad you’ve been honest, Jase. That’s what we promised each other. No lies. Now tell me, and be truthful, how much do you owe?’

‘A hundred and fifty.’

‘That’s not too bad. I’ll borrow it off my mum. You can pay her back in instalments. But promise me, never again. And promise you’ll go back to GA.’

I promised. Then I had to rush out to sign on.

Skills took the break shot, potting two balls instantly, followed by three more.

'There you go Jase,' he said, chalking his cue. Beat that.'

I potted one clean in, then messed up on the next, almost potting the black.

'Jeez, I'm just not with it today.'

'No, you're just crap at pool,' he smiled and went on to wipe me off the table.

We sat and had a drink, the hall quiet today.

'So,' I said, leaning in. 'Do you think we'll get away with it?'

'I'm pretty certain. They've got nothing on us, there's no evidence. And our alibi's sorted, we were all around Biggie's.'

Just then Biggie strolled in dressed in his mechanic's overalls.

'It's the devil himself,' Skills said, patting the seat next to him.

Biggie seemed confident we were safe too.

'If it was a murder investigation,' he said, 'the feds would be pulling out all the stops, but a failed robbery and a victim who's virtually back behind the counter? It'll soon be forgotten.'

'I doubt it,' I said.

'Thing is though,' Biggie continued. 'I was expecting large notes on that job and fixing the odd car ain't getting me nowhere. I say we start planning another earner. I know this place in Neasden yeah...'

'Count me out,' I told him. 'I don't want to know.'

'You got any better ways of making money then?'

'Listen, don't you think that last job is saying something?'

'Like what?'

'That you're pretty crap at robbing. So leave it alone.'

Scraping back his chair he stood up. 'You fucking insulting me, bro?'

'Sit down,' Skills told him.

'No I won't,' he said, pointing his finger at me. 'You're just a white boy pussy. You ain't got the balls for this kind of thing.'

I grabbed the neck of a bottle. Biggie pulled a spanner from his overalls and Skills said, 'Whoa, whoa, whoa!'

There was only so much of his bullshit I could stand. My dad was half-black but obviously that wasn't enough for this prick.

Skills told us to grow up, allow it, you're acting like you're back in primary school. Finally we put down our weapons.

I shook my head and headed for the door.

'You're a prick, B.'

'Fuck you,' he said, kissing his lips.

I came out of the job interview, walking past the waiting room where eight others were competing for the same office position, and knew I didn't stand a chance. Look at me, all suited and booted, and for what? The interviewers had been looking down their noses at me like I was polluting their breathing space, and I don't even know why I turned up. My CV was full of makebelieve, but it was as if they'd already done their research. Those few months inside a while back were like a mark for life. But I had a family to feed and I needed a decent job. Whatever happened to giving people a chance?

On the tube home I could've done with a happy pill. Then on the street I got a call from Skills. He told me to get over to the pool hall pronto, he had something for me.

'What's with the get-up?' he smiled as I walked in. 'You been to a wedding or something?'

'Job interview,' I said, sitting down. 'Though I might as well have told them I was a crack dealer.'

'Listen up, I've got something that's going to brighten your day. You ready?'

'Try me.'

He reached into his pocket and slapped a wad down on the table.

'Seven hundred notes, my man. Enjoy it.'

'What the fuck?'

'Let's just say I promised you a payday on the Cricklewood job. And when Skills makes a promise, Skills delivers.'

He explained. He and Biggie had gone on a little money raise last night. 'A shop in Neasden. A clean transaction, no complications. You know me J, that's how I roll.'

I felt the notes in my hand. 'I don't know if I can take this. I mean, it's yours, you earned it.'

'Call it a bit of compo. Now put it away. You need it, I know you do.'

He wasn't wrong. I tucked it in my pocket, smiling now. Then I gave him a little hug. 'What can I say? Thanks man.'

'One thing though,' he said, leaning over the table to take a shot. 'We had to retrieve the gun.'

'What?'

'We had to dig it back up. We needed a tool.'

I'd spent most of the day changing nappies or trying to fix our useless boiler, and now I was walking home from a Gamblers Anonymous meeting and all I wanted to do was put my feet up. As I neared the flat, Skills pulled up in his car, looking stressed.

'Get in, Jase. I've been trying to call you for the past hour.'

We drove and he told me the news. Trey Smith and the Daley brothers had been pulled in for the Cricklewood job. They were released on bail and most likely wouldn't be charged, but they were pissed off and wanted a pay-off. Four figures.

'How did they know it was us?' I said. 'I thought you told nobody?'

‘I didn’t, but you know how it is, word gets around.’

‘You mean Biggie opened his mouth as usual?’

‘Look, I don’t know about you but I’ve already spent all my cash, so basically we’re going to have to go to work again.’

‘I don’t believe this... Look, what if we just tell them to fuck off?’

‘Stop dreaming, Jase. Trey and the D brothers are on a different level, you know that. You want me to remind you of their previous?’

I shook my head. I knew full well. We had no choice.

‘Listen up, Biggie has got a job lined up for Thursday. A late-night betting shop in Kilburn. That should be our problem sorted.’

Mel had just got Kellie off to sleep, so at last I could play *Grand Theft Auto* in peace. I was just getting into it, finally ridding my mind of the D brothers and the forthcoming job, when Mel started smooching up next to me, no doubt wanting to head to the bedroom. I subtly shrugged her off, but she kept on.

‘Not now,’ I shouted, and she jumped to her feet.

‘You hardly look at me these days. It’s like you don’t even want to be with me anymore.’

‘I’m sorry,’ I told her. ‘I’ve just got a lot on my plate.’

‘Like what?’

‘Work. I want to provide and I can’t find any. It’s doing my head in.’

She stared at me. But this time she wasn’t so easily fooled.

‘You’re up to something. And I’m going to find out what it is.’

I sat in the car counting the seconds. Then Skills and Biggie burst from the bookies, each carrying a loaded bag. They jumped in – ‘Go!’ - I put my foot down and we were out of there.

Back at Biggie's lock-up, we counted the cash. Separating Trey and the Daley brothers' four large, we each had three hundred to play with. Not bad.

'So you're sure they're going to be off our back then?'

'Guaranteed,' Skills said. 'Me and Biggie are going to drop it off tomorrow. It's good as done.'

I stayed for a beer, Biggie showing us his latest stash of dodgy goods. This time it was perfume.

'Rogue by Rihanna. I've got four full boxes of this shit. Smells pretty rank though. Here, Jase...' He tried spraying me with the stuff.

'Fuck off man!'

'You want one for your woman? Ten quid.'

'I wouldn't take that shit gratis.'

Skills was laughing as he lit a blunt. He offered it over but I wanted to keep a clear head tonight. I was in the doghouse at the moment and needed to get back in Mel's good books.

Back home I walked in holding a bunch of flowers and a box of sweets. After a few seconds Mel started to smile. Finally she got up and hugged me. I had a feeling this would work. Then suddenly she pulled away.

'You've been with a girl … I can smell her... I can smell the bitch!'

She threw the flowers and Quality Street across the room.

'Trying to butter me up after seeing your bit on the side, are you? That's it, I've had enough.'

She was charging about throwing things into bags. 'I'm going back to my mum's and you can go fuck yourself – and your bitch - any time you like!'

I kept telling her it was just Biggie messing about but she didn't want to know. Within fifteen minutes her mum's car pulled up outside, and with Kellie in her arms and some bags she was off.

'Come back, please!' I yelled as the car pulled away. Then I turned to notice the neighbouring spectators that had gathered, enjoying the entertainment.

I spent the next few days on the phone trying to persuade Mel it was all a misunderstanding. Her mum was slagging me off non-stop in the background, but in the end I won Mel round.

'Okay, maybe I'll come back this evening,' she said. 'But don't forget your GA meeting tonight.'

'I won't, I promise, I'll be there.'

I sat back in relief. Then Skills phoned.

'Bad news,' he said. 'Trey and the D brothers want one more pay-off. The cops are watching them and it's affecting their business.'

'Right, from me you can tell them to fuck off.'

'Reality check, Jase. These guys won't just target you, they'll target your family. You want to risk that?'

Another job was lined up for Wednesday.

At the GA meeting a new guy was sitting in the circle, cap and hood covering most of his face. When the leader introduced him and he looked up, I got the shock of my life. It was Trey Smith. Noticing each other we both looked embarrassed. Then when it was Trey's turn to tell his tale he hardly spoke, saying he'd prefer to just listen this week, and I wasn't surprised.

'Jase man,' he smiled, tapping my fist when we broke for coffee. 'I ain't seen you for an age.'

Back at school he'd been well known for his skitzo temperament, nice as pie one minute, lethal the next, but considering the circumstances he just seemed too friendly. Was he playing a game?

'Between you and me,' he said quietly, 'I don't even have a gambling problem. I mean, I use the machines just like the next guy, but you know how it is...' He looked at me. 'You okay, bro?'

'Yeah, I'm fine, I just…' Then I got straight to the point. 'Trey listen, I want to apologise for all that shit lately. You lot being hassled was the last thing we wanted. If it was up to me...'

'Hang on, you've lost me,' he said. 'What are you chatting about?'

Skills and Biggie weren't answering their phones, so I headed straight down the railway to Biggie's lock-up. It was cold and late but there he was, working under a car. I had a good mind to let the jack down on him.

'Get up you fat fucker, now!' I said, kicking over a box of tools.

He wheeled himself out and stood up. 'What's up with you?'

I pushed him with both hands. 'Playing me for a fool, yeah?' Then I swiped some shit off a shelf just to piss him off.

He lunged for me and we started thrashing it out, wrestling to and fro, something that should have happened a long time ago. Before long he was huffing and puffing and I was getting the better of him, until he grabbed a brace and got me a good one across the head. Seeing stars I staggered to the floor. Biggie stood rooting through a drawer. Then next thing he was standing over me pointing the Glock.

'You wanna die, Jase?' he grinned, wiping blood from his face. 'I could shoot you right now, get rid of your body and nobody would ever know.'

'Go fuck yourself.'

'Still full of it, yeah?' he said, stepping closer. 'You know, maybe what you need is a fucking lesson. A nice little kneecapping. Cripple you up so you won't be strutting round so cocky anymore.'

I sprang for him. A shot hit the wall as I grabbed his arm, my fist hammering at his face until he crashed back into some car parts. The gun clattered across the floor and I leapt for it.

Pointing the gun at him he just stood there, out of breath and laughing.

'Fair play, Jase. You win.' Then he edged closer. 'Come on man, let's call it quits. I was only fucking about anyway. Put the gun down.'

'One step more and you're dead,' I warned him.

He shook his head, feigning laughter. Then suddenly he lunged for me. I pulled the trigger - one, two, three. Biggie dropped to his knees, his shocked eyes staring at me until he finally slumped face-downwards.

I watched as a pool of blood appeared by his side. Jesus Christ, I'd just killed him.

I looked around. Then I thought of the money box where he'd stashed his share of the cash the other night. I went over to the desk and opened it, several grand staring back at me.

Mel and Kellie were back home where they belonged, and Mel and I made sure to have a nice early night to make up for lost time. Things felt back to normal again. I woke up the next morning with my phone buzzing next to me.

'You're not going to believe this,' Skills said between sobs. 'Biggie is dead... someone shot him.'

'No way.' Then unable to resist it I said, 'Was it the D Brothers?'

Later that day he picked me up in his car. He told me the police were saying it could have been a robbery, but were looking at all angles. Then he said:

'Listen, about Trey and the Daley's...'

'Forget it, Skills. I already know.'

He looked at me. He was about to say something, then he turned away. We pulled in by Biggie's mum's house to give our condolences.

With little to go on and no witnesses the police hit a brick wall. It was a cold misty night and Biggie's lock-up was tucked round the back of nowhere. Me and Skills were soon questioned, but so were a lot of people. Biggie was a dodgy guy who had obviously upset somebody. These things happen. They happen all the time.

DO YOU NEED A LIFT?

The best time is when the clubs kick out; you can charge what you like. You might get people telling you to shove it, but five minutes later they're back because the other drivers are even worse. Just watch they don't go and puke in your car, that's all. Because kids today, fucking lightweights. It's all slammers and shots, then look at the state of them.

I sit there watching them. Big groups out on the razzle. Girls staggering about in mini-skirts, stack heels, a right mess. Once when I was parked outside a club in Romford, a girl stumbled into my car and fell right across my bonnet. She was slumped there not moving. I had to actually get out and pull her off. Then what happens next? Up comes some pissed-up runt with his mates accusing me of touching her up.

'Touching up my girlfriend, are you?' he says to me. 'I'll fucking knock you out.'

The girl is standing there swaying, not knowing what planet she's on and Mr Dutch Courage is pulling the belt from his trousers, threatening to whip my arse, his mates jumping about cheering him on.

I played innocent, all humble. 'Look mate,' I say, putting out my hands. 'It's a misunderstanding, I don't want any trouble.'

Then just when it starts calming down – bang – I nut the cunt and he's seeing stars, clutching his busted face. Then I'm back in the motor and out of there before you can say wanker.

It's funny with kids today, it really is. They think they can talk back, give it all the mouth and you'll just stand there and take it. Not me. I give back, I don't care who you are. That night I drove away laughing. The bloke didn't know what hit him. He learned a lesson though.

I'll be straight with you. Youngsters, they piss me off. Like the time I picked up this girl on her own. She'd just had a row with her boyfriend and was walking along carrying her shoes, in a right state. I was driving by and pulled over, asked if she needed a lift. It must have been four in the morning. She climbed in, sat in the back and I checked my mirror now and then to check she was okay. At one point I noticed she was crying. Are you alright? I asked. But she didn't answer. I asked her again and she shouted at me to piss off and mind my own business.

You see what I mean? A simple question, a bit of concern, and look at what you get back. I wouldn't mind but she was dressed like a total fucking slag. Again, kids today you see. Walking round in a come-fuck-me uniform then crying when something happens. The girl looked hardly even out of school. This was somebody's daughter here. Where were the parents? Did they know she was out at four a.m. dressed like a tart and climbing into cars? Did they even care?

'Stop asking questions and just get me the fuck home,' she said.

But who was she to tell me what to do? Did a few quid in the pocket mean she could talk down to me like I was a piece of muck? It makes you wonder. I mean, what's happened to this country? Can't people talk a civil word to each other anymore? No manners, no respect, nothing. I could see the top of her tits all pushed up like a whore. The bitch needed a word. I pulled the car over and got in the back. Didn't she realise how many sickos were out there? People who would strangle her and cut her up in a second? Was she slow in the fucking head or something?

She was screaming now, trying to claw at me, and I was holding her back. But I was just filling her in on a few simple facts, stuff her mum and dad should have taught her, stuff her boyfriend should have said instead of leaving her drunk and alone stumbling down the street carrying her heels at four a.m. like a cheap little scrubber. She was screaming and swearing at me and I put my hand around her neck. Watch your fucking mouth, I told her.

Then I left it. I got back in the front and left it there. I know what some people would have done, a lot of people, but I'm not one of them. I restarted the engine and drove her home. Okay, she'd wound me up and I was angry and maybe I pushed things, shouldn't have got in the back at all, but people like this need a talking to. Pissed to the eyeballs, laying it out like meat. I just told her to be careful. Look at the news. Every other day girls disappearing, murdered, found buried in the fucking ground. Tell me I'm wrong. It's all you ever hear about.

I drove her home. I pulled in by the new estate that had replaced the big industrial works.

I gave her a tissue. 'Come on love, stop the crying.'

She got out, slammed the door and hurried in towards the flats. It was then I realised she hadn't even paid me. Six, seven miles as well. But I was hardly going to go running after her, was I?

I got home, straight into bed next to Jill, and the next thing it was Sunday morning and she was telling me to get up, she had a Full English ready. I ate my breakfast, watched a bit of telly and then there was a knock at the door. I heard Jill going to answer it. Next thing two police were standing in my living room telling me I was being arrested on suspicion of rape.

Jill had gone sheet white, fretting like she always was, but I told her not to worry – it was bullshit, the whole thing. And the police, barging in like that? What with Jill's nerves and everything I could have killed the cunts. But I played it calm. I hugged her and told her not to worry – I'll be home in a few hours, trust me.

I couldn't believe it. You're out trying to earn a few extra quid to get by, and then this happens. In the interview room they told me the girl had bruising all over her. I told them she was a liar. If they couldn't see it was the boyfriend that did it then they must be idiots. Then I said nothing. No comment all the way. Why dig yourself deeper?

They were trying to wind me up, dragging up my past, stuff from years ago, but I just sat there looking at my watch.

'Where'd you put the condom, Geoff?'

I'd had enough of this. But when they see you getting agitated they love it, think they're breaking you and you're going to start spilling all. No chance.

Another five hours in the cells and it was interview number two - and led by a woman for Christ's sake. Here we go, real chip-on-the-shoulder stuff.

'Come on Geoff, you did it, didn't you? You got into the back and raped her. Just admit it and save yourself a lot of hassle.'

I looked her in the eye. 'Go fuck yourself.'

In the end I was bailed.

When I got home Jill was worried sick, actually sitting there shaking. 'I can't live without you, Geoff. I need you… need you here with me.'

'Jill, listen,' I told her. 'I'm not going anywhere. I've done nothing wrong. Some people just love going round spreading lies. It'll blow over, you watch, I promise.'

'I could kill the lying bitch,' she said. 'Actually kill her.'

'Don't do that darling,' I laughed. 'We'll be in even more shit.'

I wasn't worried. Or at least I told myself I wasn't. But to be honest I had only myself to blame. I never should have picked the girl up. A girl on her own, drunk, who'd just rowed with her boyfriend? And then hey, there's me, the male punchbag.

For the next couple of months I had to wait and see if the Crown Prosecution Service would accept the case, meaning I'd be charged, and most likely banged up awaiting trial – which was a bit of a headfuck to be quite truthful. By now, of course, I was dreaming of doing more than raping her, I wanted to strangle the bitch with my bare hands. I had to sign on bail at the nick weekly, and by now Jill was on the verge of a nervous breakdown.

'What if they put you away again, Geoff? What if it happens? Tell me, who will be here for me?'

'As I said, love,' I shouted. 'I'm not fucking going anywhere.'

I made her go to the doctor to up her medication. She was doing my head in.

Then one week when I went to sign-on they told me they had some news for me.

'Sit there,' they said.

An hour later back they came. The case had been dropped. The victim was an unreliable witness. No charges were to be brought. The CPS had rejected the whole thing. I was in the clear.

'Thank fucking Christ for that.'

The female copper stared at me. 'Don't be too thankful, Geoff. You did it and we're going to be watching you.'

At this point the male copper next to her looked a little embarrassed. Here I was, innocent until proven guilty, and there she was giving it all the verbal.

'I saw the state of that girl when she came in,' she continued. 'I interviewed her. You've ruined a young girl's life and you're going to pay for it, one day, mark my words.'

'Are you threatening me, detective?'

She looked me up and down. 'Get out of here.'

I walked away, and out on the street I laughed.

'Good news, Jill,' I said, returning home with a takeout Chinese and a bottle of wine. 'Let's celebrate.'

I filled her in on the score and she was ecstatic, hugging me and crying.

'I told you things would work out,' I said. 'Play things straight, be honest and you can't go wrong.'

It was a joy to see her face.

MISBEHAVIOUR

I roll in drunk for the umpteenth night running, flopping down on the sofa where Jess is hunched forward, fag in hand, staring at the TV. She is ignoring me.

'Give us a pull on that,' I say, holding out my hand.

She shrugs me off so I reach for the pack on the table.

'They're mine,' she says, grabbing the box.

Primates are jumping about on the screen, a measured voice explaining the hierarchy of the troop. But I know that Jen isn't into nature programmes. After a bit I stroke her back.

'Come on, let's go upstairs.'

Suddenly she puts her face in her hands and starts to cry.

I sit up. 'What's going on?'

She turns to me. 'It's over Andy, you've got to go. I've found someone else.'

I laugh. 'You're joking me.'

'What are you laughing at?'

'You, because you're talking shit. Now come on.' I stand up and take her hand. 'Let's go to bed.'

'Are you not listening to me? I've found somebody else, another man.'

'You, another man?'

She grabs her phone and shows me a Facebook mugshot. He is swarthy and smiling.

'If that isn't one of the blokes from down the kebab shop then I'm a monkey's uncle.'

'It's not actually. He sells cars.'

'Are you sure he doesn't want to sell you?'

'Shut up. You just think I'm too ugly to get anyone else – well this time you're wrong.'

'Whatever, I'll be upstairs. I'm too tired for all this shit.'

'Go on then, piss off. I'm sleeping on the sofa tonight, I don't even want to be near you.'

I stop at the door. 'Do what you like, meet your psycho off the internet. But when you're used and dumped like a piece of meat, don't come running to me.'

She picks up a glass and I close the door just in time. Mad cow.

I wake up with a foggy head. Jess has gone to work and it's only when I'm eating my breakfast that I remember the row. Things haven't been good between us for weeks. Since getting my redundancy pay I've been out drinking, giving her hardly any time, but the last thing I want is for her to go off with another man. But she wouldn't do that to me. Surely she wouldn't.

Around lunchtime I head down to the Wetherspoon's.

'Oi, oi.'

I look up from my drink to see my mate Big Dave settling down next to me.

'Cheer up Andy, it might never happen. But then again it might,' he laughs. He takes a good look at me. 'Let me guess. Women trouble. From the state of you last night I can't imagine Jess being best pleased.'

'She wasn't. But can't a bloke have a few pints these days?'

'Of course not. Not if you want to be in a happy relationship with a woman, we all know that.'

'What, a few poxy pints down your local?'

'No, it's not allowed, not nowadays.' Then he says, 'But let's be honest, with you it's rarely just a few pints is it?'

I turn to him, give him a look. But I suppose he's right.

'I bet she's giving you hassle about not working as well.'

'Tell me about it. But I've got my pay-off. A few weeks of doing what I want, is that a crime?'

'How about spending a bit of it on Jess?'

'I offered her a holiday but she couldn't get the time off. Truth is, I don't think she wanted it anyway. You know what, I don't think she even likes me anymore.'

He leans in. 'Look, when was the last time you two, you know?'

'None of your fucking business mate,' I laugh. Then I say, 'It has been a while I suppose.'

'Well there you go.' And he pulls out a bag of blue pills, pouring a few into my hand. 'Tonight my friend you'll be doing the horizontal mambo. These ain't no ordinary Viagra, these are dynamite, rocket strength. A couple of these fellas and you'll be going all night long.'

'Look Dave, that's not really the problem,' I say, but he puts his hand up, won't even hear it.

'Listen, not getting any is always a problem. Now do things right. Prepare a romantic meal. Dim the lights, set the mood. Candles, wine, oysters. Women love all that. Then afterwards… I mean, look at me, do you know that new blonde little number I've got in the garage office?'

'The young girl?'

'I'm in there mate - wham, bam, thank you very much ma'am. I had her over the bonnet last night and believe me, she was loving it.'

I pause for a second. 'You mean you're cheating on Angie?'

'What's that got to do with it?'

I'm surprised at the bloke. Angie has been my younger sister's friend since school and it feels wrong somehow. They've just had their second kid together.

'Listen, all I'm saying is those little fellas will bring back your love life, big time.'

I watch him strut back to work, bursting out of his Barnet FC top, more fat than muscle these days. Young blonde number? Lying git.

Still, I take his advice.

With Jess due home the table is all set, ambience just right, dinner almost ready. She hasn't answered my messages but it's not a problem. I'm in the dog house, but coming home she is sure to appreciate the effort I've put in.

Six o'clock comes and goes. So does seven. I'm pacing the flat now actually nervous, when suddenly Jess texts me.

Meeting the girls tonight, don't stay up.

I message her back but she says she's already made plans.

Fuck this. I start in on the wine, necking it straight from the bottle. Then I hit the Stellas, staring at the TV, the same old politicians preaching. Bollocks to them. I grab my jacket and head to the pub.

'What's up, fam? You've got a face like a slapped arse.'

Young Ryan Jones pulls up a stool next to me. We call him Kanye because he walks and talks black. Mention it though and he says we're just old school, living in the past.

'I was chatting to Big Dave earlier,' he says. 'And basically, he told me your predicament.'

'Did he now?'

'Yes he did.'

'And what predicament was that?'

He catches my eye. 'No pussy blues.'

I stare at him. Then I pull back and laugh.

'But this, my man, is your prescription right here,' he continues, showing me a bag of weed. 'Too much drinking just brings you down in that department, you get what I'm saying? Smoke some of this hydroponic herb and watch that sweet loving flow.' And straight away he's talking prices.

'Come here.' I lean in. 'Number one, I don't smoke that shit. Two, my equipment is in perfect working nick, so you can tell Dave to shove his fairy-tales up his fucking ring piece, got it?'

Half an hour later in walks the man himself. I get up.

'You,' I point. 'I want a word.'

Dave stops. 'What are you doing here? You didn't take my advice. Typical.'

'What's the idea of talking shit to people about me?'

'What people?'

I point across the pub. 'Him. Kanye fucking West.'

Just then Dave is joined by the girl who works for him. 'Go on sweet, run to the bar, I'll be there in a minute,' he says and dutifully she obeys, sauntering along in short skirt and heels.

I shake my head in disbelief. 'And why should I take the advice of a bloke who cheats on his wife with a tart young enough to be his daughter?'

'Now listen here you fucking pisshead,' he says, coming close.

'Come on then, what are you going to do?'

People are watching now and he shakes his head.

'Sober up Andy, you're making a fool of yourself.'

I sit back down and finish my drink.

Then I walk up the road to the next pub.

As soon as I reach the bar, Dougie the landlord places a pint in front of me.

'On the house,' he says.

'Now that is what I call hospitality.'

'Enjoy it because it will be one of your last in this place. As of next week this pub will be no more. The brewery have sold up to developers. Luxury flats.'

'No way. My dad drank here – my grandad drank here.'

'They're not messing about either. The bulldozers will be in Monday next. A hundred years of history thrown into the skip. That's money for you – ruins everything in the end.'

I bring my pint to a table wiping a tear from my eye.

'Are you alright love?' a woman says, shifting along the seat next to me. She is mid-forties, dark hair, attractive. 'You don't mind a bit of company, do you?'

'Of course not, sit in. I just heard the pub's closing down. I got a bit emotional. I've been coming here for years. My grandad used to play on that old piano over there.'

'Don't be sad darling,' she says. 'Think of it like this, a building might disappear but the spirit of the place lives on,' and she places her hand over her heart: 'In here.'

We get chatting and soon I'm pouring my heart out to her and she seems to have an answer to my every problem.

'Come here you,' she says after we've had a few drinks, and I lean in as she gives my head a cuddle. 'All you men need is a little attention, a little love.'

She takes my hand. 'Come on. Let's go outside.'

We head out, but instead of stopping for a fag she leads me across the car park and towards the bushes. When I show surprise she says, 'Well, you want business, don't you?'

I stop. 'Hang on a sec…'

'You're right, before we go any further we should really get the money thing over with. What do you say, forty for oral, or sixty for oral and full, half and half?'

'But I thought…'

'You thought what?' Then she puts her finger to my lips and smiles. 'You're a sweet man Andy, you really are. I've enjoyed having a natter with you, but we've got to be realistic here. I've got to pay the bills just like everyone else. So come on, do you want business or not?'

In the bushes she is down in front of me on her knees, head going back and forth. After a bellyful of booze it takes some effort to get the flag full mast, but by then she's up by the fence and I'm banging away. I still aren't exactly rock hard and at one point I even slip out, but I stuff it back in and finish the job.

'Now I bet you feel better,' she says as I pull up my jeans and lean by a tree getting my breath back. 'You run back to the pub while I clean up and I'll see you in a minute.'

I walk back. I might be a mug but I'm not stupid. She won't be back. With money stuffed down her bra she'll be off to her next punter. By the bar Postman Pat and his cronies are talking about me, sniggering.

'You were quick,' he says.

'Doing what?' I ask.

'Doing that prossie.'

'What prossie? I walked that woman to the bus stop.'

'She blew you at the bus stop then?'

'Fuck off.'

I sit on my own with my drink. I feel sick. Disgusted with myself. The world is full of bastards, people with no morals, no standards, but even worse I'm one of them. I go to the gents and vomit into the bog. That fucking wine earlier. I splash my face with water and look in the mirror. What a state.

Back home I sit in front of the telly. Jess still isn't back. I message her and get no reply. After a midweek one with the girls she's usually home before midnight, but when midnight comes and goes I'm worrying. It's 2am before I hear the front door, then she staggers into the room drunk and crying. She plonks herself down next to me but I fold my arms, staring at an old re-run of *Bullseye.* She is pawing at me and finally I turn.

'The state of you and you talk about me? How many shots have you had tonight?'

'SHUT UP,' she yells and I jolt.

'Calm down,' I tell her. 'Now why are you crying?'

'I… I met someone tonight.'

'Who?'

'That… that bloke I was telling you about.'

I jump to my feet. 'No way, you didn't. I don't believe this.'

'I'm sorry. But we've hardly been much of a couple lately, have we?'

'Maybe not, but still. What happened?'

'We went for a meal.'

'Then what?'

'Then we went back to his place and…'

'Well go on then, spit it out.'

'Then he raped me,' she says, bursting into tears.

I'm pacing back and forth in shock.

'You went back to his place? What the fuck did you think was going to happen!'

'Well not that! It wasn't what I wanted… and I'm covered in bruises.' She shows me her arms and legs.

'Right, that's it, where does he live?'

'I don't know exactly, we drove there.'

'Where does he work then? You said the fucker sells cars.'

'Don't do anything Andy, promise me. It was all my fault.'

'Flaming hell,' says Dave in the pub the next morning once I've filled him in. 'But the thing is, how can you be sure it was forced? Basically she went on a date with the bloke then went willingly back to his pad. In a court of law it would be thrown out, I know that much.'

'I don't do courts of law, Dave.'

'Nor do I. But there's no point losing our heads until we learn the facts. And no offence, but if your bird is seeing other men do you really think it's a job worth pursuing?'

I lean forward. 'We're all seeing other people. You're banging that blonde bird, I knobbed a woman behind the White Horse last night, Jess is meeting blokes off Facebook, the whole world's gone fucking mad mate – but the bottom line is this, Jess was raped and I want to get the bastard.'

Two old boys look around and decide to find another table.

'Listen, go easy – and what do you mean you knobbed a woman last night, who?'

'It doesn't matter, it was just a mistake. The same way Jess made a mistake. We've been going through a bad patch, but she regrets it and so do I. Now I just want to get this thing sorted.'

'Fair enough. But the question remains – was Jess coerced or does she just feel guilty now?'

'She's covered in bruises Dave. The bloke's sick and he's not getting away with this.'

'Okay. I'll see what I can do. Stay where you are. I'll bell you by lunchtime.'

He leaves and I sit there feeling drained. I've had all stress and no sleep and it's left me feeling like two sacks of shit. Then I notice Kanye by the machines. I call him over and he's all smiles.

'I knew you'd come round,' he says.

'You can put your puff away,' I tell him. 'I need a pick-me-up.'

He does the amphetamine run and in no time I'm wide awake. Then Big Dave phones.

'It's all planned,' he says. 'You're lucky, Andy. I know some fellas who owe me a favour.'

It's 6pm, dark, four of us in a van opposite CYPRUS USED CARS. Jake and Black Dwayne are ex-top boy Yids, well versed in the art of punishment. Dwayne did time for armed robbery, while Jake spent four years in the forces.

‘So what happened next?’ asks Dave as the squaddie tells an Afghan war story.

‘Well, I got the raghead on the ground and pulled out his fucking teeth, didn’t I. Later made a necklace out of the little cunts.’

‘That’s like ‘Nam,’ says Dwayne. ‘They used to bring back shrivelled ears, dicks and that.’

‘I met a bloke who brought back a whole fucking head. Listen to this…’

Suddenly we notice the Greek locking up shop. It’s time for action. Jake and Dwayne pull on balaclavas, step out and stealthily make their way over. They’re up behind the man before he can sense a thing. With a firm gag over his mouth they march him to the van and lob him in.

‘Go go go!’

We drive to a lock-up where he is bound to a chair. Jake removes his gag and blindfold, and with a light in his face he’s struggling to see us standing before him.

‘Who are you people? Where am I? Why are you doing this?’

I step forward as the others recede into the shadows.

‘Where were you last night mate?’

‘Go fuck yourself.’

I raise my hand to slap him.

‘Okay, okay!’ he says. ‘I was entertaining a woman.’

‘Right, so we’re getting somewhere. Are you married?’

‘Well, yeah – but it’s not against the law, is it?’

I lean in. ‘Raping my missus is against the law though, believe you me.’

‘This is bullshit, I haven’t raped anyone.’

The two hooligans motion me aside and start in on him, thumps and grunts echoing off the grubby walls. Satisfied with their work they retreat back into the gloom.

I step forward. ‘You’re a liar because I’ve seen the bruises.’

'I swear to you,' he sobs, lips bloody and a black eye forming. 'In the restaurant she drank two bottles of wine, spirits too, and afterwards she was falling around on the street. I helped her to my car, helped her to my flat.'

'Flat? You think I haven't done my research? You live in a four-bed semi, you liar.'

'Yes, but I have a flat for, you know, extra-curricular. And the woman was drunk. She even fell down some steps. And she was begging me for sex. Then afterwards I made her coffee, ordered a taxi. She'd told me she was single and looking for romance. Check her messages on my phone, it's all there to see.'

I'm almost beginning to believe the fucker. But no way. I motion the boys forward for another beating, but Dave halts the proceedings. He nods me to the corner for a word.

'I'm not liking the sound of this, Andy,' he says.

I stand there for a moment. 'Nor am I,' I admit.

'Nothing against your bird but I think he's telling the truth.'

Dave goes over and checks the man's phone. All three of them are gathered round reading the messages.

Head in hands I sink down against the wall.

He comes over. 'Andy, listen,' he says gently. 'The whole thing is a bit different to how we thought I'm afraid. We've got no choice but to call things off.'

The return journey in the van is silent. The two nutters have gone, the Greek in the back.

Dave turns from the wheel. 'How much of your redundancy have you got left?'

'Almost a grand, why?'

'You better give it to the Greek as compo. To stop him from blabbing.'

'But that bastard shagged my...'

'I know, but the circumstances are different now.'

I sulk for a bit, then say, 'The most I can get from the wall is two hundred quid.'

'Not enough,' he says. 'I've got some dough in the safe at work, but I'll want it from your bank first thing.'

We drop the bloke off a grand richer. As for the bruises, he agrees to tell his wife that he was mugged.

I climb into bed next to Jess, turning my back to her, but after a while I feel her hand.

'You lied to me,' I tell her.

'To be honest, I can't fully remember now…'

'It wasn't rape, just admit it.'

'Well, maybe it wasn't… but it wasn't what I wanted either, not really. I was angry with you and men were saying they liked my pictures and… but I shouldn't have done what I did.'

'Forget about it, let's just sleep.'

'I'm sorry,' she sobs. 'I just want things to be good with us again.'

'We'll talk in the morning.'

The next day I look for a job. Then around five I stop into the pub for a pint, perhaps two, but definitely no more. Dave comes in and I pass him his grand, the last of my dough.

'So how are things with Jess?' he asks.

'Not bad. We talked, made some promises. There'll be no more funny business from either of us.'

'Good man,' he says. 'I better run. But one thing, good job you paid the bloke off, I tell you. I asked around and his car place is a front for some well dodgy business.'

'Doesn't surprise me,' I shrug. 'Everyone's got some kind of scam going these days. It's the only way you can afford to live.'

'Yeah, well, you paid him a pretty penny so I'm sure there's nothing to worry about. Anyway, catch you later.'

Then up walks Kanye. 'You want more stuff?'

I shake my head but he keeps on. 'Come on, it'll get you in the groove, get your mojo rising.'

'Uh-uh,' I say, draining my pint and putting on my jacket. 'My mojo will be rising tonight just fine.'

Dinner is all set for seven. Oysters, candlelight, the works. Walking out I drop two of Dave's magic pills. Then turning up a side road a motorbike pulls up alongside me, the pillion rider taking aim with a handgun.

I leg it, the shots following me up the street.

RIOT CITY FALLOUT

Three weeks later when the cops burst through my door, yeah, I had my regrets, but during the riots I didn't think about being pulled and I didn't care either. You're living for the moment, alive in the here and now, not giving a fuck. I still can't believe it all kicked off like that. It was like a chemical reaction, all these ingredients got together then, boom, we were running the show.

All along Tottenham High Road cars, buses and buildings were on fire, and the feds cowering behind their shields. Down the backstreets things were just as lethal. Smaller groups roaming in the shadows; ambush tactics, guerrilla warfare. I saw this TV crew get beaten to shit, all their gear nicked, every last piece of it. Any stray police were being run left and right, and this one cop got himself trapped. He took a flying brick to the face and was lying unconscious on the ground.

A group of seven or eight ran in for the kill, and I could hear this guy chanting head-on-a-stick, but that fed must've had a guardian angel because just then these robocops flew in, batons flying, dragging the guy to safety. That was close. He was lucky. In fact the most surprising thing is that no policeman was killed that night.

By morning we ended up in Tottenham Hale retail park. By

now there was no police in sight and all the stores were being cleared out. I saw people loading fifty-inch TVs into their cars like they were out doing a day's shopping, but fuck if I was carrying one of them down the street. We had a look in Carphone Warehouse and the shelves were already empty. I did get a pair of Nikes from JD Sports though. But the funniest thing was McDonald's. People had broken in and were frying themselves burgers.

The madness went on for three nights. Afterwards I was buzzing for weeks. Quite a few people were getting lifted but I just hoped I'd be lucky. Then one morning I woke to the sound of a commotion downstairs and my mum shouting, and I knew they had come for me. Within seconds I was in cuffs.

I did four months inside. I'd been nicked before, done a few nights in police cells, but I'd never been to prison. What can I say? It's not nice, but what do you expect? You just try to get through it the best you can.

Before going inside I'd been doing college. I hadn't taken it too seriously, but at least it was something. Coming out though I didn't even have that. I was drifting along, getting up late in the afternoon, and before long my whole life felt directionless. And that's when I bumped into Leon.

I'd met Leon in jail and he'd been good to me. He was slightly older and had a serious rep, so once I got in with him I had pretty much no worries about being hassled in there. I was in for a short stretch whereas Leon had two more years, so returning favours on the outside was something I thought I wouldn't have to worry about for a while. Until he strolled up to me in KFC only two months later. 'What's happening, Bones?' He'd been given early release.

Some nights I'd go out helping him on money raises. Stuff like nicking items from cars or breaking into shops at night. But lately things were escalating, getting hot.

There was a dealer he wanted to rob called Lonestar. He operated from Northumberland Park. We sat in a car spying on his flat for a while, watching him come and go. His name was fitting as he was always on his own. One night Leon said he'd got some info that he'd be carrying two grand to a deal going down in Stamford Hill. We'd have to get at him between the time he left his flat and reached his car. It was a small window of opportunity and we'd have to be sharp and swift.

We sat looking over at the block, the old type with outside communal balconies, front doors visible. Lonestar lived on the second floor, third door along.

Leon passed me a lumphammer. 'Hide in the shadows then get up behind him and give him a good bash with this.'

'Hammer him over the head?'

'That's right. You'll only get one chance so knock him out then go through his pockets and grab the prize.'

I didn't like the sound of that. 'I thought you said you had an imitation gun.'

'I couldn't get hold of it so we'll just have to improvise. You take the lead, I'll hang back and keep watch.'

'No, let's be together on this.'

'You're a fucking pussy Bones, you know that? I'm a veteran of this type of thing. How are you ever going to earn your stripes if you don't get out there and show me some action. This mentoring shit is becoming a real pain.'

I'd never asked him to be my mentor in crime, but neither did I want to get him any more riled. Still, I wasn't keen on his methods. They were crude and dangerous. Whacking a guy over the head with a four-pound lumphammer could end badly for all of us.

'Okay,' I said. 'But I'll do things my way.' I pulled out a blue carrier bag and placed the hammer inside, wrapping it tight.

'I'm going to hold this like a gun and tell him to hand over the cash.'

'And you think that will work?'

'It's better than your idea. A guy like Lonestar probably has eyes on the back of his head, I'd never get near him. Then what? With a gun, or at least what he thinks is a gun, I'm more in control.'

'Go on then, do things your way. But if you fuck up it means I'll be going home tonight skint, and I've put precious man hours into this one.'

We checked the time. Lonestar was due for the meet in half an hour. Suddenly his door opened and he appeared. We watched him head along the walkway and disappear as he took the stairs.

'Right, get to work B.'

I pulled down my balaclava and hit the street. I hid behind a wheelie bin and when he appeared I jumped out pointing the tool. I ordered him to throw me the cash or I'd shoot.

Lonestar stood looking me up and down. I was wielding what could very likely be a firearm, but he didn't look scared. He took some steps towards me. 'Are you having a laugh, you little dick?'

I found myself backing away. I had the feeling he might snatch the tool if I allowed him to get too close.

'Just give me the fucking cash or I'll be forced to use this thing,' I warned him.

'What thing? You think I'm some kind of clown? That ain't a gun.' He whipped out a knife, slicing it through the air between us. He was laughing now, a real sadistic cackle and his eyes looked pure heartless. I knew right then that Leon had underestimated this guy. 'I'm gonna carve you into pieces and send them in the post to your mother.'

Backing up I tripped on something and almost fell. Lonestar burst out with laughter, then Leon appeared to his rear and whacked him over the head. 'Ahh!' He doubled up clutching his scalp. Leon bashed him again and he dropped.

Leon threw aside the half brick he'd used and began tearing through his pockets. 'Where are you hiding the funds, big man?'

'There ain't any,' Lonestar managed, face twisted in pain. 'None you'll find anyway.'

'What are you on about? Give me your drug cash man! You've got two fucking grand on you.'

'I've plugged it,' Lonestar moaned.

'You what?'

'It's up my fucking arse.'

'Well take it the fuck out then,' Leon ordered, but Lonestar was dazed and fast losing consciousness.

Faces were peering down from the flats and suddenly three guys burst from the entrance, running towards us.

'Let's split, quick,' Leon said.

We dashed to the car and jumped in. Leon was trying to start the engine, the men running closer, one waving a machete in the air as he went. This wasn't our part of Tottenham so getting caught in the act didn't bear thinking about. We were fretting and panicking for the car to start, then just in time the engine revved and we screeched away down the street.

Our assailants were left standing in the middle of the road and Leon was laughing now.

'Did you see the faces of those pricks? See the fat guy running with the long blade? And the tall skinny one hopping on the spot?'

I laughed along adding wisecracks, but I knew Leon well enough to know his merriment would inevitably fade, and fast. Minutes later we were driving along in silence and sure enough he slammed the wheel.

'That operation was a piece of shit,' he said. 'How come the man was backing you up when you were brandishing what could've been a gun? Didn't you scare him at all?'

'I don't even think a real gun would've scared him.'

'Prick deserves a shanking for that, I swear. He'll have a sore head for a good while so that's one thing I suppose. But it ain't going to put notes in my pocket, is it?'

'Would you really want those notes considering where he was storing them?'

He looked at me, then he turned back and we both laughed.

We carried on driving, then on a backstreet off West Green Road he suddenly hit the brakes. 'Watch this. I'll show you how to rob somebody.'

He jumped out of the car, heading for a black guy who was walking along laughing on his phone. On seeing Leon approach, he put his hands out in a gesture of peace. Leon punched him to the ground, then got down and grabbed his wallet and phone.

He ran back to the car and we were off and away.

'Now that, compadre, is how you jack somebody.'

He threw me the man's wallet and told me to count up the spoils. It contained a hundred and fifty in cash which Leon snatched from my hand. 'That will do me nicely,' he said, pocketing the notes. 'Next time it's going to be you bringing some paper to the table.'

Getting involved with Leon on the outside wasn't working out. I didn't want to be roped into these kind of things. I didn't want to live like this. I wanted to distance myself, maybe even move out of London completely, get a job or some shit. But what job? I was an ex con and that left me with few options. I wanted out, but instead life carried on along the same lines.

One evening I was walking to my girl's place when Leon pulled up in his car next to me. Scorpz, one of his crew, was in the front beside him. The man had big unkempt hair and snakey-looking eyes, and I didn't like him. There were two versions of how Scorpz earned his name. Some said it was because of the tank of pet Scorpions he had at home. Others said it was due to the Skorpion sub-machine gun that he kept loaded by his bed. Both were probably just talk, but the repellent name suited him.

'Hey, Bones,' Leon said. 'Just the man I want to see. Get in the car blud.'

'Nah, not tonight Leon. I'm a busy man, I've got a few things on you know.'

'I know you have,' he said. 'And top of the list is me showing you the next job we got planned. The fucking big one. Now get in.'

I climbed into the back and we set off. Scorpz turned round, showing me his fist and I tapped it.

'Heard you pulled in some Ps last night fam,' he said, gold molar glinting.

I nodded, gave an affirmative smile, but last night was something I didn't want to be reminded of. Me and Leon were up Edmonton and things had been messy to say the least. And more, Leon had only passed me twenty percent of the earnings.

'That's right,' Leon said. 'You should've seen my boy out there last night. Trying to target some guy for his phone and the man starts fronting him up, fists flying. The two of them were rolling about on the street like back in the school playground. I was cracking up.' Then he kissed his teeth. 'I had to interrupt my laughter to step out of the car and kick the guy in the face. Otherwise Bones would've got his arse whipped and been crying to his mum, ain't that right B?'

Scorpz laughed and Leon continued his yarn. 'I grabbed the prick's wallet and I ain't lying, the man was carrying a wad this thick. Serious notes, fam. But that's me, I've got a radar for shit like that. I can just sense it in the way somebody walks. See a man strutting along looking para and you just know he's got something to hide.'

'I shoulda been there bro,' Scorpz chuckled as he built a spliff.

'I love watching people get fucked up.'

'One kick, you should've seen it. I probably snapped the man's neck. Did more in one second than Bones did in two full minutes bitch slapping and rolling about on the pavement. Jeez, I'll have to check on the grapevine on that one, see if there's any dead niggas been scraped up N9 sides.'

Scorpz took a deep toke and slowly exhaled. He turned round to me.

'Yo, Bones,' he said. 'You ever kill a guy?'

'Him?' Leon laughed. 'He couldn't kill a puppy.'

Scorpz kept staring, eyes cold now. 'No seriously, you ever wasted someone? Because far as I knew, rolling with this crew I thought that was a pre-requisite.'

Leon shook his head. 'Bones ain't even in the crew. He's just on training. Work experience, like someone who makes the fucking tea. But seriously though, that's fine, because the way I see it, it's stepping stones. One day at a time. You never know, the boy might just make a master criminal yet, ain't that right B?'

We drove into Chingford. Leon pulled over on a leafy street of semi-detached houses and turned off the engine. He pointed to a house across the road, a Merc and Beemer in the drive.

'That's the one,' he said. 'Right there.'

He had all the info. It was an Indian family with a stash of gold. Mum, dad, one son currently residing there. It would be simple. Ring the bell, take control and liberate the goods. The job was on for tomorrow night.

'What do you reckon?' Leon said, turning to me. 'Think you can handle it?'

I didn't really have a choice.

Later at my girlfriend's house the job was all I could think about.

'Are you alright?' Keisha asked as we sat up in bed.

I told her I was fine, but I wasn't. My mind was fretting. At the riots I might have thrown a few rocks at the police, did some naughty stuff, but this? Leon was bringing a loaded shotgun. This was something else. All I could see before me was prison, years and years of it this time. Some people could handle that kind of shit but I wasn't one of them.

'Are you sure you're okay?' she asked, snapping me from my thoughts.

'Yeah, course I am... come here,' I said, and for a while we kissed.

When she got on top for a second round I knew I'd better appreciate it, as this could be my last bit of intimate fun in quite a while.

In the flophouse Leon was pacing up and down, imparting his wisdom. He stopped to tap the side of his head.

'Intelligence man, that's the thing. This is next level crime we're carrying out here. Big, big earnings. You've got to be sharp, on the ball, you gotta use your brains for shit like this.'

He'd already filled us in on the plans and we had a re-plated car all lined up and ready to go. Finally he picked up the sawn-off shotgun, cocking it into action.

'Remember, I don't want to use this thing, but if I have to I will. And I'm not talking about on the job either, I'm talking afterwards. I'm talking about gossip. Nobody outside of this room knows anything about this job,' he said, turning his gaze to me alone. 'So if any leakage gets to the feds.'

'Come on Leon, you think I'm some kind of snitch?'

'Maybe not, but go round bragging to men and I'll get trigger happy, you understand what I'm saying?'

'I won't tell anyone, I swear it.'

He shouldered the gun and turned it on me, squinting one eye as he took aim. 'You better not or I'll shoot the head from your shoulders, you hearing me?'

'Okay, okay,' I said, raising my arms. 'Put the gun down.'

Scorpz was laughing, but Leon wasn't joking. 'Just remember what I'm saying.'

Power asserted he threw me some gloves and a balaclava.

'Right, all set. Let's hit the road.'

Driving to the target house my knees were shaking the whole way. Leon was at the wheel cool as ever, Scorpz next to him chewing gum and nodding his head.

'Shit, feds!' Scorpz suddenly said, losing his cool as we travelled the elevated North Circular at Edmonton. Blue lights were flashing in the distance, the traffic slowing.

'Calm the fuck down, it's just an accident.'

Nearing the scene, Leon was right. A mangled car lay blocking a lane, lights and cops guiding the flow.

Leon kissed his lips and turned to Scorpz with an evil eye. 'You been smoking?'

Reaching Chingford we headed through the neat suburban streets. Leon pulled in near the house and turned off the engine.

'Okay guys, everyone fit?'

We pulled on our masks.

'Right, let's hit it.'

We rang the bell. When the old guy opened up we burst through, Leon holding the shotgun to his face, backing him inside. His son, athletic and in his twenties, came rushing down the hall, followed by his mother, a stout woman in a coloured sari, all of them shouting in a mix of English and Punjabi.

'CALM THE FUCK DOWN!' Leon yelled, loudly cocking the gun.

Suddenly there was silence. Everyone stood still.

'Okay, now we can get down to business.'

He ushered the three of them into the front room and ordered the older guy to his knees. His wife and son started pleading and Leon shouted, 'I said down on your fucking knees!'

The man did as he was told.

'Now, you,' Leon told the son. 'Show my two boys where the gold is. Any funny moves, this guy dies.'

'What gold?' he said.

'Don't play games with me man, I'm serious,' Leon said, pressing the gun against his father's head. 'I'll use this thing, I ain't jestin.'

The guy said, 'It's upstairs.'

His mum began to wail in tears.

'You, shut the fuck up bitch and stop that blubbing.'

The son led me and Scorpz up the staircase.

'Get the fuck up there,' Scorpz tutted, pushing him. 'Frickin' pussy.'

In the bedroom the guy opened a drawer and pulled out a jewellery box. 'Here it is,' he said. 'This is all we've got.'

Scorpz inspected it, holding up several pieces. He laughed and swiped the whole lot to the floor. 'You think I'm a fool? This ain't the family gold, this is just cheapo Argos shit.'

He began rummaging through more drawers, then the wardrobes. Finally he grabbed the guy. 'I want the fucking gold man!'

'I swear to you, there's nothing here.'

Scorpz punched him to the floor, then started kicking him.

'Okay!' the guy said, putting his arms out. 'There is some gold...'

'Where is it?

'It's at my dad's workplace.'

'Your dad's workplace?'

'It's in his office, stashed in the safe. But only he knows the combination.'

Scorpz pulled him up. 'You better not be shitting me.'

The three of us headed downstairs. In the room the mother

was crying and pleading, and Leon shouting at her. The old guy was still on his knees, but clutching his chest now making a wheezing sound.

'He's got a heart condition,' the woman begged. 'He needs his medication, without it he'll die.'

'I said no-one's leaving this room,' Leon insisted, then to Scorpz: 'The guy's bluffing.'

Scorpz quickly explained things about the safe and the combination number, that if the old man keels over and croaks it we might as well leave. 'So let her get the meds Leon, come on. We need this guy.'

Scorpz escorted the mother to the kitchen. When they returned Leon was still holding the gun on him and she said, 'Get out of my way.'

We stood watching her apply an inhaler to his mouth, then feed him some tablets with a glass of water.

Leon kissed his teeth. 'Here, you take over,' he said, handing Scorpz the shotgun. 'I'm having a look round this place. I ain't convinced by all this shit.'

Just then I turned left and right and realised the son had disappeared, but Scorpz beat me to it. 'Leon, where's the young guy?' he said.

'Shit!'

We rushed out to the hallway. 'Where the fuck is he?'

Scorpz cocked his gun. 'This ain't looking good.'

We checked the next room, then the kitchen. Scorpz was beginning to panic. 'He's left the house, I just know it, he's getting help and that means we're fucked.'

'Shut up,' Leon told him.

We reached the back room and the light-switch wouldn't work. Leon paused for a second to gather his thoughts and I actually saw him gulp.

'Okay,' he said, 'let's not be too hasty with this...' And right then I knew what he was going to say next - Abort – because that's what he'd told us in the plans. No risks. One thing goes wrong then it's job over, we exit. No point getting a stretch of bird all because you ignored the danger signs. There's always more jobs, he told us, no shortage at all.

But he never got to say another word because just then from the dark doorway sprang the son, sword in hand, roaring as he thrust the blade clean through Leon's guts. He retracted the weapon and struck him again, this time across the neck, throwing him to the floor.

Scorpz jumped back in terror, gun trembling in his hands as he attempted to fire off a shot, but the sawn-off was jammed. The guy came straight at him.

I bolted for the front door and running down the garden path I could hear Scorpz's pained screams behind me. The man was really going to town on him. I raced down the street and didn't look back. I must have run a whole mile before I stopped by a wall to catch my breath. Jesus Christ. All I can say is I was in a state of shock.

Back home I went straight to my room. On my phone I kept checking the news. Sure enough it eventually popped up.

Breaking news: Two men have been killed during a burglary in Chingford, East London. It is believed they died from stab wounds after holding the residents at gunpoint. A man, 22, has been arrested. More to follow...

The man wasn't under arrest for long. In fact, he was released the next day and never faced any charges. You might have even heard about it, because the story made the headlines and created quite a debate, which these things always do. Questions about self-defence: should it be legal to attack/kill intruders in your own home? Or in this case, should you be allowed to disembowel and near behead one of them, then stab the other so many times that even his own family can hardly identify him on the slab?

As for the third youth involved, he was luckily never found. Not that I wasn't pulled in and questioned. But the police must have questioned every man Leon and Scorpz had known from year dot. They got nothing.

Since then I've changed my ways, my whole outlook. I could have been murdered that night. But all in all, the sword guy did me a favour. He got Leon off my back, and likewise a lot of pressure. Occasionally friends still say to me, 'Come on Bones, it was you there that night, wasn't it?' And once or twice I've maybe even cracked a hint of a smile, but I say nothing. My lips are sealed.

KO'd

Cathy has stopped answering my messages, so I have no choice but to go round there. I've been sleeping on a mate's sofa for too long and she's made her point, punished me enough. I was out of order being rough on her, but I've got my head together now.

She opens up in her bathrobe, shocked to see me.

'Easy Cath, I just want to talk.'

'Get away from me or I'll call the police,' she says, trying to close the door.

'Look, I haven't come for a row,' I say, when I hear a noise from inside.

We stop and stare at each other.

'You've got a bloke in there, haven't you?'

Again she tries to close the door, but I force it open and charge past her down the hallway. Sure enough, the bedroom door closes just in time and I hear the lock. By the time I've booted it open all I see is an empty room and an open window. Outside there's a drainpipe hanging off the wall and a man in white briefs running off into the distance.

'I'll rip your fucking head off,' I yell into the night.

I tear through the flat looking for Cathy but she has disappeared, so I return to the bedroom. With a roar I flip the bed and smash my fist into the wardrobe mirror. I soon end up on the floor in tears. First I lose my boxing career, then my marriage falls apart. What's happening to me?

When the police storm in I jump to my feet. I charge at them giving all I've got but before long I'm face down, cuffed and getting a kicking for good measure. As I'm dragged to the van, half the estate are out cheering and jeering and I swear to God I want to kill every one of them. I'm thrown into the back of the van yelling and kicking and with the cage door firmly closed the sergeant leans in for a word.

'If you don't shut your gob I'm going to ram my baton down your throat.'

'Fuck you pig,' I say bitterly, then I start to insult his family, the words coming out of my mouth pure filth.

Sure enough, back at the station they take it the whole way. I'm told that I'm facing charges for not only harassment of my missus, but assault on a police officer. I'm bailed the next day, but facing untold shit.

'Don't worry about it,' says Frank, finishing his pint. 'The most you're looking at is a fine I reckon.'

'With my record?'

'Yes, even with your record. You nicked a few cars, had a few scraps when you were younger. Hardly makes you Ronnie Kray, does it?'

'No, I suppose it doesn't.'

'I'll make some calls, get my lawyers onto it. The police assault charge will likely be dropped. They always try that old one. I'll see what I can do.'

I watch him head to the bar for another round. Frank is a good mate. A bit of a father figure if I'm honest. He was my cornerman in the ring on and off for years, has been inside, divorced three times, basically knows what he's talking about. Still, I'm worried.

'Just be thankful you didn't get your hands on the bloke,' he says, returning to the table with the drinks. 'Because then you really would be heading for the big house.'

I take a lug of my pint then place it back down.

'I'd say you're right,' I nod.

'You know I am. Now chin up, Trev. Women come, women go, you've got to accept that. And it's the same with anything - jobs, careers, money. Look at me, I've been rich, I've been broke. It's all about this,' he says, tapping the side of his head. 'Success, failure, it's all up here. You've achieved things. Ninety-eight fights in the ring. How many other blokes can say that?'

The next day he's off for three weeks in Marbella and I'll be looking after his flat for him. But on one condition: that I stay positive. And another: that I behave.

'I hope I can trust you on that,' he says.

'You've got my word,' I tell him.

After dropping Frank off at Stansted Airport I drive back down the M11 then head through the East End to Bethnal Green. I pull over within sight of York Hall, the place where it all started for me. My first pro fight against a hard hitter from Essex who'd had eight straight wins. I thrashed him. Since my teens, boxing had been a major part of my life. It was my way out. The big dream. Out of the backstreets of the Cally to somewhere that mattered.

But for me championship wasn't to be. Boxing pro I soon realised that fighting for titles wasn't worth it. Contending was all about flogging your own tickets, filling halls; it was more lucrative fighting in the away corner. Without big backing that was the truth and I could keep dreaming or accept it.

I got into the swing. Have gloves, will travel. Turn up, get paid, go home. And if it means letting the prospect win, so be it. I was fighting regularly, making money, and though I'd never be a champion I was doing what I loved doing. Jumping in the ring and putting on a show. Even with the shouts and abuse I felt alive. Felt life was worth living. Then just as I was looking forward to reaching my hundredth bout, I lost my licence and it was all over.

I'm about to drive off when there's a tap at the window. I turn to see the local Crombie-wearing spiv known as Billy Bother. He cracks a grin, revealing a full set of broken teeth. I let down the window.

'Trev mate, I thought it was you,' he says. 'How's things?'

'Could be better, could be worse.'

'I heard about your licence. But you can appeal you know. Plenty have.'

'Come on Billy, I failed a CAT scan, it's game over.'

'No way, you could train, do all sorts of things.'

'If you say so.'

Then out come the tickets. I was waiting for this bit. He tells me about a new prospect, fucking dynamite, the next Carl Froch, and he'd get me on the guest list but you know, business being as it is. How about a night out with the wife?

'What wife?' I say.

'Eh?'

'Nothing.'

I tell him I'm skint and the tickets go back in his pocket.

Then he says, 'You know what, you need cheering up. Have you seen any of the boys lately? Bonzo, Tommy and that lot?'

I shake my head. 'I've been keeping a low profile.'

'I'm going to phone Bonzo. You need a night out, to get out to a club or something, have a reunion with the boys.'

'No, I've got too much on my plate. My life's a bit of a nightmare at the moment to be honest.'

'Even more reason,' he says. He bangs the top of the car. 'Listen, I better run. But look after yourself. I'll be in touch.'

Driving back to Frank's empty flat in Finsbury Park, I think of all the messages I've received over the last few months, few of which I've answered. In truth I've been playing the self-pitying melt for too long. After all, maybe there are other options. And maybe a meet up with my old boxing mates wouldn't be a bad thing.

But fuck it. I'm not going anywhere. I'm just not in the mood for it.

What was sold to me as a few beers indoors between pals has escalated into a full-blown party. The flat is packed with mates, mutual friends, but mostly people I don't know from Adam. Johnny 'Bonzo' Bonham is the life and soul, cracking open the bubbly and wrapping his arm round me saying I might be a bit of a moody git on occasion but I'm one of a kind, so let's hear it for North London's finest, he shouts. Up goes a cheer.

Later in the kitchen he says, 'Have you seen some of the birds in here tonight?' while chopping out lines of charlie with a bread knife.

'Yeah, but are you sure everyone's sound?' I ask, noticing three more bods being let in through the front door. 'It's not my flat you know, it's Frank's.'

'No worries, I invited all sorts. Everyone knows me, relax,' he says, leaning down to sample his wares, then indicating for me to follow suit.

'Fucking hell,' I say, coming up holding my nostrils. 'This is some strong shit.'

'It's 89% pure. You can't get better. The gear on the street is 30-40% at most, if even that. This is shipped direct from the beautiful Columbian jungle.'

'How do you know all that?'

'Let's just say I've got insider knowledge.'

Just then his bird comes along, blonde, short skirt and heels. She kisses him on the mouth then leans down and gets snorting. He slaps her on the arse and she laughs, blows him a kiss and vanishes.

'The good life, Trev,' he says. 'I'm making more money now than I ever did in the boxing game. When I retired I went through some difficult shit myself. Obviously it's not the same thing, but it's not far off. A big part of your life has ended and you feel empty. Cheated too. I spent years being bashed around in the ring all for businessmen to make money off me. It wasn't their body taking the knocks, it was mine. And for what? You make big packets now and then but it's not as if you can put your feet up. I was pro for ten years and still driving a skip lorry. You're best out of it Trev. You had a long run, but that's all it can ever be, a run. Nobody can fight forever. It's not worth dying for.'

I can see his point, but only partly. I still miss it. Miss the buzz.

'Listen,' he says, hand on my shoulder. 'Any problems we're here for you, so don't be a stranger. If you're feeling down give us a call. Any of us.'

I follow his eyes to see Tommy and Declan standing there as if by magic.

'Come here you soppy cunts,' I say, group-hugging the three of them.

Back in the lounge everyone's chatting and dancing, and I get talking to this fit black girl. She's drinking red wine straight from the bottle and a little tipsy, but aren't we all. Her name is Ruby and she lives up the road.

'Are you a friend of Bonzo's?' I ask.

'Who?'

'Never mind,' I laugh.

'Someone told me you were a boxer,' she says. 'Are you a champion?'

'No. Journeyman.'

'What's that?'

'We're the bad boys of the sport.'

'I like that,' she smiles, leaning in.

We're smooching a bit to the music. Then kissing. Then she's asking if there's anywhere private we can take this.

I produce a key from my pocket. 'How does the master bedroom sound?'

We're on Frank's king-size bed going at it like dogs. I'm coked off my box and in all fairness it hasn't turned out to be a bad night. I'm getting my end away, praising the merits of a bit of optimistic thinking, when Ruby starts gagging, and suddenly she's puking over Frank's sheets. She wipes her mouth and tells me to carry on, don't stop, but it's killed the moment somehow.

Fuck this. I get off the bed, pulling on my clothes.

'What are you doing?' she says and rips the soiled sheets off the bed. 'There you go. It's a slight mishap, that's all.' Then she holds her mouth and hiccups.

'Look darling, you'd be best resting it off - but not on Frank Duffy's bed you're not.' I throw her clothes at her.

She stays put. 'I say you get back here and finish what you started, champion.' She leans sultrily back, trying to tempt me. But the moment's gone and my mood has turned sour.

'Er, I think I've had more than enough actually.'

Insulted she jumps up, putting on her dress.

'So I'm not good enough for you, no? Fucking prick.'

'I'm not in the mood for this.'

'Well fuck you then. Ugly bastard.'

'You know what?' I grip her by the arm and lead her out of the room. 'I think it's time you left.'

In the hallway there's an audience and she's struggling and shouting. 'You're not going to get away with this.'

'Save it for someone who cares.' I push her out the front door, slamming it closed behind her.

'What's going on?' says Bonzo.

'Just getting rid of the rubbish,' I say, wiping my hands.

Back in the main room everyone's happy and loud, but I'm not feeling it. Who are all these people? Someone squeezes by saying, 'Cheer up mate it might never happen', but he vanishes into the throng before I can give him a robust reply. I move through the room. There's a bloke asleep by the side of the sofa with puke down his shirt; three men talking loud about rugby; a bunch of girls dancing by the fireplace, one of them spilling wine on the floor. Then I spot something that makes me question if I'm hallucinating.

A bloke is standing yapping on his phone by the open window while casually pissing down into the garden below. I see red and grab him backwards. Then I hammer my fist into his face. Two men get hold of me and I throw them off. I make my way to the stereo. I pull the plug on the music and begin pushing people left and right.

'I WANT EVERYONE OUT NOW!'

I've lost the plot completely. Women are screaming and there's a rush to the exit. A bearded hipster-type urges me to chill, but I give him an almighty shove and he sees sense, heads the way of the others.

'And you lot can fuck off too,' I tell my mates.

'Come on Trev,' says Bonz, ever the leader. 'Sit down. Let's talk.'

I grab the neck of an empty wine bottle and tell him I'm not fucking about, and I'm still shouting when they're out on the street.

* * *

In the morning I wake up on the sofa with that horrible familiar feeling. What have I done? I phone each of the boys to apologise, but it's Bonzo who puts me most at ease.

'Shut up you silly prat,' he says. 'We've all been there, it's called being pissed.' We chat for a bit, small talk mainly, then he asks, 'How are you doing for money?'

'I'm doing fine,' I tell him.

'I bet you are,' he says.

Bonzo knows me well.

'Look, I've got some work going later in the week if you're interested. I'm not going to lie, it's not legit, but it's not exactly robbing a bank either. It's a bit of van work.'

'I can't risk it,' I tell him. 'Not at the moment. I'm in enough shit with the law as it is.'

'I understand. No worries. But think about it. Phone me any time.'

After a few days feeling sorry for myself in front of the telly, I give myself a kick up the arse and head out of the house. It's early afternoon and the Twelve Pins is quiet, but the barman knows his boxing and he's a good laugh as well. After a few I head over the road to the Blackstock. I play pool with a couple of Glaswegian builders bunking off work, then I sit at the jump talking to the barmaid.

Her name's Brianna and she's been over from Ireland for three weeks now. First time in London.

'What's your verdict then,' I ask. 'Shithole? That's the usual one.'

'Not at all. Limerick is much worse. More lunatics.'

'Are you sure about that?'

'So far, anyway. I like London. The men are better looking.'

'Really? Last time I looked in the mirror I had a face like a robber's dog.'

We're chatting away and there's a bit of chemistry there, but

I've still got Cathy on my mind. Which is silly because in reality our marriage was over months ago. From the day I lost my licence, to be precise. I got roaring drunk, and though she hit me first, I never should've hit her back; it was out of order. But I did and it changed things.

The barmaid finishes her shift and tells me she's off to meet her boyfriend. Fair play to her. To be honest, I'm done with women. Look at that farce in Frank's bedroom the other night. I sup up and leave the pub. I grab some notes from the cash machine, my bank balance in minus figures now, and decide to take the session down towards Holloway.

Passing the derelict remains of the George Robey, a homeless bloke asks if I can spare a quid and I pass him a fiver. Who knows, that could be me soon, pacing the streets or sitting in a hostel eating cold baked beans from a tin with nutters and drug addicts for company. Or worse, dead on the floor from a brain haemorrhage. But fuck it anyway. I head on. I stop into the Bedford Tavern, the Eaglet, the Enkel Arms. One pub to the next until closing. I end up in a dodgy little snooker club with some Arsenal faces I know, then it's 2am and whatever I've been snorting has woken me right up. Walking back home along Seven Sisters Road my head feels as clear as day.

I'm nearing the flat when two hooded figures step out from the shadows. Teenagers: one white, one black - the white bloke wielding a lump of wood.

'Come on then,' I say, spreading my arms out. 'What are you waiting for?'

The white prick comes forward swinging his timber. I duck, he staggers and a swift kick to the bollocks sends him squealing to the deck. His sidekick comes in fists flailing, shouting something about his cousin, but I bang him straight backwards and knock him to the ground just as he pulls a blade and it skids into the gutter. I'm about to kick the shit out of the pair of them, when the sound of a police siren puts me off and I run.

A few evenings later I'm walking along the road when I see Ruby from the party. She's head-down thumbing her phone and coming straight towards me. I stop in front of her.

'I think me and you need a word.'

One look at me and she's off. I chase after her down the street. She slips up a side passage towards some flats, but reaching the end the gate is locked.

I laugh, walking towards her.

'Come near me and I'll have you killed,' she says.

'You tried that already darling. It didn't work.'

Her gaze hits the floor.

'Listen. I admit, I was out of order the other night. I shouldn't have thrown you out. But you can tell your two male friends that any time they want to play, I'm willing. Because right now I'm not too bothered if I'm alive or dead so fucking bring it on.'

I toss a fag into my mouth, then on second thoughts I throw one over.

She catches it, and I lean in and give her a light.

After a few puffs she loosens up a little, looking at me quizzically. 'What do you mean you don't care if you're alive or dead?'

'That's quite something,' she says when we're sitting in the World's End and I've recounted my troubles. 'But life for me hasn't exactly been a bed of roses either.'

She shares her side of things. Growing up with an alky father, suffering an abusive relationship, then almost getting caught on a Barbados drug run which was the scariest thing she'd ever done, but never again. On a lighter note, it turns out we went to the same school and she knows my younger cousins.

Later, watching TV in Frank's bed, we have a good old laugh

about things. She tells me about the two mugs she set on me. Two local clowns from her flats. Not related and clearly good for nothing.

In the morning I wake up to see her getting dressed.

'Where are you going?' I ask, sitting up.

'Some of us have to work round here.'

'Where do you work?'

'Tesco, Stroud Green Road.'

'Oh right.' Then I say, 'Listen, are we going to see each other again?'

It sounds weird, but I think I'm in love. And love can make a man do strange things, because within a few days I'm taking up Bonzo's offer of work. I need cash fast because no woman is interested in a bloke who's skint, simple as.

Next day I'm driving a Transit van, sitting beside a pair of rough-looking ex-army bods who aren't into small talk. I turn off the A13 at Dagenham and head for the derelict power station. Finally I pull in opposite a black Audi where two Turkish-looking men stand waiting. I kill the engine. The scene is bleak and it feels like we're the only people around for miles.

'Okay Trev, here's the heavy bit,' says the squaddie next to me, eyes exuding an intense life-or-death attitude that does nothing to calm my nerves. 'The bit where it all might go off. Whatever happens, stay in the motor. And take this, just in case.'

They head out and I'm left holding a fucking handgun while they make the exchange. The whole thing is out of my league and I'm shitting it. Having a row is one thing, but this? Any second I'm expecting shots to go off or armed police to storm out from nowhere. When the squaddies return to the van I can't drive away fast enough. Back on the road they look at each other and burst out laughing.

'Your face when I gave you that starter pistol.'

'What?'

'You were cacking yourself mate. Listen, you've been shaking and sweating since the moment we set off. We've been winding you up!'

After that they seem like semi-normal half-decent blokes and we have a good old laugh, things less nerve-wracking. Over the next few days we do drops in Southampton, Ipswich, Lincoln, Milton Keynes. If I'm not in the van I'm minding Bonzo's scrapyard in Canning Town. It's almost like a nine to five except he's paying me decent money.

'Now you're on the team you might as well have this,' Bonzo says, chucking me a gold Rolex.

'Fucking hell, cheers Bonz,' I say, putting it on. 'Is it real?'

'Course not,' he laughs.

Even so, I'm chuffed.

Ruby, meanwhile, has moved into the flat, but within a week we're bickering like a married couple.

'Look at this place,' she says, snapping on the marigolds to attempt the five-day-old dishes. 'It's a mess and you do absolutely fuck all.'

'Listen, I'm out there earning.'

'And what do you think I do every day? You men are all the same, lazy and good for nothing.'

'Hey, relax,' I say, cuddling up to her. 'I'll treat you. Let's go out for a meal.'

She shrugs me off. 'Just get a takeaway and get the booze in, then you can make it up to me.'

Before long we're doing what we do every evening. Getting blotto in front of the telly.

Later in bed, I realise Frank is due back in three days' time, though maybe it could be two. I promised him I'd sleep in the box room, keep the place spotless and smoke outside, but I've broken all those rules and more. We'll have to get cleaning, do a rush job. We'll also have to find a place of our own.

Come morning we're still in bed when I hear footsteps in the hall. No way. The door bursts open and Frank is standing there livid.

I jump to my feet.

'Frank mate, I can explain...'

CHARLIE SAYS

'Did you get the money off him?' asks Dom as I walk through the door, planting myself down heavily on the sofa. He can see I've had no joy so I don't know why he's asking.

'Do I look like I got the money off him?' I say.

'Just tell me you did because that's our last chance. Benzo is the only fucker on this earth who owes us.'

'Well Benzo ain't even in the country now. At least that's what his bird said.'

'You what?'

'You heard me.'

'I don't get it. We saw him only yesterday. That's when he said he'd have that thirty quid ready for us.'

'Well yesterday ain't today, is it? He's gone to Amsterdam for the weekend. He got the ferry out this morning.'

'Great, so that's it then. We're skint. And I'm here clucking like fuck,' he says, shivering with his arms wrapped around him.

I pull a bottle of morphine sulphate out of my jacket. 'Well get a load of this – and stop moaning.'

Dom is beaming now. 'Whoa, Cheers Bri.' He unscrews the cap and takes a swig of the opiate-laden syrup. 'You should've told me. Who did you get this off?'

'I met Charlie on the way back,' I say. 'He also gave me this,' and I pull out a wad of cash. 'Two hundred and fifty quid.'

'What the fuck? You walk in looking like you're about to be cremated and you're loaded?'

I shake my head, returning the wad to my pocket. 'It's hardly free cash, is it?'

'What do you mean?'

'I mean - it's an advance. We're going to have to earn it.'

'But we've already got it. You just showed it to me. You've got it right there. A whole wedge.'

'Listen you plank. I agreed that we'd do a job.'

'What kind of job?'

'A job that isn't exactly easy or salubrious in any way, which is why in hindsight I shouldn't have agreed to it.'

'Well I'm glad you did,' and Dom takes another gulp of the syrup. 'We're rolling in it now.'

'Not exactly. I mean, it's not like it's going to last.'

'It'll last long enough for us not to have to worry about where the next wad comes from, so what's the worry? There I was stressing out of my mind, looking at the clock every minute you were gone when we're sorted here.'

'You don't know what Charlie wants us to do,' I tell him.

'It can't be worse than some of the stuff we've recently done, so to be honest I'm not that bothered.'

I shake my head, I've got no reply to that.

Then he says, 'What does he want us to do anyway?'

'He wants us to take somebody out.'

'He wants us to do what?'

I reach into my jacket and pull out the handgun Charlie gave me. 'He wants us to fucking shoot somebody.'

Dom looks shocked.

'You're not so unbothered now I see.'

'Is that thing real?'

'Of course it's real, he'd hardly give us a fake piece and tell us to ice somebody with it, would he?'

'*Ice* somebody?' Dom gulps.

Then a few seconds later he says, 'How much money did Charlie give you again?'

'Two hundred and fifty poxy quid.'

'And who is it we're supposed to be targeting?'

'Well, this is the part that worries me, that makes me wish I simply walked away and said no.'

'Who is it?'

'You're not going to like it.'

'I'll have to like it, there's not much choice now. Tell me.'

'Geordie,' I say. 'Geordie Woods.'

There's a moment of silence, then Dom shakes his head. 'No – no way.'

'Exactly. I'm glad we're on the same page.'

'You agreed to shoot Mark 'Geordie' Woods for two hundred and fifty minging quid?'

'I was desperate. Well, we were both desperate weren't we, you here clucking for a fix and all? You've been doing my head in all day about it. Why didn't you just go out and shoplift something? How come it's always me who has to bring in the readies?'

'I don't know why you agreed to this, Brian.'

'I did it for you, you cunt. How's that for an answer?'

'You've got to go back and tell Charlie the agreement's off.'

'I'll tell you what, why don't *you* go and tell him that, see how he reacts?'

'Charlie doesn't like me in the best of times. In fact, last time I saw him he knocked the fucking shit out of me.'

'He gave you a punch because you were begging off him. He doesn't like that. When he says no more credit, he means no more credit.'

'Well what are we going to do then?'

'We're going to have to keep to the agreement. Go around to Geordie's door and put one in him.'

'That's impossible.'

'How, when we've got a gun?' I take it out and wave it at him. 'We've got the tool right here.'

'Doesn't matter. We can't do it.'

'We can and we are going to do it. The both of us. We've already been paid.'

'Let's give the money back. I want nothing to do with this.'

'Too late. You've sank back half the bottle of morph he supplied. Now give it here.'

He passes it over and I take a soothing swig. Then another.

'We've got to return the money Bri,' Dom says to me. 'Tell him we're not the right men for the job.'

'Charlie is not going to accept that. Besides, we're in his good books now. He'll look after us, give us credit galore from now on. If we have to do a dodgy deed for him let's just make sure we do it professionally and don't get caught.'

'Professionally? I've never done anything professional in my life.'

'Well maybe it's time to start.'

'Me? I've fucked up everything I've ever tried. Back at school you were the clever one, not me. Then you were the one who got the postie job, up with the birds each morning, whistling as you walk. After leaving school the most I did was some labouring and it didn't last three weeks.'

'Three days more like. You told me you were so bad at mixing cement, the brickie said if you don't get it right this last time he'd stick his trowel up your arse.'

'That's exactly what happened.'

'What, he stuck his trowel up your arse?'

'No, he chased me off the building site wielding his trowel and that was the end of me.'

'Sounds about right, I suppose.'

'So what are we going to do then?' Dom says.

'I told you already. We're going to stick to the plan. You know what Charlie told me tonight? He said we were two trustworthy blokes and from now on he'd give us regular freebies, but on one condition.' I raise my finger for emphasis. 'Only if we complete the job.'

'Freebies? Must admit, I understand now how you got tempted.'

'Exactly.'

'But why does he want Geordie taken out anyway?'

'You know how long Charlie and him have been at loggerheads. They don't get on. This time Geordie dissed his girlfriend or something, and apparently it's not the first time.'

'His girlfriend, which one?'

'Hayley I think.'

'So it's not Mandy then? She's a looker. I remember back at school everyone fancied her.'

'Did they?'

'Yeah, she was well nice. Still is. Shame she's with Charlie though. She's got a kid by him, hasn't she?'

'Yeah, along with several of his other baby mums. I bet he raises his fists to the lot of them, the power-mad fucker.'

'I hope he doesn't beat Mandy. At school she was one of the very few girls that talked to me.'

'That's because you had bad hygiene. You didn't wash enough.'

'I still don't. But what does it matter now anyway. I'm a fucking junkie aren't I, so it's not like any girl's going to look twice at me these days, is it?'

'Stop feeling sorry for yourself. I don't like to hear all that.'

'Why?'

'Because you're my brother, that's why. It's not nice to hear your own brother talking like that.'

'It's the truth though, isn't it?'

'Well sometimes the truth is too much. Even for me.'

I pass him the bottle back.

'So what's going to happen then?' Dom asks.

'About the job?'

'What else?'

'We're going to plan the best way to get it done without leaving a single shred of evidence. That way we don't have to worry about doing a twenty-stretch in prison.'

'I'm not doing a twenty-stretch for Charlie or anyone.'

'Nor am I,' I tell him.

'But what I'm saying is, I'm not doing the job either.'

'You are doing the job,' I tell him.

'I've just told you I'm not.'

'And I'm saying I'll kick your fucking arse if you don't.'

'And I'm saying I'll retaliate and fuck you up if you try it.'

I laugh at that. 'Fuck me up - you?'

'You heard me.'

'Have you gone fucking batshit? You've never beat me in a fight in your life.'

'Doesn't mean things can't change.'

'Look at you. You couldn't run to the end of the street without getting out of breath. Ten seconds in and you'd be reaching for your inhaler saying you're about to die.'

'I can't help it if my health is all messed up. Times have been hard, I haven't had an easy life.'

'Yes you have. Mum always treated you way better than me. I had to get up and go to school every day, rain snow or shine, while half the time you stayed at home watching TV, keeping her company, a nice cup of tea in your hand, warm and snug.'

'That's because I was ill so often.'

'Ill my foot. You're just lazy.'

'No I'm not.'

'Yes you are. Who had to run out of Tesco arms-loaded the other night all to have two African security guards try to rip my limbs off?'

'You just told me. You.'

'Exactly. Muggins here. Always me.'

'I do plenty of grafting out there. I got all them shaving goods from Sainsbury's the other day.'

'Two weeks ago more like.'

'I do my bit. When I can, that is.'

'Yeah, course you do.'

'But anyway, about Charlie,' he says. 'You'll just have to ring him up and pull out of it. There's plenty other ways we can make some quick dough.'

'Go on then,' I say. 'Enlighten me.'

'Shove on a balaclava and rob a shop.'

'What shop?'

'An off licence, a grocery or whatever.'

'A big lucrative payout then?'

'Exactly.'

'I'm being sarcastic. These shops hardly even have any paper cash these days. And for an armed shop holdup you're looking at six years inside, maybe seven or eight. And if you mean me on my own then I'd be outnumbered by staff, and we're talking immigrants who aren't scared of a fight.'

Dom shakes his head. 'Do you know what your problem is?'

'Go on then, I'm all ears.'

'You're not ambitious. Nothing's worth it, every idea's pointless.'

'You can flippin' well talk. You've never got off your arse in your life.'

'As I say, I've got health complaints - and mental health

issues.'

'I definitely agree with that last one.'

'I suffer from anxiety. Do you know how debilitating an affliction that can be?'

'Duh. I get anxiety every time I have to go out earning your crack and smack.'

'Not just mine, yours too.'

I shake my head. 'You go through way more than me, you always have.'

'So I'm the junkie crackhead and you're mister clean?'

'That's not far wrong. I dabble to be sociable, that's about it. For you it's a lifestyle thing.'

'So is that why you lost your job with Royal Mail then? Because you smoke to be sociable?'

'Not exactly, no.'

'Oh, I was just wondering why you aren't delivering letters anymore?'

'Because my supervisor was a cunt, that's why.'

'Also because he found your crack pipe in your locker.'

'He shouldn't have been looking in my locker. Everyone deserves some privacy, even a nine-to-five wage slave.'

'It was more like six in the morning to four in the afternoon, wasn't it?'

'Whatever. I'm not talking to you anymore. You're a cunt.'

'So much for brothers then.'

'Yeah, so much for brothers.'

My phone goes. I pull it out and read the message.

'Shit,' is my instant reaction.

'Who is it?'

'Who do you think?'

'Is it Charlie?'

'Yes. Asking if we're all set for the job.'

'You mean he wants us to do it tonight?'

'Why do you think I'm so pissed off?'

'You better fob him off. Tell him tomorrow night would be more suitable. Anything.'

'Me again, always me? We're in this shit together.'

'Just do it. We can't have a nightmare like this hanging over us tonight. By tomorrow we'll have thought of a good excuse to get out of it.'

'Okay, listen. I'll tell him we'd prefer to do it tomorrow. I'll say you're too bad with the asthma tonight.'

'Good idea. And it's not as if you're lying.'

I text him. *Dom is ill. Bad with asthma. Tomorrow night will be better. We'll both be fighting fit for the job.*

Instantly he replies: *Tell your fool brother if he thinks he can swerve this I'll get my boys to cut off his head and leave it out for the crows, you feeling me?*

'Oh crap.'

'What did he say?' Dom asks.

'You really don't want to know.'

'I do, so tell me.'

'Basically he said no.'

'In what fashion?'

I show him the phone. He reads the message, eyes widening with each word.

'Don't act all surprised Dom, you know what Charlie's like. He's an intolerant fucker. He doesn't give an inch.'

Dom sits back looking deflated. 'So that's it then.'

'What do you mean?'

'We're one hundred per cent fucked.'

'That's exactly what I've been thinking since taking money and a bottle of meds off the prick.'

'You shouldn't have taken fuck all.'

'Right, and return home to watch you going through cold turkey?'

'It's not just me, you were desperate yourself.'

'Not true.'

'It is fucking true.'

'Whether it's true or not is a moot point. We're going to have to pull our socks up tonight, get round to Geordie's and put one in him, I'm telling you now.'

'No way. Geordie is a hard bastard. He's friendly enough but when he's angry it's no laughing matter. If he opens his door and grabs the gun from your hand he'll batter you to a pulp.'

'I know that. But what am I supposed to do?'

'There is something,' Dom says.

'What?'

'We could always sub the job out.'

'To who?'

'Fingers or Juicehead or one of them lot.'

'Those wasters wouldn't know how to hold a gun let alone shoot straight. They'd end up shooting themselves.'

'You don't know that. They'd definitely agree to it. For two fifty in the hand, people like that would agree to anything.'

'That's right, they'd agree then simply spend the cash and sell the gun and we'd be back to square one.'

'There's got to be someone we could sub it to?'

'There isn't.'

Then Dom flicks his fingers. 'I've got it.'

'Who?'

'Marie.'

'Mad Marie? Are you off your fucking box?'

'She killed her husband, didn't she? Pushed him down the stairs after years of getting battered. The judge and jury let her off and everything.'

'So what?' I say.

'That means she's got experience. Means she isn't scared to kill and knows how to get off the rap when she does.'

'You've got a point there, I suppose.'

'It's the perfect idea. She'd probably even enjoy it. Remember the time she bashed One-Ear over the head with a brick after he nicked her stash. He was slumped there leaking blood and she was laughing at him. To Marie, putting a bullet in Geordie would be like a walk in the park. He lives just up her road as well, they're practically neighbours.'

'True enough.'

'Give her a bell, go on. Tell her there's two hundred in it.'

'Only two hundred?'

'Of course. We'll keep the fifty for more supplies.'

'And you think she'll agree to it?'

'I'll bet you a can of Skol Super she'll agree to it.'

'Alright. I suppose it's worth a try.'

I message her. *Want to earn two hundred smackers tonight? A job involving a gun. Can't tell you more unless you agree.*

Half an hour passes.

Then another half an hour.

We're sitting in front of the telly waiting but there's no reply.

'She's not interested,' I finally say. 'We're out of luck. Even Mad Marie isn't crazy enough.'

Just then my phone goes. It's her.

'You want me to shoot Geordie?' she says before I can even say hello.

'How the hell did you know?'

'Charlie told me he's paid you two to take him out.'

'He told you that?'

'It's hardly a secret,' she says. 'Charlie and Geordie have been locking horns for the past year.'

'So what do you reckon then? Do you want to do it?'

'Not sure. Why are you passing the buck?'

'Because you've got form with this type of thing and we haven't.'

'I've got form? What's that supposed to mean?'

'You killed your husband, so compared to us that makes you a dab hand.'

'You what? Like fuck I killed my husband. He had an accident, he fell down the stairs.'

'Come on Marie, you were on remand for it. Everyone knows you killed him. You've admitted it enough times when you've been off your head so come on, yes or no?'

'You're a prick Brian, do you know that?'

'Yes I do, so what's the answer?'

'The answer is... okay, I'll do it.'

'Thank fuck, I was hoping you'd say that. So should we go round yours to hand over the tool for the job?'

'No need. I don't use guns. I've got a more appropriate tool in my kitchen drawer.'

'You're going to stab him?'

'For two hundred and fifty quid I'll carve his heart out if you want,' she laughs.

'Well that's the thing. We were thinking of making it a square two hundred. We need the rest as we're skint.'

'No deal. If you're broke that's your problem. The contract is for two fifty. Charlie says.'

'Okay, if you insist, two fifty it is.'

'Bring it round to my gaff pronto. I'm talking right now.'

'Hang about, we want the job done first. Then we'll hand over the money.'

'Are you saying you don't trust me?'

'I trust you alright, but what if you run off and spend the cash on drugs? Then I'll have trusted you and been wrong.'

'Spending it on drugs is exactly what I intend to do. I'm clucking right now. If I don't get some gear into me I won't be able to hold a knife let alone commit murder with it. So bring me the cash, no delay.'

'Okay, will do.'

She hangs up.

'So are you going to bring it round to her then?' Dom says.

'No, *we* are going to bring it round.'

We grab our shit and hit the street.

Walking along Dom's teeth are rattling.

'What's wrong with you?' I ask.

'I need more sorting out – the real deal. You'll have to give her only two thirty. We need the rest for gear.'

'Marie won't relent, she's a stubborn bitch.'

'Maybe she'll give me some of her gear then, after she buys it.'

'Maybe. If not don't worry, we'll sort something out. Let's just get this transaction done.'

Reaching her block, she buzzes us in. We head up the stairs and she's waiting for us at her flat door.

'You got all the cash?' she asks as we head inside.

'Every penny.'

In the living room we halt at the sight before us. Sitting there with his curly mullet and tash, jumper and faded jeans, fashion sense circa 1986, is Geordie himself.

'Alreet lads,' he smiles as he casually rolls a fag.

'What the fuck is going on?' I say, turning to Marie.

'Sit down and do not be alarmed,' she says. 'I'll explain everything. But first,' and she holds out her hand: 'Money.'

I pass it over and we sit down, Dom next to me white as a sheet at this new state of affairs.

Geordie begins to speak but Marie says, 'Leave it to me,' and takes over. 'Now here's the lowdown. Geordie knows all about what Charlie's got planned, so we're going to turn the tables. Turn the situation back onto Charlie himself. He's been getting too cocky lately, causing all kinds of problems for a lot of people, so we're taking him off the street.'

'You're going to kill Charlie?' I ask.

She nods. 'Now you're getting the gist.'

'But hang on a minute, Charlie is connected. He knows people. He'd murder the four of us if he could.'

'Not if he's lying in the morgue he can't.'

'True, but how are you going to kill him without anyone else knowing? If his boys find out we're all brown bread.'

'They're not going to find out,' she says and points to Geordie. 'Because this man here is going to put a knife in his heart.'

'That's right Marie,' he says, licking his roll-up. 'Couldn't have put it better myself. Anyone who thinks they can get my own good friends to turn on me,' and he nods to me and Dom, 'is not going to survive the night, put it that way.'

'Well said, Geord,' Dom pipes up, sucking up to him now. 'Charlie was out of order telling us to do that. I mean, what a prick.'

This new situation isn't making a lot of sense to me. And has Geordie really got the balls to take a gangsta like Charlie out? Then I remember the time Geordie pulled a knife on a man during a fight, slashed him up pretty bad, then afterwards stood pissing down on his writhing body, laughing like a loon. With this memory in mind it's suddenly not too difficult to imagine him taking things a step further.

'So you're actually going to do it?' I say, needing to hear the fact reiterated.

'I certainly am,' he replies. 'Charlie boy's time is up, I can assure you on that score.'

'And there's a bonus,' Marie smiles, waving the wad of readies. 'All of us get to sit back and have a nice long celebration.'

A cheer goes up, everyone including me happy with that. The idea of Charlie not being around anymore *and* having an evening on the pipe is something I can't dispute.

'Yep,' Geordie says. 'Don't worry your heads lads, I'll sort him out. He called me a fucking whiteboy northerner the other day, taking the piss out of my accent, trying to impress the other black fellas he was with, can you believe it? From tonight onwards you'll have no more worries from the wanker. Good riddance, that's what I say. His supplies are crap anyway, cut with absolute shite. There's much better dealers out there.'

Marie makes a call and a courier arrives with a stash of crack and heroin. The party begins and we're pulling on pipes, getting high, laughing at crazy cartoons on the TV. At one point I notice Geordie spread back in his chair looking like he's settled in for the evening, and I say, 'So are you sure you're going to do him tonight then?'

'He certainly is,' Marie answers for him. 'So come on Geord, don't you think it's about time you got a move on?'

He puts down his crack pipe and lifts himself up off the chair. 'Yeah, no time like the present, I suppose.'

We watch him check his pocket for his blade, then make for the door. 'Mission on. I'll be seeing you boys and girls later.'

'Good luck,' Marie says.

'No need,' he replies, showing the crucifix on the chain outside his jumper. 'I've got God on my side.'

He laughs and leaves the flat.

Hours go by as we smoke more crack and watch blooper shows on TV. Time, reality and consciousness can play tricks when you're on the gear, and at one point I see Geordie back on his chair sucking on his pipe and realise he must've returned at some point. Everyone else is staring avidly at the mad antics on the screen, Dom guffawing as a dog in a spider suit chases a man through a subway.

'Hey Geord,' I ask. 'What's the score with Charlie?'

He takes a sip from his can of Kestrel Super and looks at me with a satisfied grin. 'You should've been there man. It was beautiful. I've wanted that wanker out of the picture for many a moon, I can tell you now.'

'So you actually did him?'

'I did indeed. He's no longer walking among us. I got him straight in the solar plexus. Bang, take that you twat,' miming the stabbing motion. 'Loved every moment of it.'

Marie cuts in, 'He had him down on his knees begging and saying sorry, didn't you Geord?'

'Certainly did lass. The cunt was crying and pleading for his life. It wasn't Charlie's lucky day I'm afraid. Not once I stuck an eight-inch zombie knife through his ticker.'

Everyone laughs and I'll be truthful, the sense of relief at this news is something else. No more Charlie. No more threats, insults and bullying from the bastard. I'd been worried earlier, fretting away thinking I'd got us into a right pickle. Now I feel like throwing my arms in the air with delight.

'So where did you do it?' I ask. 'Did you get him on his own?'

'He was waiting down the alley behind the shops, expecting Marie to turn up for a buy. You texted him, didn't you love, said you were on your way. Then who turns up and jumps out on the fucker?' he laughs.

'I told you,' Dom smiles, turning to me, high as a kite. 'There was nothing to worry about after all Bri, but you didn't listen.'

My memory slightly differs on that, but what the hell. I tell him it's a weight off my back and that's all that matters.

The crack supply runs out, leaving everyone a little worse for wear. Then the smack gets introduced and we're busy chasing the dragon, levelling things off. With Pink Floyd's 'Dark Side of the Moon' LP on rotation it's chillout time.

I wake up many hours later. Marie is poking me saying it's time for us to go home. Geordie has already gone. I shake Dom awake and we're both sitting up on the sofa feeling well rough.

Marie puts two cups of lukewarm coffee in front of us.

'Two minutes lads. Sorry but my mum is due for a visit any minute now.'

'No worries,' I say, taking a thankful sup.

'Marie,' Dom says. 'You couldn't sort us out with a small bit of gear could you, hair of the dog kind of thing?'

'Kidding aren't you? We caned the full two fifty. It's gone, the whole shebang. The party's over I'm afraid.'

'Take no notice of him Marie, we're grateful for you bringing us in.'

'I know you are love – but come on, chop chop, the two of you.'

We head out, eyes squinting in the painful daylight, traipsing the streets wishing we were home.

We're almost there, one minute from our gaff, when behind us a car door slams.

'Yo!' a voice says. 'I've got a bone to pick with you two.'

We turn to see Charlie standing there alive and well.

'I've been texting you for fucking time,' he says to me. 'How come you've ignored my messages?'

I'm shocked and confused, but I check my phone and the power is dead.

'Er… my battery's gone,' I say, holding it up.

'Fuck your phone,' he says, stepping closer, gold teeth snarling. His words are quiet but firm. 'If you don't complete that task we agreed on then heads are going to roll round here man. Nothing's free in this life Bri, and you and your fool brother are going to have to earn that wedge of dough I kindly put in your pocket. You understand me?'

I hear a low hissing sound, and look down to see Dom is wetting himself.

ON THE ROADS

Rocks could stare at the scene for no longer. He stood up.

'No, this shit's too fucked up for me, I'm out of here.'

He made for the door but Monsta put a heavily bicepped arm out to stop him. 'Start all that pussy running away shit and I'll slap you, you hear me?'

Rocks kissed his teeth and slumped back down on the sofa next to Natmare and Phats - Teefman over on the other seat puffing on a stick of weed.

'And that goes for the lot of you,' Monsta continued, eyeballing each of them with the mean stare of a gangsta who'd just killed a guy stone dead on the floor. 'We're all in this shit together, and until we find a solution to this matter that's the way things stand. You listening to me? So start exercising those brain cells or I'm going to start getting angry round here.'

Rocks swallowed as Monsta's eyes lasered into his. 'I'm already pissed off with one fucker here... yeah... but I'll deal with that dick later.'

Shit. Rocks wished he'd just stayed in tonight. Stuck indoors listening to his mum and sister nagging, anything... the body spread out on the floor before them.

'Hey,' said Natmare. 'If feds catch a whiff of this shit we'll be heading down Feltham way quicktime. Fucking lifers.' Laughing as he passed the skunk to Rocks. But Rocks wasn't smiling. He didn't want to hear crap like that. Being sent down was no laughing matter.

Earlier Monsta had said he had some business to sort with a guy called Juju and wanted some of the younger crew along for the show. He said he had some minor beef with him, but it was nothing, just routine. But when Juju answered his door Monsta charged through hitting him hard. Bam bam bam. Then he was shouting at him to get his arse off the floor, but Juju wasn't moving. Blood pooling round his head where he'd cracked it off a side table.

Monsta sent Teefman out to jack a car, which he did promptly. He parked it outside the block and phoned up. A spanking new Beemer. 'Can you believe this shit?' remarked Natmare. 'That new yuppie estate is becoming like a free supermarket. Go in there and take your pick, bare wealth being spread round the community.'

But now was the hard bit. They had to get the body down twenty floors without anybody noticing.

'Yo!' Monsta appeared with a duvet and ordered everyone to their feet. He got them to roll up the body. 'Come on, chop fucking chop, let's see some work done round here.'

With Juju rolled up nice and snug they gathered by the front door, checking the communal corridor left and right. 'Okay - quick.' They carried him into the lift. Counting the flights... come on, come on... until halfway down it stopped and the doors flew open. What the fuck? An old foreign guy standing there expecting to step in.

Monsta pushed him back: 'Use the fucking stairs.'

'But I have bad leg!'

'I said use the stairs or you'll have two bad legs.'

Jeez... they continued on. 'Okay, all clear.' They carried the body out to where Teef stood in a pose next to the open boot, and slung it in. 'Right,' said Monsta, checking the coast for any prying eyes. 'Let's roll.'

Phats stood running his hands over the bodywork entranced.

'Wow, this Beemer's the dog's knob bro.'

'Yeah yeah, get in.'

Monsta sat up front next to Teefy at the wheel. Off they went.

'So where are we dumping him?' asked Phats.

'We ain't dumping him, thickshit, we're burying him.'

'Oh right, but where?'

'Epping Forest. Nuff dead bodies up that way. Now there's gonna be one extra, you get me.'

After a bit he said, 'Yo, pull into those streets there.'

'But this ain't the forest,' Teef said, confused.

'Don't care, pull in.'

They stopped by a set of quiet semi-detached houses.

'Rocks, get yourself out of the car.'

'Me?'

'Yeah you, get your arse into a shed or some shit, we'll be needing tools for this job, shovels and that. And Phatboy, you go with him.'

They got out, Phats looking at the houses, entranced: 'Look at these cribs bruv. Bare wealth. One day I'm gonna live like this man.'

'Yeah well, come on,' Rocks said, helping him over a side fence, into a back garden.

They hurried down to the shed, Rocks working on the lock as Phats kept watch... Done... He passed a spade and took a fork for himself. Then a dog started barking in the next garden. 'Let's go!' They ran for the fence, Phats struggling over until the whole thing came crashing to the ground. Shit! Lights went on, someone shouting from a window. Rocks helped him up, grabbed the tools and they dashed for the car.

All in, they hit the road. Man... Both were leaning back out of breath and Monsta laughing away. 'You two crack me up.' He put his fist out to them. 'Nah, safe though, you got the job done.'

They journeyed on. By some lights Monsta eased down his window and smiled at some girls outside a chip shop. The girls all smiling back and blushing and shit: Monsta showing teeth and nodding away... 'Yeah, check this, they're well impressed.'

'Hey, Teef,' he said as the car cruised on. 'You remember this spot yeah, cos once we're done I'll be stopping off to collect me one of those bitches. So you pricks in the back will have to budge up or hit the road cos I'll be spread out back there, you listening? Yeah, have one of those bitches sucking on the end of my dick. Buff up my bone, you get me,' he said, hand adjusting his crotch with a snigger. 'That's right, ram it down her fucking throat.'

'Shit, Feds!' said Teef.

To the left a police car was stalled right there next to them. Two of the pigs staring straight in.

Monsta smiled, did a little wave...

'No, don't!' everyone stressed.

Monsta turned. 'Shut your teeth, I'm just being friendly. Act all bad and these racist fucks will definitely want to pull us. Chill!'

But Rocks could see their unimpressed faces and was waiting any second for the dreaded signal to pull over. Then suddenly the cops turned away - a miracle - put their siren up and revved off.

'See?' Monsta said. 'Pussies the lot of you. It's not like we're the only badmen in town, is it? Bare thugs on the prowl, even up in these wannabe ends. I'm sick of you lot... Gimme that,' he said, snatching the spliff off Natmare. 'Vexing me up to the hilt.'

Passing some road works they were forced to slow down, a policeman standing in the road directing traffic. Monsta kissed his teeth.

'Look at that. Fed's a fucking blood, man. Well, half a blood anyway,' he said, shaking his head in disgust. 'Pig should be capped, blow the fucker away, boom.' Then Monsta's eyes met Rocks's in the rearview. Those eyes man: cold.

'Hey Rocky,' he said as the car moved on. 'You only half-black innit? Fucking halfie, ain't that right? White blood running through your veins, that's why you be a pussy.'

Rocks turned to the window, tried to ignore the prick but he kept on taunting. Then Phats spoke out to defend him. 'That's out of order,' Phats muttered. But somehow it sounded loud. Too loud.

'Fuck you, you fat fucker, I'm talking to Rocks so shut your mouth before I mash it up for you!' He swiped for his face but Phats moved back. 'Tsss.' Then he turned to Rocks.

'Now what was I saying? Oh yeah. You might be a pussy but your sister's not bad though. I seen her the other day, carrying her books and shit. She's a right goody two shoes. Don't like to talk to the bad boys. But she got the looks, man. Yeah. And I like my coffee that way. Lots of cream and ting.'

Rocks was silently boiling up, then Monsta started laughing.

'I'm joking! You thought I was serious? Nah, I'm just testing you. But guess what? You came out on top. You kept it all inside… I like that. Shows you're wearing a real coat of armour. And you need that for this life, believe me.'

'So listen up, all of you,' he continued. 'I might say shit but I don't always mean shit, you understand me? I'm just hardening you up for the road. That's my duty. If you want to be real soldiers you gotta take the rough to get tough. You'll thank me one day, guaranteed.' Everyone nodding their heads except for Rocks. Guy talked nothing but bull.

'Look at that!' Natmare said, pointing out a group of girls walking along, all short skirts and orange tans. Natmare and Phats were in awe.

'Yeah fam, nice...'

'They're hot, I like that…'

'Rah, I'd bang all of them in one go.'

'Listen to them wanking pricks back there,' Monsta tutted. 'Dreaming. You two have never even had any pussy. And I'm talking ever. Only ever sucked dick, ain't that right, Natmare and Fatty Boy? You'd run a mile if you even seen sight of a real pussy. Only ever seen the ones on your phones when you're wanking together like a couple of batties.'

'I ain't no virgin!' Natmare tutted. 'Nuff pussy been round my dick and nuff times.'

Monsta turned quicksharp: 'You being facety you little dickhead? You're talking to an elder here. Experienced in the world, living on my wits alone, living on the edge, you hear me? You lot are fucking lucky tonight. Privileged getting an education like this. You should be calling me sir on this job. Yes sir no sir, three bags full of shit sir... Jeez.'

For a while they watched the world going by. Checking the female scenery. Checking for other mandems and that. Eyeballing a couple of bro's in a GTi trying to look all badass until they caught sight of the BMW and Monsta's demon eyes.

'You see that?' Monsta said, perking up. 'Bruthas know not to fuck.'

'Yo breds, check that,' Natmare said as a slim brunette clicked along, head-high in a business suit. Asian or something. Looked moneyed.

'That's my kinda thing,' Monsta stated. 'See that and take note. Class. Not like you lot, chasing round cheap little skanks on the estate. I'm sophisticated. Man of the world innit. Different flavours. I like to multiculturalize in the sack,' toking hard on a spliff and thought threading fast. 'Taste the whole menu. I'm global man. World player. Peace and harmony between the sheets and ting... until I get my dick out that is.

Because then the bitch always screams out in fear cos it's so fucking big. That's why they call me the Monstaman, because I make 'em screech! AAAHH, HA HA!... But listen up, what they should call me is Snakeman, cos when I'm pumping some bitch in the pussy it goes so far up I'm surprised it don't come out her mouth... Yeah!' - clicking his fingers in the air, impressed with his own wit. 'Ain't that for real?' Other voices laughing along.

Soon they approached the forest. They took the car along a quiet lane and turned in until they were deep in the woods. Stepping out of the car the air was misty, full moon shining through the trees, the whole deal.

'Right bluds. You got your tools, now dig.'

Monsta and Teefman leaned by the headlit bonnet smoking blow, while the others got stuck in.

'I want to see six feet at least. In fact, yo, make that ten. I want this fucker buried deep, you hear me. Deep! Want all the worms and maggots to have a feast down there tonight... Want to see you working off all that lard and grease your mothers serve up to you. Cos you lot still clutching those apron strings for real. Specially you Phats, work off those man-tits!' Laughing as he passed the spliff to Teef: 'I should have brought a whip with me man, get some progress out of these three.'

'Yeah I know,' Teefy said, shouting over. 'Come on, work that ting! Fucking pussies...' Thinking he was well in with the Monstaman, top Gs together and that, looking down at the minions sweating away.

Then Monsta turned and looked at him hard.

'What, blud?' Teef said, suddenly worrying he'd overstepped the mark.

Monsta looked him up and down, creasing his eyes: 'You be resting enough. Now get that body out of the boot and help these fuckers.'

'Yeah sure man, no probs,' he said, handing back the spliff

and heading round to the back of the car.

Teef lifted up the boot.

Then something inside grabbed him round the neck...

Monsta heard the boot slam down. 'Hurry up, bring that body here...' Seconds passing... 'Teefy! I said bring that pussy body round here!' – kissing his teeth. He turned. 'You not answering me you fu..?' Suddenly he screamed in shock: 'AAHHH!!'

It was Juju. He was standing there. Alive. Pointing a gun at him. An open gash on his forehead and his face smudged in blood.

'No...' Monsta put out his hands. 'No man, please...'

'Shut up nigga!'

By the grave all three diggers turned and were stunned motionless.

'You three, carry on working!' Juju shouted, not taking his eyes off Monsta who was quivering at the mouth, hands in the air.

'I don't get it, you're d-d-dead!'

The Juju-man smiled and widened his eyes. 'I know I am. I be the LIVIN' dead, star. Your LIVIN' NIGHTMARE,' he laughed. 'You tried to waste me. But let me tell you this, nothing can kill me, no-one, you listening? Plenty men have tried, but I be like a messiah innit. I RISE, BLOOD, RISE! No fucker on this earth can kill me!... now as for you, it be your lucky day, because you're gonna take my place in the grave... I'm burying you alive nigga!'

Rocks, Phats and Natmare were digging more frantically than ever, Rocks without a tool and shovelling dirt with his hands. All of them panicking, knowing this hole was likely to be the first of several.

Phatman began sobbing as he worked his fork. 'I don't want to die like this. I don't want to die...'

'Look,' Rocks tried. 'Keep it together, there might be a way out of this.'

Phats was inconsolable. 'What are you on about? We're gonna die, we're digging our own graves.'

'That's deep enough!' Juju called over. 'Now get out of there and stand in a line. I'll deal with you fucks in a minute.'

'Okay,' he said, turning to Monsta and pointing his gun. 'You fucked with the wrong mutha tonight... the wrong fuckin' mutha... NOW GET IN THERE!'

'No man, no...' Monsta said, arms out, pleading.

'I said get the fuck in.' Juju pistol-whipped him and pushed him towards the grave. 'You're getting buried alive, I swear it.'

'Please, I never meant it... it was those pussies, it was them!'

'Shut the fuck up,' Juju said and kicked him down into the hole. He turned to the boys. 'Now fuckers, get to work and bury this shit.'

They began piling the earth over him. Monsta clutched a twisted ankle, crying and pleading. 'No, please,' he begged, the soil filling fast. 'How can you do this to me? I'll kill you. All of you! Ahhhh...!'

Juju stood over him smiling and waving, 'Bye bye bye,' he said as Monsta's face disappeared.

Once the earth was levelled Juju yelled, 'Now down them tools!'

He was leaning against the car bonnet, silhouetted in the lights.

'Right... now stand in a line so I can see you all,' he ordered.

He looked rough. Every now and then clutching his bloody head in pain.

Suddenly a knocking sound came from the boot.

'Wait there,' he told them as he went around to open it.... BAM!!! A shot cracked out and birds flew out of the trees. Juju slammed the boot back down.

'Sorry about that,' he smirked, wiping Teefy's blood off his gun. 'Little interruption there.'

Natmare and Phatman turned to Rocks for an answer, but what could he say?

'Now,' Juju said, inspecting them as they stood there in a line. 'Which one of you pussies wants to die next?'

'Me!' Phats broke the silence. 'Just do it! Get it over with!'

'Oh right,' Juju said, nodding his head as if impressed. Then he said, 'Well you die last then. I'll make sure of that.' Smiling as Phats broke into a fit of sobs.

'How about you?' he said, pointing the gun at Rocks. 'What have you got to say on the matter?'

Rocks looked at him and found himself summoning up some front. Where from he didn't know.

'Do what you have to do,' he shrugged.

Raising his eyebrows Juju looked him up and down. 'I like that,' he said.

Then he moved on. He trained his gun on Natmare. 'How about you, pussy?'

Nat flinched and shook his head, speechless.

'I seen you before, yo,' Juju continued. 'You're the one they call the Nightmare boy, ain't that right? Well, now you know what a real one is like.'

He fired his gun: BAM!!! – taking off the top of his head, brains spraying three-sixty. Nat's body dropped backwards like a dummy.

'Ha! You see that? I'm loving this, man, loving it!... Now who's next?'

Phatman was wailing away, wiping Natmare's brains out of his eyes... 'No, spare us, please.'

'Ah,' Juju came close, cocking his head. 'You change your tune boy. One minute you want to take the bullet, next you don't.... Look at you,' he said, getting angrier. 'You're like a big baby. Big batty baby! But earlier you thought you were a big man, wanting to bury me in the shit… Me? THE FUCKING JUJU MAN!'

He fired the gun, opened up Phat's arm. Phat clutched his bicep, screaming in pain.

'Look at you man! You call yourself a gangsta? Call your bunch of pussies a crew? Nobody even had the brains to frisk me and Juju carries his nine 24/7, you get me!' He walked towards him. 'Fat lump of shit.' He shot him straight in the crotch.

'Phats doubled over, turning to Rocks in pain.

Another shot – BAM! – straight in the skull and it blew his face away.

'No!' Rocks couldn't bear that. He'd known Phats all his life.

'Ha ha ha! You see that? How many slugs did it take to kill that fucker?' Laughing as he blew the tip of the gun. 'But kill him I did.'

Then he put the gun to Rocks's forehead.

'I got the taste for killing now, boy... and I don't like the look of you. Think your something special. Smarter than the rest. Well I'll teach you a thing or two about that… Now pick up that shovel. A grave for each of you. Now dig!'

Rocks started digging. What else could he do? He was fucked.

'Four graves, you hear,' Juju said, gun pointing at him. 'And your one I finish myself. And that's going to be fun because you're going in alive, just like that pussy leader of yours.'

Rocks was digging away, spading up one pile of earth after the next, death staring him in the face, when he noticed Juju clutching his head again, the guy looking almost dizzy.

This was it. He took his chance. He swung the shovel and batted him in the face as hard as he could.

Juju flew to the ground and a shot cracked into the air.

Rocks ran. He dashed into the trees and tore through the woods.

Juju was floored but firing shots into the dark and screaming away. 'I'll find you, man! You'll never get away with this!'

But Rocks wasn't listening. Rocks was gone.

BLACK AND TANS

'Get your fucking hands up now, the pair of you!'

We climbed out of the ditch, holding our rifles, the element of surprise a winner every time. The two shocked Paddies – father and son – had clearly had a skinful in the village, the old boy looking like he hardly knew what day it was. But they knew to hold their hands up high and had done so with no hesitation.

They knew the drill and we had our orders: to crush not only the Irish Republican Army, but the will of the population that supported them. Ernie, a South London boy, six feet tall and fearsome-looking with it, looked them over as we held our guns.

'Well well well, what do we have 'ere then?'

The older man had dropped his violin case as he'd thrown up his hands. Ernie opened it up.

'Fiddle player are ya?'

The old boy nodded, blinking wildly, all of two teeth in his head.

'Well, I say Paddy here plays us a little ditty so we can all have a jig, what do you say boys?'

Laughter went up, then Wilf stepped forward to try and impress Ernie. 'That's right, play us a song you dirty Mick!'

'You leave this to me, Wilf,' Ernie said, brushing him aside.

'I'll get some music out of this cunt, don't you worry, but first I reckon his instrument needs a little tuning.'

He dropped it to the ground, crunching it beneath his boots.

'That's better. Go on then, Pat, pick it up and play – and you better be good I'm telling you.'

The man picked it up, the fiddle hanging in pieces.

'Don't just stare at it, you thick cunt – play!'

'I can't, it's broken,' the Paddy muttered.

Ernie leaned in close. 'You'll be fucking broken in a minute, I'll tell you that.'

'Leave my father alone,' his son said.

Ernie doubletook, then turned to us. 'Did I ask this cunt to speak?'

'Don't think you did, Ernie,' Wilf giggled.

Wilf was drooling at the mouth, spit running down his chin. This always happened when he was excited. Half his face was scarred from shrapnel he'd taken at the Front, and his mind wasn't all there either. George, his sidekick, wasn't that far behind. We'd all taken knocks, but with those two it showed.

'That's right, Wilf,' Ernie replied. 'Sharp boy.'

He punched the young Paddy hard in the face. Another whack and he hit the deck. Wilf and George stepped forward with glee, kicking him on the ground until Ernie pushed them back.

'Enough. Get him up – let's search them.'

We quickly found a bottle of clear liquid. 'Aha!' Ernie said, lifting the cork and smelling it. 'Nice bit of moonshine here lads.' He took a swig of the poteen, then creased his face. 'Christ, that could strip the paint off a battleship that could.'

He took another lug then passed it to me.

'Here you go, Alf, get some of that down your neck - wake you up a bit, you dozy cunt.'

I faced him eye to eye. We were the same height. 'Less of the lip, Ernie.' But he just laughed.

I took a lug. I didn't like Ernie, never had. He was a Bermondsey boy and thought he was the bees knees, the king of the garrison. Two weeks ago we'd battled out our differences on the barracks floor and I had come out worse. He'd been pushing things ever since, little remarks, trying to get my goat. But I was no Wilf or George and he knew it. I was waiting for my chance to get the bastard good. One of these days, mark my words.

Wilf and George had several swigs, then Ernie snatched it back necking the rest.

He belched in the younger man's face, staring him down.

'What do you say we all go back to yours, eh? Meet the women. All have a nice little tipple together?'

Both men stared at him with hatred.

'So where do you live then?' he said. 'Come on, answer me.'

They dropped their eyes to the ground, said nothing. Then Ernie pulled out his side-arm revolver, holding it to the son's cheek and suddenly the answer was a cottage a mile away.

'That's better. Destination your gaff then. And there better be a warm welcome.'

We headed along to where we'd parked the Crossley tender behind some bushes, Ernie kicking the men up the arse as they went.

'Get a move on you fucking animals!'

The old bloke kept dropping his arms slightly and Ernie grabbed him. 'You keep your hands high in the air where I can see them, you bog dwelling cunt.' He gave him a belt in the kidneys and the man doubled up.

Suddenly the son lunged for Ernie's throat, taking him by surprise, other hand going for the pistol. A shot rang into the air as they toppled over, wrestling on the ground.

'Shoot the bastard!' Ernie screamed as he struggled. 'Shoot him!'

Wilf and George were hovering over, scared to pull the trigger in case they missed, the men rolling to and fro, the Paddy's fist pumping like a piston into Ernie's face.

He almost had a hold of the gun when I stepped forward, motioning the others aside. I aimed my gun, pulled the trigger. The shot caught the Paddy in the head, missing Ernie by an inch. The struggle stopped.

Ernie freed himself from the dead man's grip and stood staring at me, blood across his face, eyes wide as saucers.

'That was pretty fucking close, Alf.'

'No word of thanks then?'

Ernie rolled his shoulders. 'Nah,' he said stubbornly. 'Not really. If you hadn't done it I'd have done it myself.' Then he turned to Wilf and George. 'And as for you two spare pricks...'

I looked up the road. The old man was limping away, emitting a wail.

Ernie laughed and lifted his gun to take aim. Then he changed his mind. 'No,' he said. 'We're going to have some sport tonight.' He ordered the other two to run up the road and get the bastard. 'We're bringing him home. Nice little family get-together.'

Ernie kicked his dead son into the ditch, the man shaking so much we almost had to carry him to the van.

The moon had gone in now, heavy clouds blanketing the sky, the kind of lighting that brought out the rebels in force. I felt we were taking chances now, pushing it.

'Ernie, listen,' I told him. 'Best we just drop this old bloke home and get back to the barracks. Let's have no funny business tonight. We've been out long enough.'

Ernie stopped and looked at me.

'Where's your guts, eh? You'll shoot a man when he's down but that's about it. Gone all coward on us now, have you?'

Ernie was trying to wind me up. Maybe get a punch out of me so he could whack me back harder. But I wasn't falling for it. I had bigger plans for old Ernie, don't you worry, but I was playing a slow game. He'd get his.

Driving to the cottage I sat in the open back keeping guard. We passed two houses that had been burned out by the forces. Then we came to the fork in the road where a few weeks back some of our men had taken the brunt of an IRA ambush, the rebels appearing from the ditches, throwing an explosive then raking all four with gunfire. Movement on the road was risky, an ambush could happen any time.

Ten shillings a day – that's what had brought me here. After returning to London from the Front, finding work was harder than I'd expected. I went to see my old gaffer at the factory in Camden Town but he didn't want to know. Nor did anyone else. I was misbehaving around the pubs, getting into scrapes with the coppers and the way things were going I'd be ending up in the clink and I knew it. When I heard the government was recruiting for ex-Tommies to bolster the forces in Ireland, good pay but dangerous work, it seemed a good option.

Back home from the war I was a bit of a walking mess to be honest. What I'd seen in the trenches didn't bear thinking about. All through my time away I'd written to my sweetheart Flo – all for us to soon break up. She told me I seemed different, like a different person. But I laughed it off. Then one time, instead of kissing and cuddling I tried to take things further. Come on Flo, you're a big girl now, my hand going up her leg and under her drawers. She struggled from my grip and ran back home.

The next day her butcher father came at me with his cleaver. 'Touch my daughter again and I'll chop you like liver!' I told him he had nothing to worry about because I was on my way to sign up to fight the Irish. 'You do that,' he said, 'and I hope they blow you to kingdom come.' I laughed and gave him two fingers. But Flo was right. I had changed. War does that.

We reached the cottage and got out of the van. That moonshine had been strong stuff and we were pretty pissed now. Ernie hammered at the door. 'Open up!'

'Mary mother of God!' the woman cried as Ernie pushed her husband in towards her.

We charged in, turning the place upside down. But it was clean, no arms.

'Right, everyone outside and up against the wall or we'll burn this place to the ground!'

The man, woman, three daughters and a son were lined up outside.

Ernie marched straight up to the son, a farm boy of about sixteen. He grabbed him by the hair, interrogating him about any local Sinn Feiners, then gave him a belt across the face. The boy dropped to his knees and Ernie was about to put the boot on him, when he noticed Wilf and George drunkenly harassing the girls, trying to pull up their skirts.

'What the fuck are you two up to, eh?' Ernie going over and slapping Wilf across the head. 'And you, ya little bleeder,' giving one to George.

Ernie stood towering before the girls, all of them petrified, not knowing where to look. He smiled.

'Please, leave my daughters alone,' the mother said, reading his intentions.

'Shut up, you silly old mare!' he shouted in her face.

Then he was back surveying the ladies.

'These are some nice young daughters you've got here missus. Very nice indeed.'

'Please, I'm begging you, leave them...'

Ernie pulled out the youngest, a girl of about fifteen. She struggled and cursed him, spitting in his face, but it only excited him more.

'We've got a wild one here, have we?' He tossed his rifle to me. 'Look after that, Alf. I'm heading to the barnhouse to teach this young madam some manners.'

The girl's brother ran for him. 'Get your filthy hands off her!'

Wilf and George grabbed and held him back, both wild-eyed and cackling.

Ernie was out of the picture now, the sound of laughter and muffled-screams coming from the barn, but I'd had enough of these games. If the rebels got wind of what happened on the road back there, they'd be packing their guns right now. Ernie was trying to get us killed.

Wilf and George were jeering at the family, poking them with their guns, when I had an idea.

'You two,' I said to the cretins. 'Bring the women and the old man inside – leave the boy. And sober up for God's sake.'

'Hark at him,' George said.

'Get the fuck on with it, now!' I ordered. 'Bring them in and don't touch them, either of you. They're hardly gun-toting Sinn Feiners, are they?'

It was just me and the boy now. I walked up to him. He was staring back at me with hatred.

'What's your name?' I asked.

'Sean,' he said.

I nodded to the barn. 'And your sister's name?'

'Bernadette.'

I showed him Ernie's rifle. 'Well, Sean, you see this? Walk towards the barn and this is yours - to use.'

He probably thought I was winding him up, that I'd shoot him in the back or something. But slowly he walked, taking his chances. When he reached the barn I threw him Ernie's gun.

He ran inside and the sound of Ernie's begging was satisfying to say the least. Two shots and Ernie was dead.

The girl came out with him in tears, and he sent her back into the house. Then he stood staring at me, the gun down by his side.

'Thanks for that.' I said, keeping my gun on him. 'That was Ernie O'Hara by the way. That's right. A London boy but Irish just like you. Strange old world, isn't it? But there you go. You did well there. You see, we're not all bastards us English, are we? Some of us just want our pay, a bit of ale now and then, and a body that isn't in parts by the time we get home. All the rest is just complication. That's the way I see it anyway.'

He thought I was playing with him, taking the piss, trying to push the humiliation further – which I well might have been. I was an Englishman in a land of enemies that wanted me dead. I was fighting in a war I didn't even fully understand, and it wasn't the first time either. I'd fought for Britain in the trenches tooth and nail, knee deep in muck, watching my mates get blown to smithereens, all to return to a country that had no use for me. Didn't fucking want me.

I was rambling now and he probably thought I was going mad, which wasn't far wrong.

'Do you know how that feels,' I asked him. 'Your own country not giving a shit?'

He raised his gun to shoot me, but I got there first. No choice. I shot him and he dropped.

Wilf came out of the house.

'What happened, Alf?'

'Our young friend here is dead,' I told him. 'Oh, and he just shot Ernie in the barn.'

'What...? The bastard!' He ran over there.

I followed him in with a flashlight. Ernie was flat on his back, half his head shot away, and I couldn't help smile seeing him with his kecks down.

'Alright, now get George and carry Ernie's body to the van, and let's get the fuck back to the barracks.

Will stared at the scene, his face twitching in shock.

'Another thing,' I said, slapping his shoulder. 'Make sure to pull up his britches before you do.'

He ran back inside wailing.

Setting off in the van, Wilf and George were in tears, badgering me about what exactly happened. After umpteen times spinning them a yarn, I shouted:

'THE KING IS DEAD YOU CUNTS, NOW FACE IT!'

'Ernie was a great man,' Wilf blubbered. 'He was the best there was.'

'Rape isn't in our rulebook, Wilf – Ernie's no hero.'

'What rulebook?' he said. 'We don't have a rulebook.'

The van was rattling up and down on the stony road, the rain falling now, and suddenly the vehicle jolted and the engine packed in. We rolled to a halt. Christ, this was all I needed.

I got out and had a look under the bonnet. It was no use. The engine was dead.

'We'll have to walk, lads.'

'But the barracks is miles away.'

'So be it.'

Twenty minutes along the road a light began approaching behind us. It could have been army or police, but I had a bad feeling.

'In the ditch, everybody, now!'

The vehicle came to a halt a little way up and my fears were confirmed. It was the IRA. A dozen of them jumped out with their rifles, carefully edging forward in the darkness.

'Guns ready,' I said, trying to fire up some courage, but Wilf and George were cowering by my feet, useless now.

'Come out ye Black and Tans!' a voice bellowed. 'Out with your hands in the air!'

This was it, I was about to die.

No way. I scampered up, took a chance, tearing through the hedge as the bullets began to fly. One tore into my shoulder, another my thigh, but I made it into the field and ran. Wounded badly, I stopped to hide behind a bank of heather as two of the rebels searched for me, but they thought I'd escaped across the bogs.

'We'll get you next time ya blackguard, you're a dead man!'

George and Wilf were surrounded and dragged out of the ditch, up onto the road. Both were kicked senseless, their cries and pleas ignored, then shot in the head.

I heard the vehicle drive away, the men cheering as they went, two out of three of their quarry eliminated.

How I made it back to the barracks that night, heavily injured and with the rebels on high alert, is a story in itself. But by the time I got there nobody could understand a word I was saying.

Those few miles took it out of me. Or maybe my whole Irish experience did. The lack of discipline, the looting, burning, indiscriminate killing.

War can bring out the worst in a man, and I was no exception. I physically recovered, but that was my last active night as a Royal Irish Constabulary man in the 1919-21 War of Independence. I was sent back to London, my adventure in Ireland over.

KENTISH TOWN BLUES

Every morning Tommy McCabe used the same Kentish Town cafe for his breakfast. Over ten years he'd seen the management change and waitresses come and go. He'd also endured a divorce, the death of a son, and had dipped so much into his savings that one morning putting his card in the wall he realised he didn't have enough money for his breakfast. He stared at the screen: No Funds Available. Out of all his life's calamities this one seemed to hit him the hardest.

He walked back home in the drizzling rain like a man stunned. Passing the cafe he saw waitress Karina giving him a quizzical wave, probably wondering why he wasn't coming through the door to take his usual place by the window. But no, paying for food on tick wasn't Tommy's style. He'd rather starve than get out the begging bowl. No chance.

He returned to his flat and sat in front of the TV eating corn flakes with tap water, as he hadn't even had enough change to buy his daily pint of milk. Finishing his paltry meal he stood by the window looking out over the estate as the rain fell down. There used to be a woman in the block across the way who'd put on a show each night, strutting about her flat in the buff. Eileen used to tell him to close the curtains and put his tongue away and Tommy would laugh.

Things were good back then. He didn't quite realise it at the time, but he knew now. He used to make a good few quid on the lorries. Quite a lot of money. Pat Mahon used to pass him a bag to hide with his cargo over to France, shoving a wad into his pocket for good measure. Fuck knows what was in the bag because Tommy didn't dare look, but he had a feeling it was undeclared cash. Though who knows, it could've been drugs or guns for all he knew, but it wasn't his concern. It was the money in his pocket that mattered. Luckily during those runs he was mostly waved through at customs, and the odd time when his load was given attention it was only a rudimentary check.

Those were great days. He'd still go out drinking with the boys back then. Holidays with the wife. His three sons were doing okay too. Kevin a fireman out in Cheshunt. Peter an estate agent in Finchley. Even his youngest Micky had been doing well for a while selling timeshare in Spain and he'd got himself a nice Spanish girlfriend. Until of course he started on the hard stuff and it all went tits up. He remembered having a local drink with him one Sunday afternoon. The boy coming in and out of the gents rubbing his nose. Tommy wasn't stupid.

'What's wrong with just having a drink?' he asked.

'Things are different nowadays,' Micky told him. 'Times have moved on since your day.'

Micky moved back to a flat in Somers Town leaving his girlfriend and child in Spain. He was a wreck by then. Out shoplifting, breaking into houses, always getting himself nicked. When it ended badly it was no surprise. The boy had long enough to try and pull himself together but it never happened. Tommy would never forget the time he returned home to find his front door had been kicked in, the place turned over. A neighbour mentioned he'd seen his son earlier rushing down the communal stairs. Tommy's mother's wedding ring was gone along with four hundred quid saved for a rainy day. Tommy repaired the door, kept the theft quiet from his wife and told his neighbour not to say anything. When Micky died, Eileen never got over it, and Tommy wasn't happy either, not with all his memories of when the boy was young and innocent, a smile on his face as he played in the park, but you can't cry forever.

Their marriage faltered after that. Things went quickly down the pan. In a row Eileen blamed him for Micky's death, saying he'd been too harsh on the lad when he was young, his punishments too severe. It was a question that haunted him. Had he been too hard on him? Maybe once or twice after he'd been drinking, but it was nothing compared to how he himself was brought up. It was savage back in those days. In his house anyway. But maybe Eileen was right. Micky was more of a handful than the other two. Once he reached twelve or thirteen he was never up to any good. Misbehaving on the streets. Bringing angry neighbours and the police to the door.

One day Tommy came home from a session in the pub. The day was seared in his memory. Old Paddy Flynn was heading back to Ireland after forty-five years on the buildings and they gave him a good old send-off. He was a character, part of the local furniture, everyone loved Paddy. A lot of old faces turned out and it was like a reunion of sorts. It was in the George IV, a pub gone now. Tommy remembered walking home that night knowing he'd probably never see some of those faces again. But at least they'd had a good old craic. When he got back there were bags and suitcases in the hall.

'It's over Tommy,' she said, matter of factly. 'I'm moving out.'

He didn't shout. He sat with his head in his hands.

'Look at yourself,' she said. 'I've had enough.'

If he wasn't at work, away for days at a time, he'd be in the pub. And even just a few years ago it seemed there were pubs on every corner full of inviting faces, and he was never one to say no to the lock-in. Eileen had met another man at the bingo. A man older than him, but a lively man, into gardening, walking, outdoor pursuits, able to have a joke and a laugh without a drink in his hand.

They moved to the man's place up in Barnet. His sons and grandkids visited; Tommy didn't. He stared from the window, the rain falling heavier now. Those corn flakes hadn't done much to relieve his hunger, his belly rumbling for some solid food. Tommy went to the kitchen, rummaged in the cupboards and found a tin of Spam. The top was covered in dust and he wiped it to check the use-by date. Three years out. It'd do, it wouldn't poison him. He stood forking in the fatty meat, aware of its inferiority compared to his breakfast down the cafe, a meal that set him up for the day, seeing Karina and having a chat with the usual faces. It was his daily routine. Service with a smile and maybe a catch-up on local gossip with roadsweeper Fred, a man who could talk for England.

If there was a local story Fred knew about it. All the ins and outs. A planning application for a block of flats on a patch of green where people walked their dogs, he was on it. A local councillor keeping suspect company or fiddling expenses, he was spreading the word. Nobody pulled a fast one on old Fred. Then Tommy remembered what someone had once told him about Fred. That he hadn't swept the roads in years. That he might still wear the council jacket but Camden laid him off years ago. Tommy told the man it was bollocks; he'd chatted to Fred enough times on the street and he'd had his broom with him, but the man shook his head. Pride reasons, he said. The council let him go. Tommy didn't believe it. The bloke was a liar. And even if he wasn't, why was he going around telling tales on people? Whispering in his ear with a smile on his face. Divulging other men's business.

It's like when Tommy lost his job on the lorries. He didn't

shout about it either. If people asked, he said he was still working away, business as usual. Adapting to a life of no more work hadn't been easy. It made him feel old and used up. But that was then. He actually was old now I suppose, so things were different. But he was still strong, still had his health more or less and these things matter. But adapting to a new routine is never easy. Look at now for instance. Scraping the last bits of jellied meat from a tin of Spam.

He returned to his seat in front of the TV. Two presenters chatting to a celebrity he'd never heard of. His pension money wasn't due until Thursday and here he was, unable to afford to feed himself. Having said that, he knew this day was due to arrive so it was hardly a big surprise. But he hadn't wanted to think about it. Chose to stick his head in the sand. Probably because he knew there was nothing he could do. Or at least nothing he'd be prepared to do. The thought of queuing up for the food bank was just that, a thought; he wouldn't do it, no fucking way.

On the screen smiling faces were nattering on but Tommy wasn't listening. He sank lower in his seat and felt a weary tiredness descend. He contemplated heading for the bedroom and climbing under the sheets. Giving up. Letting the day pass him by. If life was a daily battle then he was on the losing side, that much was obvious. Losing the battle, losing the war. Fuck it, he walked to the bedroom, took off some of his clothes and got into bed. He remembered his dad used to do this. Every time he was out of work you'd find him in bed. Don't wake him, his mother would say. His dad's depression was no laughing matter. But bed was better than when he'd hit the whiskey bottle. That was something else altogether.

His father was brought home by the police one time, his usually-red face ashen white. He'd been gone all day, all evening, and his mum was worried. When he turned up with the police in tow the kids were sent upstairs, but they crept down to listen from the bannister. The police had found him loitering on Suicide Bridge. The whole thing seemed odd at the time, like one big misunderstanding, but later in life Tommy understood the feeling. Also why his dad would take to his bed. Wanting to switch off, give up existing for a while, abdicate all responsibilities, float into the black and disappear.

Tommy fell asleep and his dreams were nostalgic. They were surprisingly warm and glowing. It was the 1970s and he was a young man again. Back then motorbikes were his thing and a gang of them would ride down to the coast. Sometimes they'd get into fights, battle it out with another mob. He remembered a sunny weekend in Southend. The girls looked amazing and there was this lovely bird called Jeanette. Leather jacket, boots, long blonde hair. He'd see her every time he went. His gang were drinking in a snooker place where the bikers hung out; the London boys had taken over for the day and the locals weren't happy. A group got mouthy and it turned into a brawl.

Down in the car park fists were flying. One of Tommy's mates Frankie got a razor across the cheek from a bloke who was as wide as he was tall. His name was Mick the Fish, a known face down that way. It all kicked off. Tommy knocked the shiv from his hand and the Fish battered him into a corner, jeering as he rolled up his sleeves saying he was going to pummel the living daylights out of him. He worked as a butcher and rode a Norton. Tommy took his chances. Quick as a whippet he leapt up and threw an almighty punch into the centre of his chest, knocking the wind out of him. The Fish dropped to his knees clutching his heart. Tommy followed with a brutal kick to the face and Mick the Fish was flat on the floor.

Des Madden tried pulling Tommy away, saying it was time to scarper, but Tommy knew he'd gone too far and kept staring down at him, the big man's lifeless eyes wide open, glaring at the sky. The fight was over and some of the boys gathered round for a moment, pushing him with their feet. 'Shit Tom, I think you've fucking killed him,' said Gnasher. People were approaching and that was their cue to ton it back to London.

Tommy's right-hander had stopped the Fish's heart, but help was quick and he survived, spending a fair old time recovering in hospital. Back in Camden Tommy's brutal punch upped his standing no end, but left him lying low for fear of retribution from the Fish's firm. Luckily nothing happened, and the Fish never grassed, but no more Southend meant no more Jeanette, which was painful as he'd never known a girl more beautiful.

He dreamt of ton-ups and women and mad nights on the town. All the energy and laughter of youth, living like there was no tomorrow. He dreamt of old mates he hadn't seen in decades, some who had passed now, others who for all he knew could have earned a packet and be living in the lap of luxury. Once more he dreamt he was back in that scruffy Southend car park. His dream turned dark. Chains and knives were swinging, except this time his side was losing badly. Several of his friends lay on the ground taking the boot or a lashing, his best mate Kevin flat out, his skull split open from a cudgel. Once again Tommy was floored and cornered with Mick the Fish closing in on him, a broken bottle in one hand, skinning knife in the other. Your choice, Tommy boy.

He woke with a start, heart banging in his chest. His dream had been so life-like, so vivid. He dropped his legs down and sat at the edge of the bed. It was dark outside so he must've slept the day away. Heavy footsteps and shouting sounded from the flat above; the couple who lived there were rowing again. The volume increased. They were attacking each other now for definite. He'd heard it all before, the woman no pushover, giving as much as she took, if not more. He'd seen the man in the lift once with a black eye. The noise intensified and a bang that shook the room indicated at least one of them had toppled to the floor. With further yells and shrieks it sounded like they were killing each other. Which was no unknown thing in these flats either. Six months ago a man in the next block had strangled his wife to death. Then he carried her over his shoulder to the car and drove out to the country to bury her. He was stopped after driving erratically on the A1. In the boot they found his deceased wife and a shovel. Upstairs the riot continued. It peaked and began to subside. Then he heard the bedsprings on the go, the usual culmination to their rows. Tommy felt a sense of relief.

He shoved on his jumper and jeans and went into the living room, his empty cereal bowl and Spam tin still sitting there on the table. He cleared up. His belly was growling and there wasn't a bite to eat in the house. He drank some water from the tap then stood meditating on how best to proceed. He'd actually have to go out and nick some food. Enter a supermarket and shoplift. Shove some edibles under his coat or into a bag. It was either that or go hungry. He saw people shoplifting from time to time. Slipping in a jar of coffee or a bit of meat perhaps. Then there were the runners. Grab and go. They always caused a scene, the staff running about in a fluster, most people carrying on their shopping oblivious. Whenever he spotted someone on the take, he'd turn away, pretend he hadn't seen a thing. If someone fancied a shave in the morning or a piece of protein with their dinner, how they obtained it was none of his business.

Tommy got his jacket and put on a cap and gloves as the nights were chilly out there. He checked his pocket for his keys. Noticing the small meat knife on the counter, he stopped for a moment. He picked it up and slipped it in his back pocket. Why had he just done that? He hadn't carried a knife in years. Not since his early twenties when he'd fallen out with one of the Vella brothers. A mouthy fucker called Johnny. Half-Irish, half

Maltese. They lived up the Clarence Road Estate. Fall out with one and you'd have the whole clan after you. Tommy was standing drinking with a mate outside the Halfway House one night when Johnny Vella walked past and shouldered him, spilling half his drink. Fraught words were exchanged and Tommy decked him then and there. Now they were after him and word on the street was Tommy was due a striping across his face. He treaded carefully for a while and made sure he always had a weapon on him. Two of the brothers screeched up in a van one night and chased him on foot halfway across Kentish Town, but nothing more came of it and in time the grudge was forgotten. But now after all these years, why had he just pocketed a knife?

Was he losing his marbles? Perhaps he was. Then again, it could be dangerous out there, so maybe it was just a sensible decision. Tommy was more of a day person at this point in life, his days of roaming wild and free in the night long gone. He hardly even went to the pub these days, preferring to have a drink indoors, if he drank at all that is. Because one thing was for sure, come nightfall you had to watch yourself out there, have a set of eyes at the back of your head, so having something sharp poking into your arse was probably a good idea.

His hunger was killing him now. He needed something to fill the hole. He reached to the top of the cupboard and took down a half bottle of Bells. Two inches of whisky remained. He unscrewed the lid and sank it down, a little fire in his belly, something to bolster him for the mission ahead. He exhaled while staring at the empty bottle. Christ Almighty, he lamented, you know you've hit rock bottom when you're necking from a bottle of whisky that's for sure. He turned up his collars and left the flat.

He took the lift three floors down, graffiti all around him. K-TOWN KILLAS ... NW5 KINGZ ... AGAR GROVE ARE

BATTY BOYS ... MALI BOYS RUN TINGS. He stepped out into the night air and walked across the estate. It had stopped raining, the wind blowing hard and cold. He turned out onto the street. Where was he even going? If he got nabbed pinching from his usual supermarket he'd be barred and that wouldn't be convenient; he'd be shooting himself in the foot. Maybe he'd find a small shop off the beaten track, a place he didn't use. Pocket a pint of milk and a couple tins of Fray Bentos. He needed some ham and cheese, some bread too, but a full loaf could prove difficult.

Walking along he shook his head, unable to believe the situation he was in. It really was the pits. But at least he had the whisky in him, warming his chest, providing a lightness of step and dulling the grief in his head. He weaved through the streets up towards Gospel Oak, a little shop in mind that seemed a safe bet. He turned up a side road, low-level blocks of flats at each side, and was only noticing how dim-lit and deserted it seemed when he heard footsteps approaching from behind. A young fella in a hoodie was walking alongside him now.

'Boss, you got a cigarette?'

Tommy told him he didn't smoke.

'How about some money then?' Suddenly he was pushing Tommy to the wall. 'Come on, what you got for me?'

Tommy's words came out as a mutter, incomprehensible, even to him. His mind was overloaded. Why hadn't he remained on a busier road, somewhere better lit?

'I'm asking you a question, old man, you fucking deaf?'

Tommy tried to move away. He was backing into a side passage leading to some flats, wheelie bins lined to his right. The boy was gripping his jacket, right in his face, so close he could smell the weed from his breath. How had Tommy got here, trapped like this? Things were happening fast, the boy insistent, and there seemed no happy ending. Tommy was scared now, the adrenaline trembling through him. His assailant's eyes were small, dark and cold and he noticed a wispy moustache.

He never should have left the house tonight. He should have stayed put. Safe in front of the telly. Guts rumbling, mind depressed, but safe at least. The youth looked about seventeen, but it was hard to tell. Tommy thought back to when he was that age. Him and his mates were no angels. When he thought of some of the stuff they did, nicking bikes, cars, breaking into places, he could only describe himself as a tearaway. They got up to naughty things all the time, but picking on random strangers on the street wasn't one of them. It wasn't the done thing. Not where he lived and not among his crowd anyway. They picked fights with their own. People who were ready and willing. If a mob from another estate came for a rumble they responded in kind. But stalking the street to prey on strangers would have been seen as low. Scumbag behaviour. Unacceptable.

The boy was slim, young and fit, at the beginning of his adult life. What had changed since Tommy was his age? Was it drugs, bad parenting, a lack of general standards, social morals?

'Why are you doing this?' Tommy heard himself say.

For that he received a slap across the face. 'Fuck you, I want your phone man.' The stranger was trying to search his pockets.

'Okay, steady on. I'll give you what you want,' Tommy said, hand reaching for the knife in his back pocket.

It reminded him of an incident back in 1973. He'd been visiting a girl on the Regent's Park Estate. Susan was her name. It was a short-lived romance, and afterwards he was walking back towards Camden Town. He badly needed a jimmy and slipped down a backstreet to go up against a bridge wall, the Euston rail line running below. His dad had worked on those tracks for several years. Repairs at night. He'd tell him stories of the mighty railway's history. It was built in the 1860s and much of the workforce were Irish navvies, but there were English, Scottish and Welsh crews too. They dug out the deep track with picks and shovels. Back-breaking work. The story went that four local pubs were built for the labourers to drink in, keeping the warring groups at bay. The Irish used the Dublin Castle, the English the Windsor Castle, Scottish the Edinboro Castle and Welsh the Pembroke Castle. The drinking was fierce and nothing could quell the fights, battles so prolonged that occasionally the army was called in. The men were worked like slaves, shifts on the shovel long and gruelling, and with no safety standards many lost their lives, the true number a lot higher than the official records.

Tommy was pissing by the wall dwelling on a harsher past when a drunk bloke came up, tattered suit on him, hand out asking for some change. Tommy didn't warm to him. 'Can't you see I'm busy?' The man called him a wanker and walked on. 'Come here and say that,' Tommy said, but the man kept going. 'You heard me,' he said over his shoulder. 'You're a fucking wanker mate.' Tommy caught up and pushed him. The bloke turned round and flicked out a blade. They grappled, Tommy knocking the knife from his hand and it slid to the gutter. Both went for it, but Tommy got there first. He remembered holding it in his left hand as he punched and kicked the bloke but he kept coming back for more, then suddenly Tommy was stabbing him repeatedly. The man fell moaning to the ground, blood coming from his throat, jacket a mass of blood. Tommy looked left and right. The road was deserted; scruffy four storey houses that years later would be tarted up and sold for millions, but for now the tone was low and money tight on these streets. Tommy was feeling the pinch too, his pockets empty, not a penny to hand over even if he wanted to. The man was struggling to sit up, blood stringing from his mouth. Finally he exhaled and lay back against the wall. He was still now. Out for the count. No longer breathing. Tommy was incensed, a bloody knife in his hand, fuming at what the man had just made him do. A long stretch in prison would be a certainty if he didn't think fast. He hefted the man upwards, his body surprisingly light. He heaved him over the bridge wall and then he was gone, a thud sounding from the tracks below.

Tommy had taken a drink himself that night. Some Martini around Susan's house, a bottle she'd swiped from her mum and dad's drinks cabinet, the two of them knocking it back in her bedroom, and it had left his head fuzzy, not quite all there. The street was empty, Tommy the only man alive and breathing on that stretch and he slipped off into the night, rain clouds gathering overhead that would wash the blood from the paving stones, and the stranger's body sure to be torn apart by an oncoming train. His dad would tell him of the regular one-unders, how the rail workers would have to help in the clean-up, because if they didn't who else would. His dad a man with problems himself, cleaning up after those suicides, a task he wasn't paid to do, the sight potentially putting ideas into his head, sending him up to Archway Bridge with the darkest intentions. The things a man has to do for money. To just get by.

Tommy got home that night and lay on his bed. He decided to blank out what had happened by the railway bridge. Wipe it from his consciousness. Bury it so deep that even if the police pulled him in for a talk, he'd know nothing and convince them accordingly. But time passed and there was no arrest, no news of a man dead, nothing at all. It was like a bad dream, almost as if it never happened.

A year later he let it slip to a mate one night. The Grafton Arms was doing a late one and he and Ray Marney were in the corner drunk. Ray had split from his girlfriend after her bruiser of a dad, Seamus, warned him off at the door. Wielding a hammer he told him he was a thieving skinny galoot, not good enough for his daughter and to end it or he'd get a bash round the ear. He pushed him down the path and with a boot up the arse sent him on his way.

Now Seamus was in hospital after being struck from behind on the street. He was found unconscious on the pavement with a head wound and his wallet missing. He'd been off to buy some tobacco from the corner shop. A witness saw a black man running down an adjoining street so it was presumed to have been a mugging. Seamus Power was on life support and it was touch and go.

Ray was crying into his pint saying it was him, he'd done it and tomorrow he was going to hand himself in to the law. If the man died or was left a cabbage there was no way he could live with it. Tommy was drunk too and mulled the problem over, finally telling him to do whatever he thought was best. Then he confided about the man he'd stabbed and thrown down to the tracks. A down and out, probably not missed. The man had come at him with a knife, then Tommy had stabbed and killed him so throwing him over seemed the best option. Ray looked at him for a moment, confused, then he turned back to his pint and carried on rambling about handing himself in. It was as if he hadn't heard a thing.

Ray never did hand himself over. Sober he must've changed his mind, and no culprit was ever caught. A day or two later Seamus made a miraculous recovery and was up in bed talking like he'd suffered nothing more than a slight flu. He was back home in no time, soon returning to his job driving a JCB. But he got his wishes because Ray never again bothered his daughter and in fact soon disappeared off the scene, moving abroad and was never heard from again.

The streets were violent nowadays, but violence was hardly a new thing. Sometimes you imagined a past when everyone lived peacefully and you could walk down the streets without a care. Things were different now certainly, violence more random and unpredictable perhaps, but nostalgia can play tricks with your thinking. Maybe it's age. Getting old and feeling vulnerable. Wishing for your youth again, when you imagined you could handle anything. When chucking a man over a bridge was just one of those things you file away and do your best to forget.

Who knows. The only thing certain was that once again Tommy had a knife in his hand and was repeatedly plunging it into the boy. The mugger was all out of fight now and Tommy let him drop down between two wheelie bins. He was slumped by the wall, legs out, head to the side, jacket wet with blood.

Tommy's heart was hammering. He saw the bloody shiv in his hand and quickly returned it to his back pocket. He took a look around. Not a soul. Just like that night back in '73. He got down to check the boy's pockets. A knife, a phone, a wallet containing two twenty-pound notes. He took the money and returned the rest. Slipping out onto the street he distanced himself from the scene. Several streets later he felt a lot better. An energy to his stride. A sense of having righted a wrong. He noticed his gloves were a little bloody so he shoved them into a bin and kept going. With money in his pocket now he stopped at a chip shop for a bag of fish and chips, then an offy for some cans, and took a circuitous route back to the flat.

Reaching his front door he was glad to be home. He covered his meal with salt and vinegar and tucked in, a can of Fosters at the side. He was ravenous and the food was good, probably the best fish supper he'd ever tasted. Finishing up he literally licked the platter clean.

He sat back to relax. He noticed some small blood marks on his jeans. There was probably a bit on his jacket too. It would be wise to round up all his clothes and get rid of them. He changed his kitchen bin bag, added his clothes, and shoved the lot into the block's rubbish chute, the bin men due in the morning. He had a quick bath and afterwards returned to his seat feeling clean and new.

He cracked another can and flicked through the channels. A Stallone double bill was beginning. *First Blood* and *Rambo.* Which reminded him. He'd watched that first one back in the ABC on Holloway Road with Eileen. On the way out they met Marty and Anne McHale and went for a drink, visiting the Nag's Head, the Hercules and the Half Moon if he remembered rightly. Maybe they went on to the Gresham and made a full night of it. The ABC was a pub now, to this day retaining the cinematic décor. Anne was still around, but two years back Marty had a heart attack at the bar of The Mother Red Cap up by the Archway. It was lunchtime and he took his usual two pints of the black stuff then slumped down on the counter and was gone. Best way to die, someone remarked.

Tommy gazed at the TV. Army vet John Rambo and sheriff Brian Dennehy at odds and anticipating a long game of cat and mouse. Just then from outside he heard a whirl of police sirens, approaching, getting louder. He froze in his seat. He visualised the pounding of boots up the stairs and armed police storming in as he sat there in his slippers. ON THE FLOOR NOW WITH YOUR HANDS WHERE WE CAN SEE THEM. He listened to the sirens gradually fade and relaxed again. It was a false alarm, but they could indeed come for him this time. It was a possibility and quite a strong one. But somehow, despite further rounds of sirens that night, so many in fact that it seemed there must have been a prolonged riot out there, he could somehow tell, feel in his gut, that it wasn't going to happen.

The next morning in the cafe Karina asked him where he'd been yesterday. He told her he'd had a few tricks to get up to. He was a busy man. 'I'm sure you are,' she smiled. 'I'm sure your retirement keeps you very busy.' Soon roadsweeper Fred sat in for a word.

'Did you hear what happened last night?' he asked as Tommy tucked into his Full English with buttered toast and strong tea.

'You're the oracle round here mate so you tell me.'

'Kids,' he said, shaking his head. 'Knifing each other again. There's no end to it. There were two gangs on the rampage up by Queen's Crescent market. They were running through the streets, an ongoing battle, attacking each other. I'm talking knives and machetes, big poles, lumps of concrete, whatever they could find. Two are dead, six hospitalised.'

'Sounds bad,' Tommy said, forking in some sausage.

'I've heard of mass gang fights before but this one takes the biscuit.'

'You're not wrong there.'

'One boy they found flat out on the road up the top of Grafton Street, knifed in the head. Another was a few streets away slumped by some bins, out cold. Tell me Tommy, can you ever remember it being as bad as this?'

Tommy took a drink of his tea. 'Not exactly, no.'

'They're out of control. You must have heard the sirens last night, they didn't stop.'

'I heard them, yeah, but what can you do?'

'I know what I'm going to do,' Fred said. 'I'm going to have a word with the top dog at Holmes Road to finally do something about it. I can't promise anything though. This new superintendent they've got is useless. He's got them stuck in the nick ticking boxes about all sorts. Have you heard the latest? There's a hundred genders and women can have a todger. It's official. Say any different and you'll be done for a hate crime, whatever the hell that is. What next?'

'The world gets more insane every day, Fred. It's best to laugh at it.'

'Impossible. In our day the police were out walking on the streets. Out solving crimes or at least being a visual deterrent. Getting things done.'

'You should write to the local paper about it.'

'That's exactly what I plan to do. Somebody has to do it.'

'Well the best man is definitely you.'

Karina came over, rubbing his shoulder. 'Poor Fred. I'm sure things will get better. They always do. You need to stop worrying your head about things.'

He turned to her. 'I bet where you come from the police wouldn't mess about like they do here.'

'In Poland the police are much stricter.'

'You see. But over here, of course not. Not a chance. They let the thugs rule the streets.'

Karina went to serve somebody and I said, 'Here, Fred, have they arrested anyone yet?'

'For the two murders?' He leaned in, talking quietly. 'As it happens, I was speaking to one of my contacts earlier. Six are in custody, two of them expected to be charged with the two killings.' He looked at his watch. 'And by now, fingers crossed, let's hope they have been.'

'Now that is good news,' I said, putting my knife and fork down on my empty plate. 'The best news I've heard for a good while.'

'You can say that again. Hopefully the buggers will get the punishment they deserve and be kept off the streets for a long time.'

'I'm with you on that one,' I said, signalling Karina for another strong brew.

LIFE SENTENCE

The house was empty. Carol had gone with the kids and Jack was early; he wasn't due in at work today until eleven so there was no rush. He finished shaving and stared at the face looking back at him in the mirror. The couple extra hours in bed should have done him some good, but instead he looked rougher than ever, blue circles under his eyes from another night of broken sleep, mind racing, waking up in a sweat. Carol had soothed him at one point, told him not to worry, he was just having a bad dream, it happens to us all. But things were getting worse. Getting serious.

Jack was out in the wilderness. A deserted cottage somewhere. Knocking on the door with a chainsaw in his hand, all powered up and ready to go. He was pounding away, calling out, knowing if the bastard didn't soon answer he'd have to use one of the windows, smash his way in like a fucking criminal. Then suddenly the man was there. Older, greyer, but it was him alright. Standing there, scared.

'Go away, whoever you are or I'll call the police.'

He was trying to close the door, shut Jack out and life would carry on, problem go away. But Jack had his foot there, he wasn't going anywhere. Glaring into him pushing close, words slow and intense, watching his face change, skin turn white.

Finding him. Getting to him. Putting things right. Sometimes the urge was so strong he felt he was going mad. Other times he had more realistic things to think about. Work, reality, his family. He had three kids now. Ryan, the oldest, fifteen years old. God, how time moves. It's astonishing. But that's it, when you have a family you move on, leave the past behind. You've got responsibilities for Christ's sake. Got to keep your head screwed on. More pressing things to deal with. Like the threat of losing his job at the engine plant. There'd been redundancies recently, cutbacks big time. Not anywhere near management level, but even so. You've got to stay on the ball. Be aware. Have your head in the clouds and there's always somebody hiding in the wings, ready to take your place, grab everything you've got. No mercy. Got to live in the real world, the here and now. Not look back ever.

The 80s of his youth was so long ago. A different world. It needed to be buried. Press delete, watch it disappear. Jack had moved on, got sensible and done well for himself. A good home, good job, both out of town, and kids he'd die for. And Carol, she understood him, had a light inside of her, knew how to cheer him up. Knew he sometimes pushed himself too far, but understood he only wanted what was best, for her, for the kids. Carol was proud of him. She told him often enough. Assistant manager now. Sometimes he had to pinch himself. But deep down he knew Carol was in the dark. A chasm between them. Secrets. Things he would never tell.

She would never understand. Why would she? The things he'd done it was hard to believe now. The recklessness. Self-hate. Anything goes. And to make it worse, it was all his own choice. He wasn't like a lot of the other kids. Some of them homeless, landing down in the big city, living from hand to mouth. He was different. Well above all that. He had a home. Not up north in some broken-down mill town but twenty minutes away on the Victoria Line. A bit of a messed-up home, but still.

After his mum and dad split up he ran a bit wild for a while. Felt confused, I suppose. A teenage thing. Passing phase. Bunk off school and head down the West End. Burger bars, cafes, arcades. Hanging around. Making friends with other boys. A bit of mischief, earn a few quid here and there. Same old stuff any truanting kid would have done.

Don't make me laugh. Jack stared at his eyes in the mirror. Bloodshot, an unhinged look about them. At school he'd been doing pretty well, did his homework, passed his exams. But come fourteen, fifteen, forget it. Necking pills. Dumping his school mates. Getting in with the wrong crowd.

It seemed harmless at first. Easy. Sometimes you didn't even need to do anything. Just take the cash and scarper. What's a punter going to do, call the police? But even when you did have to work, you can switch off to these things. Especially when there are drugs involved. Not let it touch you. It's not real. Not really happening. A stranger in your mouth in a public toilet somewhere. Big deal. He's the one with the problem, the need, not you. You're just making some easy money, notes in the pocket, a little bit of freedom. You're the one laughing, not these cunts.

But now there were other implications. Turn back the clock and there are questions everywhere. Screaming in your face, fingers pointing. He wondered if he'd enjoyed the attention, affection, the things he'd never got from his mum and dad as they fought endlessly. Always asking for it. Taking things further. Letting them buy him things. Spend hours with him. Blurring the lines. Pushing the boundaries. Acting like a fucking little queer.

But it ended. It had to. He moved on. Crying as a teacher hugged him. He told her he'd been experimenting with drugs, had done some bad things, but it was over, a mistake. He wanted to change. And he put his trust in her – hadn't told her anything really, not even a fraction, but she helped him, got him back on track. Start afresh, get on with it, leave the past behind.

But it never goes away. Not really. It lingers dormant, seemingly under control. Then suddenly there it is full-frontal in your face when you're on the motorway, when you're lying in bed, when you're staring into the mirror seeing the youth that you once were. And Ryan fifteen now, his father's son, a near spitting image. Seeing him under the Dilly lights, hustling on the street, selling himself on the meat rack, led to a stinking Hackney tower block, predators in wait, the end of youth, fucked for life. Drawing a blade across his wrists, a darkened alley somewhere, all too much. Nobody to turn to, blood draining into the gutter, life ebbing away.

Jesus Christ. He had to cool it. He splashed his face with water, slapping the skin, rinsing away the filth. He had to stop thinking the unthinkable. He'd have to start leaving Ryan alone. Stop poking around in his bedroom, checking his laptop, his phone. Stop spying on him. Let the boy grow.

Sometimes he'd watch him hanging around the shopping centre with his mates. A safe distance, head down in the crowds, keeping an eye. For what? Bad people, bad influences. Men were out there waiting for you, sniffing out your youth, ready to pounce. One minute you're growing up, smiling, everything's normal, the next you're sniffing drugs in an underground car park, ready for anything, up to God knows fucking what.

One Saturday he'd followed his son down to London. Ryan had started going down there now and then with his mates. Jack had warned him of the dangers, but there's only so much you can say. Lecture them too much and they'll stop listening, go the other way. Jack knew as much himself. He told Carol he was putting in some overtime. Then he followed him down on the same train. Pure paranoia. What if the kid was up to things? His mates pulling him in, polluting his mind? You don't know. How can you? Look at his own youth. Ryan and his friends visited a few shops, went to a McDonald's then spent the rest of the day skateboarding at the South Bank. Kids just having fun.

Jack felt silly. He walked away. Let the boy be. Ryan wasn't stupid. The boy had more sense than he'd ever had. And Central London, it was such a different place now. Cleaned up. Parts of it hardly recognisable. Jack hadn't properly observed London in years, popped down for work purposes now and then, drove in, drove out, but saw little. He walked around Waterloo. An Imax cinema complex was down where the bull ring had been, cardboard city. Where before there'd been greasyspoons, dusty pubs, grubby little shops, there were now snazzy cafés, bars and restaurants. The blackened buildings had been cleansed and refurbed, the whole place like one big leisure park. He crossed the Thames at Hungerford Bridge. Up Villiers Street to Trafalgar Square, then over to Piccadilly and into a bustling Soho. He remembered the dark neon nights. The prostitutes, porno cinemas and arcades, back alleys strewn with needles. But now the sky was blue and the sun shining down on clean coffee shops and eateries, people out on pavement tables, smiles all round, a confident urban populace at ease with itself. No edge, no tension.

He saw a down-and-out being shuffled on by the police. He'd hardly noticed a single beggar all day; it was as if they'd all disappeared, gone, part of the last century. He imagined government-commissioned night squads touring the streets in blacked-out vans, working stealthily, collecting up the homeless, the destitute, the unsightly. A state sponsored snatch squad working for a clean efficient London, forth economic capital of the world and rising, no place for misfits or the poor, machines working the landfill, disease buried deep in the ground, radioactive vats full of crushed bone. Turn a blind eye, problem solved. A world free of drugs and decay, slot machines, seedy sex, primitive desire. A world swept clean.

But it was there alright. Just not so much in your face. It was pushed indoors. Or pushed further out to the suburbs. The run-down streets and estates he'd seen on the way in. Real London. Not this brochure version. Shunt the crap out of sight, bad for business, let it fester elsewhere. Forget it. The solution was to get away, move on from the lot of it. And Jack had done that. The city was no place to bring up kids. As soon as Carol got pregnant that was it, see you later. Taking his family to the sticks. Best thing he'd ever done.

He went home. Back to his wife, his little boy, little girl, Ryan following a few hours later. The family all together on a Saturday night. Watching the talent shows, getting the games out, father and son playing at the screen like best friends. He ordered a big take away. Have whatever you like. Told them this year he'd take them on the best holiday ever. Fuck worrying about money. Live. And fuck the past. God mate, just get over things.

But certain things, how? It was two months ago now. Sitting in front of the telly one night with Carol, the kids in bed. That bastard's face flashing up on the news. Eyes staring, possessed by the devil. *A recently released paedophile has been hounded out of his Hampshire home by angry locals who discovered his identity. The man has been moved to a secret location for his own safety.*

Jack picked up the remote and casually turned it over. Then he went to the toilet to vomit. Everything rushing back. Flashbacks of the horror. Bed early. Sweating. A flu. Days off work unlike him. Holding back the mental breakdown. Too much. Bottle it back up, wait for it to go away. Certain things you tell nobody, you keep to yourself.

He studied his face in the mirror. He looked worn out, his skin more ragged with each sleepless night. He'd aged years since that news report. Hadn't had a proper night's sleep since. He used to be out like a light, very few dreams at all. Not now. Every night feared. Every night a death trip. Murder, rape, destruction.

And last night Carol trying to soothe him. Telling him to relax, it's just a bad dream, too much coffee, stress at work, and he held her so tight, was frightened of drifting off again, falling into that semi-alive semi-dead nightmare world, because sometimes he'd wake up and he'd still be there. It was insanity. He didn't trust himself, didn't know what he was capable of. You read the papers and people lose the plot, it happens all the time, they kill their whole family, kill themselves, and when your mind is all over the place you just don't know what you'll do. And Carol was moving her hand down and touching him, saying she'd make him feel good, relax, and you had to watch out, voices in the head, forces taking over your body, somebody swinging a hammer, plunging a knife, and then you're dialling 999 and crying down the phone because you've woken up from the lunacy, blood on the walls and your whole family dead, and his wife was working on him, whispering how she loved him, loved him inside her, and remember when they used to do it all the time, whispering sweet nothings in the black night. But he had to shove her away. He didn't need that now. None of it.

And later, almost dawn. Dreaming, sweating, screaming. But not a sound, only the croaking of the rooks in the trees and the sweet song of the blackbird's early chorus. Jack standing in a disused warehouse with a blowtorch. The bastard spread-eagled, hands and feet nailed to the floor. At least the other three, the sidekicks he'd gone down with, had the decency to die in prison. Suicide. Cancer. The other murdered in his cell. Not this bastard. The ringleader free, out there somewhere, given a home and protection, living the life of fucking Riley.

But things were different now. Different rules. Jack held the man's fate in his hands, listening to the shrieks and howls, smelling the burn of melting flesh as he worked the flame to great effect. Genitals dripping away like candle wax. Listening to him plead for mercy through the horror, for a saviour to come down and pull him from the torture and pain, the hell of the demented madman getting down on his knees, sinking teeth into flesh and tearing his face off, erasing his identity, his memory, every night ripping the bastard apart.

Finding him. That was the crux. Getting the info and cutting through all the dreams and nightmares and burning away the demons with a dose of reality. It wasn't makebelieve at all. Didn't have to be. It was possible. Some rational thinking, the application of company tactics. Keeping an eye on the rivals. Money changing hands. Hiring somebody to do the legwork. Same thing. Get the whereabouts, weigh up the pros and cons, then go. Mission underway. He'd carry out the kill himself. Get the bastard out of his head, out of his life once and for all.

But it was a fantasy. Something that would never happen. How could it? It would rip his family apart. With Jack doing life in prison it would solve nothing. He thought of the boy that had been killed. He had vaguely known him, had seen him around the streets, the arcades. Quiet bloke. Broken family, sent to a kids' home, same old story. He didn't deserve any of it, but it was a lottery. It could've been Jack. He'd been over to the killer's Hackney flat for parties three four five times himself so it was just a roll of the dice. But the last time was different. Jack had never been so scared. Drugged, hallucinating, kept prisoner. The gang were getting more brazen. Different men coming in to brutalise him. Hell and reality washed into one. The ringleader watching and laughing. Hissing away. Finally they brought him for a ride and dumped him out of the car, somewhere near the forest. Must have decided a shallow grave was too much effort. Chucking pound notes at him. Money to shut up. Money to fuck off.

Jack never told anyone. He was too embarrassed. Too ashamed. He left it all behind. Never wanted to see that world again. But next thing it was all over the papers. Boy dead. Body found. Men arrested. A paedophile ring that prowled the train terminals, coach stations, the Strand, Soho, Piccadilly, Leicester Square. Preying on the vulnerable, the truants, runaways, failures of the system. More boys buried across the country. Missing. Dead. Never found.

But Jack wasn't dead. No chance. Jack was still here and doing well. Getting on. Doing his best. Alive and thriving. He rinsed with mouthwash and spat away the scum. He had to go to work. Had to get out there. Out in the world. Live. Tear himself away from all this overthinking, all this looking back and get real. He went into the bedroom and got dressed, shined his shoes. Forward was the way. It was the only direction. He headed down and had a quick coffee, a bit of toast. He got his car keys. Maybe he'd do a late one tonight, a few extra hours. Graft it out, exhaust himself. Get into the rhythm, mind working like a machine, no time to think at all. Definitely. Head down, get stuck in. It's the only way.

DEAR JOHN

Hugh was in the corner of the cell playing with Boris his pet spider, while Marty lay on the top bunk thinking about his missus. He'd spoken to her on the phone yesterday, and though she'd tried to sound normal and denied anything was wrong, things were different. He could tell. Call it a sixth sense, call it what you like, but he could feel it full and strong. Donna was taking him for a mug.

'Guess what, Mart?' Hugh says. 'Boris the spider has just told me something.'

'Oh yeah?' Marty says, playing along, glad of the change of subject before it completely battered his head in. 'What's he gone and said now?'

'He says he thinks you're not a happy man. He tells me something big is bugging you.'

'Well, on that score old Boris would be correct. Tell him he's a clever chap.'

Hugh places the spider back in his web, removes the tome he'd been reading off his chair and sits down, feet up on the lower bunk.

'It's time to spill the flava beans Marty,' he says as he builds a spliff. 'I'm all ears and I've got all the time in the world. Well, a month at least. Then I'll be back on the street and you'll be looking at a new pad partner, which could be a good or bad thing depending.'

'Knowing me I'll get a fucking spicehead ranting in my face day and night. Or some dirty smackhead who sleeps all day and refuses to wash. Or maybe somebody even more crazy than you.'

'Come on Mart,' he says. 'Fess up to Uncle Hugh. Who knows, a problem shared could be a problem no more.'

'I don't know H. I don't think you can help me with this one I'm afraid.'

'Try me.'

'I can try but I'll be wasting my breath.'

'It's Lenny Flint, isn't it?' he says, which isn't a bad guess.

Lenny four cells up had been pissing him off lately, firstly about the two tins of tuna he owed him, but also after he started wisecracking yesterday in front of Tony Williams, being sarky as Marty walked by, trying to get into the top dog's good books at his expense.

Marty shook his head. 'It's not Lenny. But I must say, the man is trying my patience. He could be in for some punishment and very soon.'

'You're going to do him?'

'Let's call that a yes.'

'Okay. But it's not your main gripe?'

'Correct.'

'Well now you've stumped me.' Then Hugh says, 'It's not women trouble, is it?'

Marty turns to him. 'You're stumped no more fella. Women trouble it is.'

'Spill it.'

'My missus is seeing another bloke.'

'How do you know that?'

'I just do.'

'Not good enough, I need more than that.' He turns to Boris in the corner. 'Marty is imagining things again B, letting the paranoia win the battle, ain't that right mate?'

'I'm telling you H. She sounded different. And she asked me if I'd got her latest letter yet. It didn't sound right. All the signs are there.'

Hugh lights his spliff, takes a couple of tokes and passes it over. 'Here, inhale some of this onto that strife of yours, then you might see things from a different angle.'

'There's no angles about it I'm afraid. It's my worst nightmare. But one that in all honesty from my first day in this dump I knew would occur.'

'You seriously think Donna has hooked up with someone else?'

'Bullseye.'

'Tell me more.'

'There's not much to tell apart from the fact that when I get out of here I'm going to murder the bastard. Actually strangle him to death with my bare hands.'

'I don't think that'll be necessary.'

'Why?'

'Because Boris just told me that your missus is still indeed faithful and true. The bloke you're dreaming of killing doesn't exist.'

'Tell Boris from me that he doesn't have a clue on the matter. And even if he did I'm not interested in his opinions. Or his advice.'

'Boris, let me tell you, is more intelligent than you and me put together. His opinions are not only valid but based on a long ancestral line of life experiences stamped into his DNA, therefore wisely valuable.'

'Wise old Boris, eh?'

'Spiders see and hear everything. They're quiet and stealthy, but great observers and cognitive absorbers. They're patient too - patience and cunning, always signs of a perceptive mind.'

'If Boris is so clever, why did he choose to live in a fucking jail? Right now he could stroll out the window, on through the yard, beam a web over the wall and set up camp in a straight-goer's nice warm living room before the day is out. If he was clever that is, but he's not. He's voluntarily incarcerated. Jail as a lifestyle choice.'

'You're wrong again, Mart. Boris doesn't see his home as a jail. To him it's a fruitful habitation where he can acquire three square guaranteed portions of flying critters in his gut daily. That means a lot to a creature like Boris. A good old feed, it's top of his hierarchy of needs. He's also got decent company, and I'm not talking about his birds either – and he does get his legs over quite often - I'm talking about you and me.'

'If you say so mate. But I'll beg to differ on that.'

'Fair enough. But wait… he's just told me something.'

'Go on then, I'm not going anywhere.'

'He's told me to tell you to stop slagging him off. He's a clever creature and his kind have survived on their wits in this world for aeons, a lot longer than we have in fact, so genetically speaking that shows a fair bit of intelligence. And in that time they've been observing us, making notes and shaking their heads at our chronically disastrous behavioural habits.'

'Is that so?'

'Humans are probably the most suicidal species on this planet. It can't be denied. So many things we do causes problems not only to others but ourselves. Other sentient beings the world over look down on us with disdain - a disdain that we deserve, may I add.'

'That's some wacky reasoning there but I see your point. I can't imagine Boris or any of his brethren doing what I did to land myself a stretch inside, so fair enough.'

‘Exactly. Man is his own worst enemy. We’re a crazy species. We think we’re clever, sitting at the top of the tree looking down on the wildlife below, when the truth is the wildlife is laughing at us. The day we’re gone, having annihilated ourselves with nuclear bombs or technology or whatever else, the green shoots and insects and animals will completely take over. And they won’t cry no tears at our demise either, I can tell you that.’

‘Won’t they all be dead too?’

‘Nature never dies. It’s seeded within the earth. It’ll build back up, eventually running the show. A human-free planet full of thriving life.’

‘You could be right. I mean, I can’t deny the possibility.’

‘Which brings us back to your predicament.’

‘Unfortunately, yes. The missus.’

‘The missus indeed. So shoot the breeze. You talk, I’ll listen and when you’re done I’ll consult our friend over there for words of comfort and advice going forward.’

‘What can I say?’

‘You can start at the beginning.’

‘You mean yesterday’s phone call when Donna sounded offish?’

‘No, right at the beginning. Let’s take it from the top. Where did you first meet Donna?’

‘It was a pub on Lea Bridge Road. Disco night. I’d had a few pints and my mate Stevie pulled me over to try and chat up these two sorts who were standing under the lights. One of them was Donna.’

‘Boris wants to know something. What was she wearing?’

‘Oi, tell Boris to watch it or he’ll end up with only seven legs.’

‘He’s only arachnid after all. He has feelings too, you know. Desires. It won’t do him any harm. Liven up his life for a change. It can’t be all fun and excitement lying in wait for a passing gnat all day.’

‘Fair enough. Absolutely lovely she was. She was wearing a tight pink top, a white mini-skirt and white heels. Her clothes were real figure-hugging you know. Showing off her shape.’

‘And the other bird, her mate?’

‘Her mate, H, would’ve been right up your street. Big blonde hair and bubbly personality. A bit like that model you’ve got on the wall there except she wasn’t showing her bare knockers. But it was Donna that really caught my eye. God, yeah. Long dark hair, beautiful brown eyes. Kind of Spanish-looking. Mediterranean good looks. I couldn’t stop staring at her.’

‘So they were standing there under the lights and you and your mate took the plunge?’

‘We certainly did. Me and Stevie Nixon. He was practically pulling me over to the other bar where the disco was going on. Raving about these two birds, how if we didn’t get in there quick they’d be snapped up in a heartbeat. So yeah, I strolled in there with my pint.’

‘And you went straight up to them?’

‘To be honest, no. There was a bit of a delay. I had to throw back a vodka to give me the courage. I mean, these birds weren’t your standard Friday night fare in a pub in Leyton, put it that way.’

‘So what happened once the magic voddy was imbibed?’

‘Action, that’s what happened H. I got my arse over there and started putting on the charm.’

‘Did you dance?’

‘Yeah, we did. We got dancing pretty quickly, which I thought might put her off because pulling moves ain’t exactly my forte. But I can always belt out some shapes if the situation demands, which I did.’

‘Can you remember what song was playing when you first hit the floor?’

‘I can as it goes. ‘You’re Out of Your Mind’ by Dane Bowers

featuring Posh Spice. Top tune.'

'How about your mate and his girl, were they having a boogie?

'Stevie, I recall, was already in the corner with his bird sharing a tongue sandwich. Yvonne she was called. He didn't mess about. Never did, Stevie.'

'How about you, did you kiss Donna in the pub?'

'Not that I remember. We talked mainly. Afterwards when we were waiting outside the cab office we might've shared a kiss. The full menu came later of course.'

'So was it back to yours or hers?'

'All four of us went back to their flat in Walthamstow.'

'You made love?'

'Oh yeah. Course. It was definitely a case of making love rather than a standard bunk-up, yeah.'

'And?'

'It was perfect. In fact I knew that very night Donna was the girl I was going to marry and have kids with.'

'You knew that quickly?'

'I did indeed. It just felt right, instantly. Like we were made for each other. You just know. And a few months down the line we moved in together.'

'And things worked out?'

'Yeah. It took us a while to get married – I mean, I had a couple of short stops inside - but it happened. And then of course little Jake and Jessie came along. What more can you ask for?'

'What about your mate Stevie, did it turn out to be a long-term relationship for him too?'

'Joking aren't you? Back then he had a different bird on his arm every night.'

'But he settled down in the end?'

'Settled into a grave plot up Plaistow yeah. The bloke died an early death. We're talking a few years later, but still.'

'Details. Where and why?'

'It was outside the Angel and Crown.'

'I'm a South London man, where's that?'

'Down Bethnal Green way. Roman Road. He was standing having a fag and a natter on the phone when a car pulled up. A bloke jumped out, masked and wielding a shooter. Fired a round of buckshot into his chest.'

'Had Stevie been balling his missus?'

'Don't think so. It was more of a money-related thing. Stevie was a professional conman. He could talk the hind legs off a donkey and did so with gusto. He drove a Merc sports, wore a Rolex, all the top labels, and was always sweet-talking people to invest in his get-rich-quick schemes. Throw money into the pot and enjoy some healthy returns. He'd deliver on his word too, then they'd toss even more money into the black hole. Then of course he'd go cold on them. It was a classic ponzi scheme kind of thing. Men were chasing him all over London in the end. Even me, a mate, I was taken in at one point. *No Mart, this one ain't a con, it's real. You're gonna collect big time.* He died owing me a grand. But there you go.'

'Did they find the man who shot him?'

'Yeah, some Essex prick. From Basildon if I'm correct. Fancied himself as a face. He got a twenty-five. Probably should've just walked away, but I suppose being taken for a mug can be hard to live with.'

'So back to Donna. She was the perfect wife?'

'Yeah… well, you know, we had rows now and then just like anyone does, even split up once or twice, but it was nothing serious, just the two of us being stubborn. In the main we were solid. Things were good.'

'Until?'

'Until I started hitting the bookie shops, that's when.'

'You were pulling in good money on the blag for a while though weren't you?'

'Not really. It's a mug's game. You'd earn a few hundred, sometimes a few thou. It's hardly a jackpot is it?'

'But you had good holidays, wore nice clothes, kitted out the missus and kids, had a decent car. Things must've been good for a while?'

'They were okay, yeah. But that was more to do with the things I was doing on the side. Stuff I was never caught for.'

'Drugs?'

'Yeah. I started helping a mate with these big deals. Joey Sparks. We'd buy gear in bulk and sell it down the chain absolutely cut to fuck. I'm talking kilos of the stuff. When the cash rolled in from those capers I was laughing. But I always spent it quick. Always spunked it in case the coppers came knocking. If I'd been clever and invested the profit legally, in property or whatever, I wouldn't be sitting here now.'

'Live fast, spend even faster?'

'That's pretty much it. I'd blow it, then be back sitting on my arse potless. That's when I'd have to shove on a mask, dust off the shooter and target another shop.'

'And then you were caught?'

'I was never actually nabbed at that. Though once I was very nearly caught. A van came flying into me as I ran back to the car. Threw me right in the air. That's why I walk with a limp now, an old man before my time. Why? Because I wanted to put food on my family's table.'

'And have a decent motor parked outside?'

'Course.'

'And good holidays?'

'Why not?'

'And plenty sniff up your snout?'

'Well, now you mention it, that's exactly where I went wrong.

At first I'd only indulge at the weekend, then it became a daily thing, and before long it was morning, noon and night. And then I was desperate and throwing on a bally and waving a shooter about more often, taking big risks.'

'What about you and Joey Sparks? I thought you had a good thing going selling kilos of gear?'

'Oh, that ended.'

'What happened?'

'We had a few disagreements. Sparksy had most of the contacts so he used to take most of the money. It wasn't fair because we both put the same work in. Then he disappeared and it all dried up.'

'Sparks vanished?'

'He took his business elsewhere. Spain probably. The Far East. Fuck knows.'

'And what happened after that?'

'I became reckless. I lost my reasoning. Too much charlie up the nose and a lack of funds can do that. I was making plans I'd never have dreamed of with a sound and sober mind. I was off my nut and it caused a lot of stress at home, I recall.'

'So homelife wasn't always so good?'

'Not at this point, no.'

'And you were dreaming up grandiose plans?'

'You're not wrong there. Plans that if carried out would've had me tugged in a second.'

'Such as?'

'I was planning to rob my brother in law's business. He had a big warehouse stocked with moody white goods. They were selling like hot cakes and he was making a mint. I was going to target him on his cash run to the bank.'

'Your wife's brother? That's a bit naughty, ain't it?'

'I know. I was losing my morals. Thinking I was the big I am. Thinking I was God, that I could pull off anything, any feat known to man. I was worse than you. You talk to fucking spiders, I was off my face talking to the walls.'

'Less of that, it sounds disrespectful. Boris has ears you know.'

'Sorry Boris.'

'He'll forgive you, but not next time.'

'Tell him thanks, I'm very grateful. But talking of you and Boris, can I ask you something? Why did you name him after that ex-prime minister mug?'

'I didn't. The man you're referring to doesn't come into it.'

'Yes he does, he's the most well-known face I can think of with that name, and you called your pet spider after him. The man's a pillock.'

'That goes without saying. All politicians are pillocks, along with those who believe in them. But let me tell you now, the man you're talking about isn't even called Boris.'

'Yes he is. That's his name, are you mad?'

'It's not his name.'

'You off your trolley?'

'His name is Alex. Which is what his friends and family call him. He made the other name up to try and sound interesting. The only genuine Boris is our eight-legged sage over there.'

'Are you telling me that mug who pushed jabs and lockdowns for a virus that didn't exist doesn't even use his real name?'

'Precisely dear Watson.'

'That makes him even more of a liar than I thought.'

'Correct. But you're misinformed on one thing.'

'Which is?'

'The big bad killer flu that could drop you dead on the street China-style really did exist.'

'No it didn't. We've talked about this before. It was whatever cold or flu you happened to pick up during that period. The common cold rebranded. And when people got jabbed they got more illnesses because it messed up their immune systems. A win-win for these evil fuckers. Culling the population.'

'I'm telling you, it did exist.'

'No it didn't.'

'Oh yes it did.'

'So you and that Churchill-wannabe are in full agreement? Go on then, tell me, where did it exist?'

'In the heads of the globalists whose friends run the highly profitable pharmaceutical industry.'

'Phew, thank fuck for that. I thought you were serious there for a minute H.'

'I am. Just because you conjure something out of thin air doesn't mean it's non-existent. The killer virus very much existed, though more as a grand concept, like the basis of an extreme religion.'

'Ah, so you've got me on a technicality there. It existed but only because a tsunami of propaganda forged it into some kind of mystic reality. A mass hallucination in the sky.'

'Not bad Mart, I like that.'

'Thanks.'

'Fake pandemics are just like wars, they make a lot of very rich people a lot richer. The magicians waved their wands and conjured the concept into existence and the public believed and responded accordingly - to the point of idiocy. So in that respect, it very much existed.'

'I see your point. Boris Johnson as David Koresh or Jim Jones. Authority figures playing cult leaders and pushing the doctrine. Getting the believers to jump through hoops and inject the Kool Aid while they themselves broke every rule and partied nightly. Livin' la vida loca.'

'Of course. It's like socialism. It's for the plebs only, Mart. The men pushing the message live like kings.'

'As always. But it still doesn't answer my question regarding old spidey over there. Why give that eight-legged freak such an obscure name, and a Russian one to boot?'

'Language, Marty.'

'My apologies, m'lud.'

'Our pad mate is named after a Who song as it goes. If you haven't heard the track there's not much to say, but The Who are his favourite band, ain't that right B mate?'

'So in a secret life he dons a skinny suit and a green parka and rides a Lambretta?'

'Of course he does.'

'Sneaks off when the lights are out, drops some purple hearts and hits a club down Carnaby Street, all eight legs on the floor, showing how it's done?'

'Sounds about right. Mod was the coolest teen movement and naturally Boris only hangs with the coolest.'

'Are you telling me Mods were cooler than the Casuals?'

'Mods morphed into the Casuals. If that's news to you, you need to sharpen up on your social history and modern youth movements. But by the time of the Casuals the rules were looser, more free flowing. The original Mods were style-conscious to a degree unknown thereafter. They were real obsessives. Sharpness of attire was their *raison d'etre.*'

'Nobody looked better than me when I was kitted out in Stone Island, Armani jeans and Timberland shit kickers, that's a fact.'

'If you say so.'

'I do.'

'So let's get back to our original talking point.'

'Oh no, my missus?'

'That is the motif of this conversation, so yes.'

'Well, in a nutshell, she's lost interest in me.'

'You really think so?'

'I know so H. Here I am rotting in Wanno unable to provide and there she is stuck at home struggling. Though to be truthful,

I don't even blame her. It doesn't mean I'm not going to skin the imposter alive though, because I am. In fact when I get out of this shithole it'll be the very first thing I do.'

'Enjoy your five minutes of freedom then.'

'I'll have to, because the thought of some other bloke in my bed… Jesus, I'll tear his fucking head off with my bare hands.'

'Don't go there Mart. Clear the image from your mind. Deep breath, into the lungs and out through the nose. Repeat until you achieve peak tranquillity.'

'What would you do then, come on? Wouldn't you want to take action?'

'I'd only act if I had evidence, not reasoning based on conjecture. But I let my bird go anyway. We said goodbye. With a stretch like mine, I had to be realistic.'

'The evidence is loud and clear and shouting in my face. There's a new bloke on the scene, I can feel it in my gut.'

'Billy O'Connor from the spur below felt it in his gut when he strung himself up in his pad last month. He had six months to go and it turned out he was imagining things. His missus was faithfully waiting for him.'

'O'Connor was a nutter. Forget to say good morning to the bloke and he'd think you were blanking him, plotting his downfall. He put a shiv to my neck once asking why I'd looked at him funny when I walked past him earlier. He was a class A mentalist.'

'That's a word to consider Mart, next time you think the missus is putting herself about.'

'Listen, I never said she was putting herself about, I said she might have another bloke on the scene. Donna's no slag.'

'You said this, you said that, but it's all words. All speculation, all fantasy. In a place like this our minds can play tricks with our mental wellbeing. We're in captivity, not in control, so our minds imagine all sorts of things. Unsound mental health is a natural by-product when you're physically caught in a trap, your fate in other people's hands.'

'I'll begin worrying when I start talking to spiders. When that day arrives I'll book myself into the hospital ward and have long conversations with the shrink. A scenario worth considering eh, H?'

'Touché. I'm just saying you're running away with yourself, letting your thoughts slide towards the no-go zone. When you spoke on the phone to Donna she was probably just having a shit day. It can happen you know.'

'Maybe.'

'Well that's an improvement at least.'

'It won't be if the post arrives and I receive a Dear John.'

'You won't get a Dear John.'

'But say I fucking do? *Sorry Marty, but I've had to move on...* I won't be able to handle that H. You do know that, don't you? I'll fucking lose it, smash the place up, probably end up strangling a screw or something, I'm not joking.'

'Ease down. Chill. It won't come to that, I promise you.'

'With all due respect H, you can't promise me jack shit. If I get a letter from Donna saying it's over, that'll be the one thing that pushes me over the edge.'

'Do you really believe that?'

'Unfortunately, yes. In fact even the thought of it leaves me feeling like I've lost my sanity already. Like I'm watching my marbles roll away across the floor.'

'We all have our vulnerabilities I suppose.'

'I know we do. My dad was mad, you know. He used to brag about it. *I'm mad as a fucking hatter,* he used to say, then laugh like a lunatic. Not that I ever saw much of him because he was mostly inside, but even so. I've got it in my family. The curse.'

'You know what I think?'

'Go on, tell me.'

'The most sensible option we have right now is to consult old Boris, see what he makes of all this. I'm not joking. In a crazy world the sanest man is king.'

'Can't say it doesn't make sense. He's definitely the sanest living being in this room right now, I know that much. Me with my fucked-up head and you with your past insane acts of violence. I mean, look at us.'

'Take it easy Mart, I never killed anyone.'

'No, but you did a fair job cutting off a man's fingers and toes and laying them out in a macabre pattern around his unconscious body. What was all that about? It's hardly the work of a sane mind, is it?'

'Fair play, conventional sanity was never my strong point I'll admit. But some would say what you did to earn your stretch was even worse.'

'And why is that then?'

'Because taking on the task of cutting up and disposing of a deceased body is hardly work for an ordinary decent criminal, is it?'

'I needed the money. I was desperate. The drug deals had dried up and betting shop blagging was getting too hot. And the body I worked on belonged to a bona fide scumbag, a total wrong 'un, I know that for a fact.'

'Many would say that's no excuse. In fact some would even suggest you took on the job because you enjoyed it.'

'They'd be talking shite then, wouldn't they?'

'I mean, I know you were charged for one body, but it's obvious you had experience, otherwise a top firm like the A-Team wouldn't have hired you to dispose of their human waste. How many bodies did you actually do?'

'Look H, I'm in no mood for this. Let's just drop the subject.'

'You told me earlier that your dealing partner Joey Sparks went missing after you had a disagreement.'

'Yeah, so what?'

'You said Sparksy vanished to Spain or the Far East?'

'That's right.'

'Well how come they found one of his arms buried in Wanstead Flats?'

'That had nothing to do with me.'

'Then a part of his leg was dug up in a field near South Mimms motorway services.'

'I don't know anything about that.'

'And finally they found his head in some wasteland by a rail depot in Barking.'

'Now look, I told you…'

'You had a disagreement, you say?'

'So what? It wasn't me. The bloke disappeared and I never saw him again.'

'Nor did anyone else. Apart from the coppers who dug up his scattered remains. It was in the papers at the time. The Jigsaw Murder they called it. The work of a professional, they said. Someone perhaps in the butchery trade. Didn't you once say that after leaving school you worked in a butcher's shop?'

'That doesn't mean I'm some kind of serial killer.'

'But getting away with it would've definitely impressed the Adams boys, I know that much.'

'Well H, maybe your little carving up session with fingers and toes would've impressed them as well?'

'Not really, because I was caught bang to rights for it. But by the sounds of things Mart, you got through quite a number before only facing the courts for one.'

'Look H, whatever.'

'Okay. But my point is that all psychopathic acts are relative. Is one man's heinous act really more heinous than another man's? To be clear on the matter, we're all in the same boat.'

'That may be. But all I can say is right now I'm feeling none too healthy in that respect, put it that way. And with all this Donna business I'm hoping the state of my head doesn't get any worse.'

'So it's over to Boris then. Spider philosopher in residence. Let's see what he thinks of your predicament.'

'Go on then, ask him.'

'What do you reckon Boris old son, is Marty's missus up to dirty tricks or is life in chokey just getting to him and he's losing his noodle? Come on Bozzer, we're waiting, we need some wise words here.'

Just then the mail arrives. A single letter for Marty, Donna's handwriting on the envelope.

'Oh shit…' He tears it open and scans it avidly.

'What does it say?'

Marty's face relaxes, a picture of pure relief.

'Boris has spoken,' he says.

'There you go Mart, I knew he would. He has his own ways but he never lets you down.'

PAYDAY

I walk out of the dole office onto a rainy Holloway Road. Reaching the cash machine I put my bank card in the wall, hoping for a miracle. Not today I'm afraid. Twelve quid to last me till Monday. What a joke. I take out a tenner and head for the Wetherspoon's.

The place is pretty busy, for this time of day anyway. I order a pint and the barmaid clocks my scar as she serves me. It's a look I've seen a million times before – ever since I was bottled outside a club six years ago - but I'm well over it now. Some people are pretty, some aren't, simple as. If some choose to judge me on facial appearance, then so be it. To be truthful though, I'd been a cocky fucker growing up, always joyriding motorbikes and asking for trouble, getting into untold scraps. Looking back it's surprising I'm in one piece.

I pay up and take a lug of my pint. It tastes good. I'll have to watch it though in case I get a thirst on, which for me is never a good idea. Not these days. I might be near-skint but it didn't stop me last time. A swift shoplifting spree, quick sell off and that was my beer tokens sorted till closing. Mad or what? Since splitting with Fiona things have been turning silly, I'm just not myself. I bring my drink to a table and a minute later a hand claps down on my shoulder.

'How are you keeping Rob?'

I turn to see my old friend Steve, who I haven't set eyes on in two years at least.

'Steve mate. How's tricks?'

'Good,' he says. 'Things are swinging along quite nicely.'

'The last I heard you were living out in Ibiza?'

'I was indeed. I'm back in the Smoke for my sins now. Well, for a while anyway.'

'You still trading, shifting powder and pills?' I ask quietly.

'Not any more. I'm in a different racket now. Different game altogether.'

Whatever it is must be lucrative because his threads aren't cheap, and as he invites me over to his table, nor is his bird. She is stunning. It turns out she knows me from school, the year below, and I really should have recognised her.

'Lisa's grown up a bit since then,' Steve says, draping his arm around her. 'Fucking beautiful, don't you reckon?'

'Shut up,' she laughs.

We sit chatting and I keep the tone positive, making out I'm doing fine.

'Are you still with Fiona?' he asks.

'Nah, that finished a few months back. Just one of those things really,' I say, but my acting isn't very convincing. He can see right through me, my whole situation. No girl, no job, going nowhere. I suppose it's obvious really.

'You still riding a motorbike?' he asks.

'Not for a while now. I had to sell my last one.'

'Always were handy on a bike though, weren't you?' he winks.

Soon they have to head off. They're going down the West End to do some shopping. We swap numbers.

'I'll give you a call in a few days,' he says. 'I'm going to see what I can do for you, moneywise. I might have something right up your street.'

As we shake hands he slips me something. 'Look after yourself,' he says, and I'm shocked to see it's sixty quid.

'Honestly Steve, there's no need,' I tell him.

'It's nothing,' he says. 'I'll be seeing you soon.'

Sure enough a few days later he gives me a call. It's a sunny day and we meet in Highbury Fields. We sit on a bench, Lisa over on the grass on her phone as we have a chat.

The question is simple. Do I want to earn myself some serious cash?

'Who doesn't?' I say. 'But it depends. If the odds involve doing ten years inside then, you know, maybe not.'

He's gazing across the park, looking philosophical.

'There's risk involved, of course there is. But the odds are in our favour. We've done several of these jobs already and pulled things off pretty nicely. I can't really tell you much more at this point, you understand that?'

'Yeah, course I do.'

'Just rest assured, it's professional. Everyone on the team knows what they're doing – including Lisa. Let's just say she's an expert in research. Knows her stuff.'

We watch as she kicks a ball back at some kids.

'You're a devil on two wheels Rob. Just what I'm looking for.'

He lights a cigarette and clocks me noticing his watch.

'That's right,' he says. 'It's a Rolex. I'm not exactly dripping gold, but a little luxury, why not?'

Lisa walks over smiling. 'You two had your little man chat yet?'

'Yeah,' Steve says, standing up. 'We're pretty much done here I reckon.' Then he turns to me. 'Listen, think about it. If you don't call me in three days I'll know you're not in. That's fair enough. But say yes and I'll have to spill the beans, and then there's no going back.'

We shake hands and I watch them walk away.

Money makes things happen and I want some of that. If Steve says the job is safe, then it's safe. London is full of chancers as dumb as they come, idiots just waiting to be arrested, but Steve is smart, in a different league, he always has been.

Still, I have to think about it.

The next morning I get a letter from the social. They're stopping me a week's money for signing on twenty minutes late. Fuck the cunts. I phone Steve. I tell him I want in.

The Yamaha Sport Steve has lined up is the kind of machine I have dreams about. I give it a spin to get the feel of it, heading out past the M25, practising turns and swerves, hitting 130mph on a straight country road and feeling the surge, the pure adrenaline, before realising it's probably best I keep myself in one piece for the job at least. I still have it though, that's for sure.

Steve is running a firm targeting designer stores and jewellers in the West End. Steve and Lisa are smart operators; they do their homework. The level of planning blows me away.

To be honest, I'm shitting it. A few days beforehand, I meet the rest of the boys in a flat off Caledonian Road, and they're good blokes. They show me footage of some of their jaunts.

'Fear not,' they say. 'It's a buzz like you won't believe.'

'You're new to this,' Steve tells me. 'But you're a mate and I want you to collect. There's wealth out there, big wealth, and all the bankers and crooks who run this country have had their paws in the till for too long. It's our turn now.'

We hit a jeweller's on Old Bond Street. Two bikes, two sledgehammers. The hammers hit the glass as we rev our engines, people steering clear, hands swiping the goods, knowing exactly what to go for, loading up, the seconds ticking, then passengers all aboard we're out of there.

Back at the flophouse my feet aren't touching the floor, a dozen arms around me.

'You did it. Welcome to the firm!'

We party all night.

Steve fences the goods and my cut is five grand. Money I've never even dreamed of earning.

'Tip of the iceberg,' he tells me.

With cash in my pocket the first thing I do is head into town to get myself kitted out in some decent clothes. I literally throw the rags I'm wearing in the bin. Then I go on the piss. I pub crawl around the West End on my own, dressed to the nines, ordering the priciest drinks just because I know I can. But nobody is friendly so I cab it back home and take the session local.

I head to the Hercules, flashing my wad and chatting to the barmaid. I'm buying her drinks thinking I'm well in there, until she tells me she has a boyfriend and two kids. Another girl starts at seven, a cracking little blonde number right up my street, but by now I'm pissed and slurring, beginning to talk shit. I switch to lemonade and have something to eat. Then I'm back on pints, but things are blurry now and all I remember is the landlord pushing me out saying I'm harassing his staff and not to come back. By midnight I've somehow sobered up and find myself knocking on my ex-girlfriend's door.

I might look a state but Fiona lets me in and we sit in her kitchen talking for hours. We haven't spoken in two months, and she tells me she's spent the last few evenings on the wine herself. She's just split up with the bloke she left me for. The news sobers me. We end up in bed.

The next morning I wake up to the sight of Fiona sleeping

soundly beside me. I'm stroking her hair and it smells beautiful, a scent I really miss. How did this miracle happen? One minute I've got nothing, the next I've got the two things I most need in life. Money in my pocket and things with Fiona back on track. I kiss her face, gently waking her.

She opens her eyes and shrugs me off. 'Oh no... Rob, please.' Abruptly she gets up, sitting at the edge of the bed.

'What's wrong?' I ask. 'I thought everything was fine with us now?'

She picks my trousers off the floor and throws them at me.

'Look, I think it's best you left. We both had a few drinks last night. I wasn't thinking straight. Let's just call it a one-off.'

I try talking to her, but soon she's yelling at me, acting as if she's made the biggest mistake of her life.

'Don't do this to me okay,' she says. 'I don't need this right now. Just go. Leave me alone!'

For days I sit in my flat, playing on my new Xbox, or watching films or fucking about on the internet. But soon I'm bored. I have no friends. No proper ones anyway. Nobody close I can chill with, talk to about things. Where have they all gone through the years? I don't want to bother Steve or any of the gang as they all have girlfriends and do their own thing, but I long for his call, to hit the road and get out there working again. That buzz, that camaraderie, I need it.

Soon enough the call comes in. 'Briefing time Rob. It's all planned.'

We meet in the same flat and run through the logistics. This one is a major one. A jeweller's in Knightsbridge.

Again the job goes bang on plan, and we're gunning out of there at 100mph loaded with designer gold. Back at the flop we party into the night and again the haul is promptly fenced. My cut this time is, let's just say, mindblowing.

I buy more clothes, more gadgets. I hit the pubs again telling myself this time I'll behave. One afternoon I'm sitting at the bar of the White Swan at Highbury Corner in a Gucci suit, open neck shirt and chain, oozing the kind of charm only money can buy. I get chatting to this fit curvy girl who is lunching with some work friends. As she waits for her round at the bar I tell her she's the nicest thing I've seen all day and she smiles and returns the compliment. After a chat we arrange to meet when she finishes work at the Islington Council building up the road. She returns to the pub at half five with a thirst for vodka and cokes, and by seven we're in the corner snogging each other's faces off.

'Let's go back to mine,' she says.

We cab it to her flat off Essex Road. She shows me the bedroom and tells me to wait for her while she has a shower; she needs to freshen up. I sit at the edge of her bed waiting for her. After drinking all day my head is spinning. I didn't quite realise how pissed I was. Then she's back, strutting in all dolled up in sexy gear, stripping me off and pinning me down on the bed, writhing all over me. But there's a problem. I can't perform.

She pauses. 'Don't you fancy me?'

'You're the hottest thing I've ever seen,' I tell her, and we carry on, but still nothing is happening. Suddenly she stops.

'Are you gay or something?'

'Of course not. It's just I maybe hit the beer too much today. I was in the pub from opening time.'

She stands up, glaring at me up and down.

'You know what I think?'

'What?'

'I think you better leave.'

I return to the pub for a bit, watching the evening crowd laugh and joke and have a good time. Then feeling reckless I head up Holloway Road to the Hercules, the pub I've been barred from. In my drunken mind I'm convinced I've got unfinished business with the blonde barmaid. I can give her my number and we can meet some other time. And if the governor doesn't like it he can go fuck himself.

I walk up to the bar and the bloke is straight over, shoving me out onto the pavement saying I'm barred for life. A barman joins in pushing me in the chest, telling me to do what the man says. I lunge for him and we're rolling on the floor. Then next thing I know the police are talking to me up against a wall. They're saying if I don't calm down they'll nick me. Further up I can see the barman getting a bollocking as well.

'We're giving you a chance to go home and get yourself to bed, your choice.'

I nod, say okay and they let me walk.

Fifteen minutes later I'm banging on Fiona's door, her flatmate saying she doesn't want to speak to me and to go away or she'll call the police.

'Fuck the police,' I shout, throwing stones up at Fiona's window.

A van soon screeches up on the road.

'You again,' the same coppers say and throw me into the cage.

I spend the night in the cells. I'm cautioned for being drunk and disorderly and warned that if I bother my ex again I'll be looking at a restraining order.

I lay low for a while. Then Steve phones and tells me to put on my glad rags because the whole crew is going clubbing.

'Think of it as a works outing,' he says. 'Something to boost team morale - not that we need it of course, but so what, let's get pilled up and paint the town red.'

Little does he know it's exactly what I need.

We hit a West End nightclub, all of us suited and booted, slamming out moves on the floor, the smartest mob there, and

I hit it off with a posh girl.

'So tell me, what do you do?' she asks.

'I'm an armed robber.'

'No, seriously,' she laughs.

'I'm not lying, honest. Armed robbery, that's my game.'

She likes my humour and calls me her mystery man.

We end up in a flat in Notting Hill putting her bedsprings through a workout. But the next day sober as she sits putting on her make-up for work, she seems like a different person.

'So you don't want my number then?'

She shakes her head. 'Last night was last night,' she says.

Posh birds can be as cold as ice. But I scored so what do I care?

Strolling along Portobello Road market I get a call from Steve.

'You get your end away then?' he enquires.

'Certainly did. Performed three times.'

'Good man,' he says. 'Because on Wednesday you'll be needed for a different kind of performance.'

We hit a well-known store in Mayfair. A night job. Same MO, same success. Revving out of there loaded and happy.

'That's how it's done boys,' Steve says as we toast the sight of the shattered windows on the morning news. We're on a roll.

I buy myself a Kawasaki Sport. Total dream machine. Handing over the cash I feel like pinching myself. It's like I've won the fucking lottery. I take her for a run, heading out to the sticks, knowing if I die right now, smash myself to bits, at least I'll be dying happy. But not everything is so good. I'm thinking more and more about Fiona.

I order some flowers to be delivered, the most expensive available. I want to say sorry. That night outside her flat I'd been an idiot. I miss her. These one night stands mean nothing to me. I have all this money but nobody to share it with.

A few days later I receive a message: *Rob, I appreciate the apology but I want to make something clear. It's over.*

I head out. I hit the nearest club. I throw my cash around and shag a fat girl in a mini-skirt. Afterwards she wants me to stay the night, but I tell her I have to go. Walking along the street, four blokes are hanging outside a kebab shop, staring at me as I pass, jealous of my smart designer threads while they stand in cheap jeans and T-shirts munching doner and chips.

Hearing the words 'flash prick' I turn round and front them, arms outstretched.

'Come on then, I'll take all fucking four of you!'

They kick me into next week and I wake up in an ambulance.

I'm released from hospital the next day and advised to rest. I feel like shit, every limb aching. But most shocking of all is my face. It's blown up black and blue.

Steve phones, wanting me to help nick some bikes for the next job. 'This one is the biggest yet,' he says. 'You're going to love it.'

'Sorry mate, I might have to bow out of this one I'm afraid. I'm not in the best condition. I went out drinking, then four blokes jumped me and used my head as a trampoline.'

He comes over to visit. The second he sees the state I'm in he says he'll get Pete to fill in for me.

'Fucking hell Rob, what happened?'

'I was pissed. I asked for it. It's just one of those things.'

'It's a shame you're going to miss out because this one coming up is due to be mega.'

'I haven't resigned Steve, I just need some rest and repair time.'

'You're right. Get yourself better and you'll be back on the team before you know it.'

That was the last time I spoke to him.

The job took place three days later and things went wrong

from the start. A member of staff played hero and took the swipe of an axe, leaving him bloodied on the floor. Then in the getaway the public waded in, taking one of the bikes down, two of the team held on the ground for the police. Steve and Pete, however, got away.

It was all over the news. *'Man seriously injured in daylight smash-and-grab raid'.* Things hadn't gone to plan and in the chaos mistakes were made. Things were hot now, and Steve and Lisa were too smart to stick around. They brought forward their long-term plans and escaped the heat for another kind of heat. Spain most likely, though I can't be sure. The rest of the gang stuck around and took their chances. All were soon arrested.

As for me, I expected my door to come crashing in any second, any hour, any day now. But it didn't happen. No one grassed me.

My money ran out and I never got back with Fiona, but at least I'm free and that's something. Several of the gang weren't so lucky. I suppose I've got to thank the four pricks on the street who gave me a kicking that night. They saved my life. Or at least a good few years of it.

NON-CRIME HATE INCIDENT

My flight lands down at Stansted at 10.07am and I'm met with the heavy grey skies that can only be expected of dear old Blighty. It's May and the sun should be shining, but every time I visit it's the same story. The summers of my younger days were glorious, all those 80s and 90s scorchers seared in my memory, solid sunshine from May to September, but something happened. Something changed. A bit like the country itself. Britannia no longer rules the waves or anything much else, and as the shuttle train heads down through a London of grey housing estates and dead industry, I get the sense of a country dying on its feet. A nation gone to the dogs. Take the flats where I grew up for example. Things weren't perfect but they were okay; people helped each other and were happy enough. Now the sense of community is history and you need bars on the windows to keep the predators out. What happened?

Back in the day Maggie was pushing optimism. To some of us anyway. A chance to go self-employed, get entrepreneurial and make some money. But relocating the manufacturing and selling off all the country's assets perhaps wasn't such a great idea. Back then I'd argue with my old man about politics endlessly, thinking I knew it all because I was getting some cash in my pocket, believing things were on the up and would stay that way. My dad worked at Ford's in Dagenham, a trade union man. In the mid-90s when Tony Blair was sliming up to the cool kids with his eyes on No. 10, my dad predicted the future. Do not trust that fucker, he said, while every other sod couldn't wait to vote for him. He said Blair was more of a greedy capitalist than even Thatcher. His lot will suck out all the wealth and bankrupt the country for everyone else. My dad didn't stick around long enough to witness the complete fallout thank God, but nor did I to be fair, I fucked off to Spain where I've been living for the past two decades.

The train alights at Tottenham Hale and I grab an Uber for the six miles down to Canning Town where I'm booked in at the spanking new Royal Ordnance Hotel. I haven't been back to the Smoke in a fair few years, and having been warned I'm prepared for surprises, but even so, the extent of the changes is quite staggering. For a start, this part of Tottenham, which to me has always been a bit of an industrial shithole, is covered in tall modern towers, some looking like they've been constructed from a kids' Lego set. But there you go. The cab moves next through Hackney and I'm spotting the changes, but I've been told the real punch in the face will strike when we reach the old manor. At Homerton we join the A12, a motorway in all but name, and head for the East End proper.

I chat to the driver. Abdul from Syria. He's been in the UK for four years after getting asylum, but fair play to him, he's a friendly bloke and we're chatting away. He lives in Forest Gate but says he wants to move somewhere safer as the area's got big problems with drugs and gangs and he doesn't want his kids getting drawn into all that; he wants them to go to college and do well. As I say, he's a decent chap and like most of us I take people as they come. Which reminds me of another thing my dad talked about. Racism. It was driven by ignorance and bigotry and he wouldn't have it, not in his house. Workers of the world of all colours and creeds unite against the bosses and take over. That was his interpretation of it anyway; Marx himself, however, wasn't too enamoured with freedom of movement as it only helped the bosses amass cheap labour, so the unite bit probably didn't mean in person, but there you go. When the revolution happens, my dad said, all the profit and means of production will be spread equally and colour and class won't mean a thing. But when my mum was robbed by a gang of blacks one evening on her way to the corner shop it must've tested him. She was in hospital overnight and his expletives, if I recall, didn't impart the same generosity of spirit towards all sectors of his fellow man. When he retired they moved to Leigh-on-Sea. Got the fuck away. I moved even further. It must run in the family.

Approaching the Blackwall Tunnel we turn onto the A13 for Canning Town, my old stamping ground by the Royal Docks. The new tall buildings hit me immediately. Corporate glass and steel. Sanitised ghost towns. Silvertown Way, an elevated dual-carriageway which not too long ago was edged with low warehouses and industrial works, is now lined both sides with looming skyscrapers that block the view and leave me dizzy. To clear my head I get the driver to turn down into the old working-class backstreets, if only to check they're still there. We cut through the encroaching new build, then drive through familiar streets of old flats and council houses. Buildings that used to be pubs stand at several corners. Since the closure of the docks in the 80s time hasn't been kind to this area. Passing a patch of green I recognise a face. It's Brian Downe who I haven't seen for a decade or more. He's standing letting his dog have a wander on the grass. I tell Abdul to pull over.

When Brian sees me he puts his hand to his chest, has a mock heart attack. We laugh and shake hands, go in for a hug. He says it's been so long he thought I was dead. Shot by gangsters and buried up in the Marbella hills. Either that or wearing concrete boots at the bottom of the North Sea. One of the other. Wouldn't be surprised at either, he laughs.

'No chance mate. You know me Bri, I'm a survivor. How's tricks?' I say, watching his dog squatting down doing its business.

'Not bad. Cracking on, getting by. You know how it is.'

'Are you the last man standing round here then? The manor looks fucking hollowed out mate.'

'Must be joking, Dan,' he says. 'I've got the White brothers up the road. They're still up to capers. The Masons are three doors away. Old Kenny Cribb is still on the scene too. He's just come out after doing a two for some road rage bollocks. He pulled a hatchet on someone.'

'Silly cunt.'

'There's still a few of us knocking about.'

I look around. 'But the manor's changed though hasn't it, something chronic?'

'Progress I think they call it,' he says, nodding to the shiny towers half a mile away. 'I call it money laundering.'

'Without a doubt.'

'Streeties pub is still going strong. I go down there most weekends.'

He's dressed in a stained sweatshirt and joggers, looks like he's seen better days. He clocks me checking out his attire and says he's doing some decorating this afternoon. It's not yet noon and I can smell the drink off him.

'You still with Vicky?' I ask.

'She died mate. Cancer. Two years back. I scattered her ashes at West Ham – you know, the new stadium. It was her wishes. You know Vick, she was more into the football than me. The rest went up Ilford, Valentines Park where we first met.'

'I'm sorry to hear that. I didn't know.'

'No worries. I've got the grandchildren at least. Five of them now. Brian junior lives up in Norfolk. Nicola's in Thurrock living with some new fella, wouldn't trust the cunt if you paid me. Still though.'

'You okay for money?' I take out my wallet.

'Nah, no need,' he says, but I ignore it, pass him a ton.

'Buy yourself a sherbet.'

He thanks me and shoves it into his bum bag. 'Maybe I'll buy you one. How long you staying? Friday night come down Streeties. We'll have a natter.'

'Nah, it's a whistle-stop. I'm visiting relatives. A couple of days at most. I don't want to lose my suntan.'

We say our cheerios.

Back in the car Abdul drops me outside the hotel and he's sent on his way with a tenner tip.

I check in at the foyer, all polished surfaces and a marble floor, and take the lift to the top level. It's a decent gaff, I've got to say. My room isn't bad either. I throw my gear on the bed and stand by the window to see what I can see. I spot a kestrel in the air, hovering on the breeze before it swoops sharply down. Bird of prey. Good sign. There's a great view along the Thames, out past the curving Isle of Dogs and into Central London. Tower Bridge, St Paul's Cathedral, Big Ben, the Houses of Parliament - all that prize architecture wasted on the cunts inside. Too many modern buildings are marring the scenery if you ask me, impressive in their own way but lacking imagination. Still, it's an amazing vista. I pull out my binoculars for an eagle eye view. It's fascinating; I could stand doing this for hours. To the right of St Paul's I can see part of the Old Bailey. Which of course brings back memories.

For years, apart from a pub fight that got me eight months, I was pretty clean, which considering how many tricks I got up to was nothing short of a miracle. But my run of luck came to an end when I was remanded with five others for a Securicor van hold-up. We had intel the vehicle was carrying two mil in readies, and we swooped in for the kill as it stopped at the lights on Mile End Road. The attack was swift and meticulously executed, every cog slotting into place, even if the sum we'd expected was somewhat inflated. We got away that time with just under £1.3 million. We'd targeted the same monthly high-stake run three times over a fourteen month period, none of the security industry's innovative tricks able to keep us away. We were flush in pocket by this point and should've put our feet up for a bit, but greed has its own momentum.

Not long afterwards we were pulled in and questioned, but it was a fruitless grab. They had nothing on us. The Flying Squad said they knew we were at it, so expect a pull any day now lads. But it wasn't going to happen. Not unless we fucked up, which wasn't our style. Then Gary Green, a friend of ours, was given a tug. He was involved in a serious VAT swindle and they had him bang to rights on that one. They sat him down and applied the pressure.

'There's big sentencing in fraud these days Greeny boy. The judges are cracking down, setting examples. Handing out silly sentences you wouldn't believe. Government orders. Dish out lots of bird, crack down hard. And you with a new-born son and all. You won't be seeing much of him in the big house, will you Gal? Especially when they send you to one of those shitholes up north. You've got form mate, so how does a nice ten rec sound? How about HMP Frankland? 350 miles away up north. Or what about HMP Dartmoor perhaps? Stuck out in the middle of fucking nowhere. Try getting the missus and little one out there for a visit. We can make life extremely difficult for you Gal. There's more connections and favours in our game than you'll ever know.'

Gary Green cracked and grassed the lot of us. He turned Queen's evidence and testified up there in court the slimy cunt, unable to look us in the eye. Three of us got a ten, but Eddie Basford took a twelve, and Pete Graves a fourteen. That is some serious bird. For his favours Green ended up with a single year for his VAT rap, but within two months he was back propping up the bar of his Stratford local. The man had no shame. He spread a tale that the corrupt Old Bill had warned him if he didn't talk they'd make sure his missus and kid suffered in some way. Then he said his evidence meant jack shit; it was just a formality and they had enough proof to put us away regardless. He made up all kinds of excuses, but the man was taking the piss. A month later a masked gunman entered the pub and fired several shots at him. He survived. A few years later, in prison for another crime, he was targeted again. The second attack also failed.

I step away from the window and have a shower. Then I order some lunch from room service, have a beer and watch a film on TV. *High Plains Drifter* starring Clint Eastwood. I get locked into the storyline, engrossed in the whole Western atmosphere and the present world around me just falls away. Before I know it, the credits are rolling and almost two hours have passed. Christ, they don't make them like that anymore.

I get under the sheets for a nap and wake up three hours later fully refreshed. Talk about luxury. This place is good for the soul. It's dark outside now and opening the bedside drawer I find a business card. CITY GENT THAI MASSAGE. *Treat yourself to the best in olde London Town.* The design is edged with bowler hats and umbrellas, and the bird in the picture isn't too bad either. I mull over the proposition before me. On the plane over I'd promised myself I'd behave in this department, but you only live once, and why not? I call the number and I'm told Jasmine will arrive within the hour to cater for my needs.

I climb into my dressing gown and potter about for a bit until I get a text from Jasmine saying she has arrived and is on her way up. She walks in the door, black bob and red lipstick, throws her fur coat aside and greets me in stockings and suspenders. We fool about on the bed for a while, take things nice and slow, then she assumes position and I'm pumping away, the sweat pouring down my chest, all cylinders on go, banging out a quality workout. I'm locked in a solid rhythm and for some reason my mind goes back to the prison gym in Full Sutton when I'm pumping hand weights, going for the burn, and small-time Peckham crook Lloyd Campbell walks in the door, brazen as you like, thinking he's untouchable. He does some skipping work to loosen up then grabs two dumbbells and gets cracking on the curls. Standing there in front of everyone, flexing away, ignoring the fact that only hours earlier he'd knocked out a high-ranking scouser in the import trade, put him on his arse, a man not known for his niceties. Campbell was warned if he wanted to live another day he better get himself transferred quicksmart, but he chose to ignore that advice. And here he was, lying flat on the bench now, straining on a three-hundred-pound bar when another black fella he thinks is a trusted bro strolls by and slams a fat dumbbell down in his boat. Boom. Campbell gets a double blow as he drops the bar onto his chest and his eyes are popping out of his head. Out comes a shiv, his paid-off pal slashing out like a loon, Campbell trying to fight him off with smashed ribs, no breath and blood and teeth all over the shop. The Peckham bad boy was taken to hospital, but more importantly he learned that you can grow your arms as wide as an average man's torso but there are still certain people in this life it's wise to sidestep. He was never seen in the nick again.

I finish up and flop aside. We lie for a bit before Jasmine

chops out a line on the bedside table. She asks if I want any. 'It's fifty quid for half a gram,' she says. 'You want to buy?' I give her a little slap on the bottom and tell her the truth, that I'm in London for work so I've got to stay on the ball, keep my head clear.

She disappears to the khazi, strutting in the platform heels she never took off, then she's back slipping on her coat and adjusting her hair and make-up.

'Busy night?' I ask.

'It's always a busy night.'

'Where are you off to next?'

She checks her phone. 'A man in Whitechapel.'

'Decent chap?'

'Not really. He likes to be whipped. Likes me to draw blood.'

'Be careful it's not Jack the Ripper. Whitechapel is his manor and he's got bloodthirsty form that bloke, believe me.'

I get a smile from her. It's only slight but shows she's human at least, not a cyborg sex doll programmed for one thing only.

'How long have you been in England?' I ask.

'Two years now. The money's getting me through university.'

'How old are you then?'

'Twenty-three.'

'That makes me old enough to be your father.'

'You don't look old,' she says, a vested compliment with an eye on further trade no doubt.

'I don't feel old. I'm fit as a fiddle.'

'That you definitely are.'

She throws her bag over her shoulder and hands me a card.

'Next time you can request me personally if you like. I'm usually available twenty-four seven.'

'Cheers. I just might. Thanks.'

She departs with a cool but mischievous eye.

I check my burner phone for any messages. None, so it's all

good. I get up and hit the shower. With the water powering over my face I think of my wife Beatriz at home in Marbella with our three kids. One boy, two daughters, aged from four to fourteen. All happy. Doing well. All used to *Papa* going away occasionally for short breaks concerning his business. I feel a twinge of guilt and for a moment I'm a little ashamed of myself. I know for a fact that Beatriz would never cheat on me. She's the perfect wife and mother and she's got principles. She's also a strict Catholic and adultery is one of the forbidden ten commandments. I'm token Church of England and though I do believe in the existence of a higher power, I follow my own rules, live by my own commandments. Not that Jesus and the rest didn't have it sussed, because Christianity preaches a good philosophy, in theoretical terms at least, but life as it's lived with boots on the ground is more complicated. Flexibility is key. Thou shalt not kill? Fair play, but what if somebody is out to slaughter you or your family, what then? Are you meant to sit back, twiddle your thumbs and wait for them to burst in wielding an AK?

Jesus was no pushover. Think about it. He was young, fit and strong, a carpenter in the building trade. At night he drank with women and criminals and, if provoked, had a hot temper. In the holy temple, when he saw the pharisees buying and selling, treating the place like a market for monetary profit, he completely lost his rag, upturning tables and wielding a whip, sending every one of them on their toes. What would Jesus have done if someone had threatened his mother? Here you go, I'll turn the other cheek for you. I don't think so. Not until the very end anyway. When Scotch Tommy Braddoch from Ilford woke up to find a masked intruder prowling about in his living room, with his four children sleeping upstairs, he shot the bloke in the eye and painted the back of his head across the fucking wallpaper. He phoned up some associates and they tossed the cunt in the back of the van and buried him out in Rainham

Marshes. It turned out the thief was a wanted man, suspected of not only several rapes but an unprovoked murder where he'd kicked a homeless man to death on the street. He was a crackhead waste of space who would have gone on to thieve and rape and kill again. Had Tommy Braddoch done a favour to society, made the streets safer and society more civil? Or had he murdered a man in cold blood for which he was owed a dose of punishment? I know the answer to that one.

I turn off the showerhead, dry myself and get dressed. Lounging in the leather chair with the TV on I peruse today's dinner menu. There's Beef Bourgouingnon, Truffle-stuffed Chicken and the chef's special Lobster Thermidor. In the end I opt for plain old burger and chips. I get a side salad for health and a low alcohol lager to wash it all down. Dinner ordered, I flick through the channels. BBC and ITV are abysmal these days, their soaps particularly tedious. I've been speaking *Espanol* and watching Spanish soap operas for the best part of twenty years, and though slightly tacky and over-dramatic, at least the storylines are coherent, the women pretty and it pulls you in. Some might disagree, but the whining, depressed faces and endless strife on *Eastenders* is all too real. Who wants to watch reality? With money in your pocket you can live the good life virtually anywhere, including here, but being working class and skint in Great Britain you really are trapped up shit street. No decent schools, no apprenticeships, no entrepreneurial spirit, few opportunities worth getting out of bed for at all. Even the few bank branches that remain stock hardly any readies. No wonder so many youngsters are selling drugs.

I think of blokes like Brian Downe, traipsing the streets with his dog like a man due for the scaffold. Left behind, bewildered in a condemned wasteland, kept poor and miserable by a system that hates him. Poor old Brian. He never got further than occasionally throwing on a bally, grabbing a long 'un and turning over a post office or betting shop, no intel, just bowling in whenever, and half the time collecting little more than beer money. Living it up for a few days, king of the manor, then you're back to square one, on the dole or shovelling muck on a site, selling knock-off cigarettes from a car boot on a Sunday. Time catches up, your heyday's gone and you've got creaking joints, a dodgy back, and it's noon and you're half pissed on supermarket cider wandering the streets in your stained Primark best.

I sound like a snob. A total cunt. And maybe I am. My thoughts are broken by a message coming in on my burner. It's Eddie Basford. Good old Bazza. He says the meet is on for tomorrow evening, 8pm Sainsbury's car park, Walthamstow. He'll have all the info and tools required for the construction job. I smile at that and reply with a simple: *Nice one.*

Dinner arrives and I tuck into my beer and burger. I tune into a nostalgia channel, watching a 70s episode of the New Professionals starring Joanna Lumley and Gareth Hunt, bloke who shook the coffee beans in the adverts. The episode was filmed in Camden Town, a kind of choreographed cat and mouse chase. As they outwit their adversaries around the pathways, locks and bridges of the canal area I note the quiet eeriness of a distinctively less populated London. It brings back memories of the vast derelict spaces, the broken-down warehouses and out-of-bounds areas of my youth, all of them gone now, most covered in housing.

I was a right rascal as a boy, but it didn't stop me inheriting my dad's love of ornithology. I used to go birdwatching with a boy up the road called Simon. He was what you'd call a geek I suppose, a boy with respectable parents who somehow found himself on a council estate, but we bonded over our shared love of nature's feathered friends. He was my mate, so I made sure the rougher kids around the flats left him alone. I'd knock for him and strapping our 8x30 binoculars we'd travel to woods, derelict rail yards, industrial wasteland reclaimed by nature all over the place, noting down the birds we spotted. Simon had a great ear for birdsong and was an amazing artist. When we'd stop for our packed lunches, he'd knock out a pencil sketch of the scenery, and his work was something else. When we reached fourteen his family moved up to Great Yarmouth and that was that. Later someone said they might've heard he got leukaemia and died but couldn't be sure. I hope it wasn't true. The boy never hurt a soul. I hope he had a good life.

I finish my meal and after watching half an episode of some vaguely remembered 80s sitcom I decide it's time to hit the sack. I pop a zopiclone – I'm no addict but like to have a supply for when need be – strip off, climb beneath the sheets and sleep the slumber of the dead.

Come morning I wake up fully rested and bounce out of bed raring to go. I'm free until the evening, so I decide to spend the day sightseeing. A regular tourist except for the fact I was born and bred here, an ex-pat Londoner with a head full of memories. I tube it to Bethnal Green and go for a walkabout. I moved over this way when I first moved out of my parents' gaff. Six mates cramming into a sublet council property, partying regularly, living fast and wild. I'd heard a lot of the pubs had closed down but to see it in the raw is painful. However, a fair few are still around and they're looking in good nick, which isn't surprising as the area's growing trendies and fashion hipsters have to drink somewhere. In fact the extent of white faces on the street comes as a surprise as I'd heard from naysayers that there were very few of us left round these parts. I make for Roman Road and begin the two mile stretch, weaving in and out of the backstreets. I notice some building work on the Bancroft Estate, regeneration going on. Then I'm back on the main drag, passing the shops and turning down Usk Street to the location where I lost my virginity. I stop outside the block where a group of us bowled into a party one night, confident and alive, basking in the banter and bravado of youth. I got chatting to a girl called Cheryl and after a while she led me into one of the bedrooms. I was almost seventeen and had never gone the whole way, so considering the regular action my mates reckoned they were getting, it was about time. Cheryl Spicer gave me a thorough seeing-to that night and taught me the ropes. 'Look at Dan,' my mates laughed. 'He's just lost his cherry.'

I'm staring up at the second floor, a space cadet mired in sentiment when I hear a shriek followed by the sound of raucous shouting. Two push-bikes tear around the corner followed by half a dozen youths running on foot. All are laughing. I step inwards, unacknowledged as the group passes by. Then I hear a voice calling out for help. I rush around the corner to see an old woman on the ground, her bags dumped around her, fruit and veg scattered. I ask if she's okay, help her up and gather her shopping.

She tells me they stole her purse. 'They're like rats. Human rats,' she shouts in their direction. 'But it's not the first time and it won't be the last, I'm afraid.' I see a crucifix round her neck; she sounds Italian.

A Muslim couple turn the corner and rush over. They say they're her next door neighbours and I tell them what happened.

'Was it that lot that just went by?' the man asks, turning to where they scarpered. 'Fucking bastards. They're cowards, the lot of them. Pussies!'

It's the third time she's been targeted by these youths and doesn't deserve this shit, he says. He gets on the phone to the police. There are more people on the scene now, a neighbour bringing out a chair so the woman can sit down. 'One hour?' the guy's saying into his phone. 'They're not going to turn up at all, are they? Ah, of course, report it online...'

Still, the police just might make an appearance and I can't risk that. The situation seems in good hands so when the guy turns his back I quietly get myself off. To say I'm livid at what I've just witnessed is an understatement. I'm reminded of the time my mum was pushed about on the street while going down for a loaf of bread and the cunts were never caught. It's not something you ever forget or feel less angry about. I'm back on the manor for twenty-four hours, taking a leisurely daylight stroll on streets I know well and this is the shit I'm witnessing. What the fuck is going on with the world?

I walk back to the tube station. Heading down the subway steps I notice a small plaque commemorating the '43 tube disaster. That's a first, it wasn't there last time I was in town.

'Site of the worst civilian disaster of the Second World War. In memory of the 173 men, women and children who lost their lives on Wednesday 3rd March 1943 descending these steps to Bethnal Green underground air raid shelter.'

I'd heard about this tragedy growing up. During the nightly blackout an air raid siren sent hundreds of families pouring down the pitch-black rain-sodden steps, when the sound of an explosion occurred. People thought they were under attack from the skies and the ensuing crush on the tight subway stairs was fatal. The media hushed up the incident, people told not to talk about it for fear it might lower morale. Years later it turned out there'd been no bomb or even any threat of one that night. The explosion was a secret new anti-aircraft rocket that had been set off by accident half a mile away in Victoria Park. That's the official story anyway. Fuck knows what the military were up to that night, but the aftermath was horrific. I continue down into the tube feeling sour.

That's another thing that pisses me off. The Second World War. Or to be frank, both of them. My dad was a pacifist in this respect, saying the only real winners of those two wars were the bankers. Again he had a point, but I couldn't see it then. I'd be in the pub with him debating, saying Hitler and the Germans deserved all they got and Churchill was a hero. How else would the working class have got half-decent housing and a free health service if it wasn't for the war?

What about the masses of working-class that were sent to die, he said, what housing and healthcare did they get? Good fucking point, I realise now. I was mouthing off, a clever-dick waving my patriotic flag, talking like an upstanding citizen, while on the side I was doing something my hard-working banker-hating dad never did: actually robbing banks.

I take the Central Line into the West End and get out at Tottenham Court Road. The station has been rebuilt and extended, and heading down Charing Cross Road I notice it's eaten up the Astoria where back in the day I'd go to banging all-nighters. Shame that. I head into Soho and it's been cleaned up even more than last time, but it's still lively and colourful enough, and I cross Shaftesbury Avenue into Chinatown, almost getting run over by some speeding div on a bike. It's all the rage in London now I've heard, hooded scrotes on wheels snatching phones. I've heard they've got it down to a fine art. Not surprising with the amount of clueless mugs walking about glued to their screens. But I know this much, if one of the fuckers tries it with me I'll take the cunt down, speeding bike or not, crack his head off the pavement, give him a stomping then bite both his ears off and spit them in his face. It's the only thing appropriate for the pricks. People don't though. They just stand there looking at their empty hand, nonplussed. But ignore me, I'm ranting now, going off on one.

After Gerrard Street's heady aroma of Cantonese roast duck, I come out onto Piccadilly Circus, checking out the hustle and bustle and iconic ad hoardings. I sit with the tourists by the Eros fountain for a spell and a Dutch girl asks me to take a picture of herself and her friends. I oblige, hand back her phone and there are thanks and smiles all round. I'm sitting there absorbing the buzz and atmosphere when a memory pops up. The time a mate snatched a businessman's briefcase just over there, under the ads by Glasshouse Street.

There used to be a donut shop on the corner and that's where it happened. It was night-time, the businessman turned up the side street and Jimmy Black ripped the case off him and ran. It was a targeted robbery, Jimmy receiving two hundred quid by some faces operating out of Ilford at the time. A couple of them had a fruit stall nearby on Rupert Street so they were familiar with the local lay of the land, put it that way, and exploited it in kind. Jimmy later found out the man wasn't a businessman at all but a member of parliament, renowned within his circles for his insatiable love of young arse. The MP frequented a notorious public toilet by St James's Park, and after a few gins of an evening at the gentlemen's club he'd head down the Dilly to blatantly pick up boys from the meat rack. Most of his chums would apply caution in this respect, preferring to send hired hands for such arrangements, but not this old vulture. His predatory night-crawling was well known among the young runaways flogging their wares, and he was said in the bedroom to be a sadistic bully. But things came a cropper for this esteemed government minister. The police raided the Regent Palace Hotel one night and he was unintentionally caught in bed with a 14-year-old and arrested. The unfortunate matter was going through his solicitors and was expected to be hushed up and forgotten. The Ilford lads now had his suitcase and inside found what they were looking for: official papers referring to his arrest. They got on with blackmailing him or they'd take the evidence to the Sunday press and drag his credentials through the mud.

A first payment was successfully collected. Then next day each of the gang had their doors kicked in at 5am. Instead of being taken to the police station for normal procedure, they were handed over to agents of a senior calibre and driven at gunpoint to an undisclosed location. After several hours blindfolded, bound and forced to endure white noise and other hellish sounds, they were warned by whatever shadowy intelligence agency had kidnapped them that if they ever dared pull a similar stunt the safety of their wives and children could not be guaranteed. Do you understand what we're saying, dear boy? I remember in the pub Jimmy telling me what he'd heard, his hand shaking as he lifted his pint. Paedophiles were running the country. They held all the power. It seemed far-fetched at the time; not so much now.

I leave the Dilly and turn down Jermyn Street, a quiet haven from the teeming hoi polloi. I enter an elite little eatery that looks like it hasn't changed since the roaring twenties and I'm shown to a table. I slot in, order up, and supping on my aperitif I tune in to the calm respectable patter around me. I actually spot a face I recognise, dining in the corner with three other gents. I won't name any names, but if it isn't him it's a dead ringer for an ex-Tory MP whose main claim to fame was an alleged fetish for having his toes sucked by high-class women. According to the *News of the World* at least. He also liked to don the Chelsea strip while on the job apparently, which is even worse. Speccy Chelsea cunt. Now here's a sleazy bastard if I ever saw one. I listen to him talking frankly and evenly, his companions all ears as he discusses the intricacies of his charity work. No, it's not him. No way. Then he smiles a toothy grin and again I swear it's the same bloke. Who knows. Who cares. My starter arrives and the waitress is a little cracker. A classy blonde with a naughty smile. As she bends over to set down my lunch I spy Tory Boy's beady eyes checking out her derriere. Dirty old bugger. I smile, say thanks, and watch the waitress stroll back to the kitchen. Shapely arse though, I must admit.

I wolf through my main course then politely decline pudding or a port or coffee to finish, and get myself back on the street, ducking down into the station as it begins to rain.

I tube it one stop to Green Park then take the Jubilee Line a further nine to Canning Town. I alight and go for a gander. I head for the pedestrian underpass, the vast flyover system looming overhead. I spot some homeless tents down there, and though it's still light there are several groups of dodgy-looking men loitering about. I imagine the area at night, a mish-mash of elevated roads and railways, a shadowy cesspit, and I remember before the regeneration when this whole plot was a bleak industrial wasteland of pylons and works, yards full of goods pilfered from lorry jump-ups, well dodgy at night. Craig McCarver's sister was raped one time walking back from the station, two men following behind and taunting her. They pounced and dragged her into a secluded corner. Two white pricks from Beckton it turned out, their mugshots still clear in my mind, spotty fuckers with odd-looking faces, nonces the pair of them. One supposedly hung himself in prison but we all know what really happened, and I wonder what became of the other because the McCarver's were no shrinking violets. I pass three men in leather jackets hanging about smoking and smirking, swarthy and shifty as fuck, and I picture my wife and kids down here, lost and stranded in the night, a group of men trailing behind, laughing and jeering, underpass echoes and nowhere to run, and suddenly I want to kill every male cunt I see, every dodgy fucker sliming about up to no good. I envisage myself with an axe running through the streets, attacking at random, an urban nightmare, the old Royal Docks lined with futuristic buildings, mirrored glass in the neon night, the flash of colours in the fallen rain, computer game graphics, a flailing berserker covered in blood, leaving a trail of bodies so deep the streets are running red with gore.

I head over to Barking Road, a main thoroughfare of shops. Back to sanity. It's stopped raining, the sun cracking through the clouds for a few seconds before slipping away. The Royal Oak, a fierce pub with a boxing legacy, has retained its architecture but it closed down as a boozer years ago, and of course the new Rathbone Market space is an empty travesty, but it's when I turn down into the backstreets that I'm hit with some real disorientation. Enormous new developments stand imposingly where there used to be small businesses, garages, scrapyards, pubs and the like. The buildings are a claustrophobic mish-mash, and I pass a massive construction site where there used to be yards of workshops and portacabins, land of disputed ownership. I actually knew some of the owners, local men battling it out in court a few years back so they could sell up and make a mint, real estate at a premium due to the corporate plan to transform the last untouched area around the docks. I remember it's where car dealer Terry Corbett had one of his legs taken off with a power saw, his privates stuffed down his throat. His torso was found bobbing in the Thames by the Tate & Lyle plant, his missing leg never found. The Hillman brothers went down for that one. For years they spread the word that an Essex firm was responsible, a row over money. Their appeal failed. Truth was Corbett was screwing one of their wives.

I return to the hotel. I'm occupying the en suite, sitting on the throne ruminating on my plans when Bazza sends me a text.

8pm sharp at stated location.

For the craic I reply with: *If I'm a minute late will you give me detention?*

Just saying, he replies.

Fair do's, I type back. *See you there. Plum.*

No reply. He never was one for the humour old Bazza. But at a time like this even I can understand. To me though it's laugh or fucking cry time. Without a bit of jest right now I'd be lost. The pressure is on, the showdown ticking closer.

I've got two more hours to kill and I'm pacing about the room fidgeting. Not good. Looking at the king-size bed I debate giving Jasmine a call, snatching a quick sesh, working off some of the tension that always creeps up on me around this point. The job is on for tomorrow. Furthermore, I can't fuck it up.

I look at Jasmine's business card then place it aside. Humping a call girl at present wouldn't be advisable. It would be a waste of energy, a distraction, when what I need at present is focus. A cool head. The clock is ticking and the stress is going to be high. One mistake, one deviation from the plan and it could all go south. I've been waiting two decades for this and there will be no second chances. If I fail in my task I won't be able to live with myself.

I sit down. Christ, I need to chill out, give the overthinking a break. I turn on the TV and flick through the channels. I settle on an 80s/90s music documentary. Madonna singing 'Holiday' on *The Tube.* Right fit little bird. Next up is 'Two Tribes' by Frankie Goes to Hollywood, Ronnie Reagan and Soviet commie Chernenko battling it out in the ring to a baying crowd. It's a good video, Frankie's music impressive when you hear it now. Then I jolt in my seat at footage of Queen's Live Aid set at Wembley. 'Radio Gaga'. I was fucking there! Me and Bazza. I won a couple of tickets in a radio competition and took Baz as he was more into music than the lot of us put together. When I called round his house and pulled out the tickets he was gobsmacked. I watch Freddie Mercury strutting his stuff, a fucking master performer, and during crowd footage I'm searching to spot us as we weren't far from the front, but I don't. Afterwards we got chatting to two girls from Mile End and went back to East London on the train with them. They were slightly older and neither of us scored. Then we were standing chatting outside Bazza's house, thrilled at what an amazing day it had been when his dad burst out the door and pulled him in by the hair. 'Where the fuck have you been? You said you'd help me on the stall today you little cunt and you do a runner? You lazy skiver. Get in there.' He turned to me, pointing his finger. 'And you can fuck off out of it as well.' Within a year Bazza had bulked out and grown up and even his old man wouldn't mess with him.

Up comes commentary and music from Bros, Kylie, Sonia and Def Leppard, then the doc heads into the rave era. The footage of young wide-eyed herberts pulling mad shapes to repetitive beats embarrasses me a little. Not surprising considering I was one of them. We all got into it for a bit. Apart from Bazza that is. He knew better. Preferred a pint in the pub, but even more liked to stay in his room perfecting his guitar licks, Saturday night in with Mark Knopfler on the stereo showing how it's done. Talented bloke Bazza. He joined a pub band, had a residency in a boozer in Silvertown, but I told him he was wasting himself, Wembley Stadium is that way mate. But what did I know, I was dropping Es in crumbling warehouses in Hackney and frying my brain cells till dawn.

The Britpop era arrives, Blur and Oasis giving it the big one and Ginger Spice packing her assets into a union jack dress, yes please. But sadly it's time to switch off and go. I grab what I need, check myself in the mirror then head down in the lift and walk through the foyer. Outside I climb into a waiting Uber for the journey up to Walthamstow. The driver is pumping out gangsta rap and strikes me as a bit of a wannabe, but at least he's got the decency to ask if I mind the racket. Not at all, fill your boots, I tell him, and we're off to E17 to a soundtrack of bitches, niggas and hoes. Each to their own I suppose. When we reach the

Sainsbury's rendezvous point I tell him to kill the volume, attention not required now. We drive up and down the car park looking for Bazza's Merc but I can't spot him. I phone the fucker and he says he's right across from me - I'm looking at you right now you cunt. I see him sitting in a black Range Rover with his phone to his ear.

'I thought you drove a Mercedes?' I say.

'I also drive a Rover.'

Fuck up number one, but it's only minor. No problemo. Ali G waits as I walk over and climb in.

'You're two minutes late,' Bazza says.

'No, you're two minutes early.'

'Anyway, how are things, you feeling fit?'

'Well up for it.'

We get down to business. He tells me the ins and outs, then passes over the tool for the job. It's a Beretta, the model I requested. There's a full clip of ammo, a silencer, and the kit feels good in my hand. 'Perfect.' I tuck it into my man bag.

'Good luck Dan, you'll need it.'

'No worries.'

I go to climb out, then I sit back down.

'I was up Bethnal Green earlier. Having a walkabout. I saw an old woman get robbed.'

'What do you expect, it's Bethnal Green. Full of muzzies. Always was a shithole anyway. Remember Tommy Fallon, he was knifed to death by some flats off Globe Road in '89. Jumped and left with about twenty punctures in him.'

'True. I forgot about that. But we used to go partying all around there. Some good memories.'

'Good and bad.'

'Yeah, suppose.'

'Anyway, it's all set for tomorrow Dan. Make sure you do a thorough job.'

'There's no doubt on that score.'

I wish Mr Happy cheerio and head back to the hotel mulling on the info, making sure it's imprinted like a tattoo on the inside of my skull. There's no referring to notes in this game. Back in the hotel room I'm pacing up and down, checking the tool, assessing the risks and possibilities, all the maybes and what ifs. The pressure is on and once again I'm thinking of Jasmine, Blade Runner sex cyborg for hire, getting her up here for some much-needed relief, but I decide some wrist action is a safer bet.

I thumb a free newspaper I picked up earlier and stop at a picture of the governing Labour Party's female deputy prime minister. I hate these cunts, I really do. Socialists with lucrative business interests and several million tucked in the offshore account. Worst government in history. Starmer more inhuman than Blair and that takes some doing. I strip down, chuck my clobber aside and jack off to the sight of the cow's gormless mug, tit job cleavage on proud display. Get a load of this you ginger slapper. I'm whacking away picturing the slag in front of me, giving it some welly, giving her what she deserves, and I think of Gary Green. Gary the cunt. Gary the grass. The fucker spent only two months inside before he was back on the street, propping up the bar of his local boozer after snitching on his mates, a man with no heart and no shame.

I think of the first attempt to take him out. We were in prison when a figure in a bike helmet walked into his Stratford local and fired several shots at him as he stood at the jump. Green ran to safety, taking no more than a bullet in the arm, while another ricocheted off the bar striking a random punter in the foot. It was a botch-job of the highest order, the gunman returning to the back of a waiting motorbike and speeding off into the night. Green was paranoid now, permanently looking over his shoulder. He moved from inner-city Stratford to suburban Harold Hill and was shoving industrial levels of charlie up his snout which not only increased his anxiety but left him in dire financial straits. Untrustworthy now, nobody would work with him so big payouts from crime were hard to come by. Friendless, his newfound drink and drug buddies were culled from the lowest of the low. He and a mate called Benson had a tip-off that a local elderly couple had secretly won a substantial sum on the lottery and kept a stash of readies under the bed. Where this rumour originated from was never discovered, but they followed the old man home from the bookies one day and tied him and his wife to chairs demanding the appearance of this elusive cash. It never materialised and both were tortured to death in a highly unpleasant fashion.

In mitigation Green claimed he'd been off his head on crack cocaine that night and couldn't remember a thing. He was out of his mind, therefore not responsible for his actions. The jury were not impressed and the pair were sentenced to twenty-five years apiece. In prison Green was once again targeted. He was slashed across the face with a peach tin lid in an attack that was supposed to have targeted his jugular and left him bleeding to death. Scarred but alive Green went on to spend much of his sentence in protection. His mate lasted four years before he succumbed to a smack overdose. Good riddance. Shame it wasn't the pair of them.

Green was finally released from jail last year, clean and drug free, and was currently working as a foreman for his brother's building firm. He lived with a council admin boss called Susie Smart in a house in Woodford. She'd written to him in prison, enclosing provocative pictures to tickle his fancy, and for several years they conducted a relationship by phone, letter and visits. Susie had history with lags, one of a breed of women with a strange predilection for jailed criminals. They write long missives to serial killers and other filth, want to court and mother them perhaps, be the saviour that redeems them.

Though more likely it's the dangerous aspect that floats their boat. Fuck knows. A few years earlier she'd shacked up with another ex-con. He'd strangled a woman to death in her bed but was rehabilitated now, as innocent as a new-born lamb. They quickly had a couple of kids, but things didn't work out. The man had been incarcerated for so long that he found freedom on the outside an alien way of life. While going for a walk one day he stuck a blade in a passer-by and was back in chokey getting his wake-up call, three-square meals and all bills catered for in no time. After this, Susie did more lag research and set her sights on double killer, snitch and all-round bad egg Gary Green. No slip of a girl, she coochie-cooed him with snaps of her more than ample assets and got her man.

On release he moved directly into her house where he was now father to her two young kids. Sometimes he went for a pint in the nearest pub. Occasionally he had a flutter in the local bookies. Most days he walked the dog through the local fields and woods, but often brought the children, sometimes the missus. Tomorrow he and Susie are holding a garden party to celebrate the announcement of their engagement. The forecast predicts a slightly humid day, cloudy with no rain.

The thought of the bastard getting his comeuppance is firing endorphins through my system like an electrical charge. I'm tossing away staring at a government slapper and drowning in feel-good chemicals. Since the day of our arrest I've wanted to carve Gary Green into tiny pieces. Put the bastard through a meat grinder. Human meat in your doner kebab and you better fucking enjoy it. I've dreamt about it. Longed for it. Been out on the beach playing with the kids, the Spanish sun shining down, imagining I'm gouging his two fucking eyes out and feeding them to the cunt. They didn't mess about back in the days of yore, I'll tell you that. In Ye Olde England you'd be dragged behind a cart through the streets, hung from a rope until you're nearly dead, then taken down, disembowelled and forced to watch your entrails get cooked on a fire. There was no pansying about in those times. And more, I'd reintroduce the lot of it. Get the crowds out on the street for a raucous Medieval spectacle. Certainly for traitorous scum like Gary Green.

He's been a lucky man in life, but his good fortune is grinding to a halt. I'm coming for him and it's an exciting time to be alive. I up my vigour, wrist working away, eyes blazing at the government cow staring mockingly back at me, the dislike and disharmony mutual. I feel the rising wave, a volcano about to erupt, cover the city in molten lead, and with a growl I splatter over the mare's baps and face, making a right mess of the slag; phwoar, take that you cunt. Get in.

Spent now I flop down on the chair. I chill for a minute or two. Then heart rate back to normal I get up, screw the newspaper in the bin and feel a little disgusted with myself. But not for long. I get under the shower, rinse away any nagging doubts then decide to call it a night. I pop a pill and climb under the cool sheets. Thankfully the medication works fast and I'm out like a light, no thoughts, no sense of time, nothing. Out like a corpse, batteries on charge for the big day.

I wake up with my travel clock saying 7.15am. Fuck me, that was a good sleep. I step out of bed and get dressed. The day has arrived and I feel no tension. Game fucking on. If anything, I feel excited which is a good sign. I've had this feeling before, tend to get it on all the best ones. After all, I've done seven now. Spain mostly. A couple in Amsterdam. One in Cyprus. This will be my eighth. But this one's different. This one's personal. A moral hit. A noble crime. Or maybe not even a crime at all. A man like Green doesn't deserve to walk this earth. Not after the things he's done in his life. Nobody forced his hand, strapped him to a rack and turned the wheel, he made his own decisions and now is pay-up time. Call it a non-crime hate incident. The British coppers love that phrase these days. They use it all the time when they're policing people's Facebook accounts. In this instance, I'm happy with it.

I cab it up past Woodford, up near Repton Park, the old Claybury nuthouse cum expensive flats. Seven miles. On the journey I sit in deep thought as Iqbal or Abdul or Mehmet takes the wheel, keeping his eyes on the road. There's no talking this time, my mind strictly on the job. I'm in the zone. Call it a death trance. It certainly feels like one. At my destination I give the driver a tenner tip and he tells me to have a great day. I certainly intend to, that's for sure. Standing on the road waiting for the car to disappear I feel a sliver of doubt, but it's only momentary. I'm only human after all. I look around. Suburbia meets country. Houses nearby, but not too close. I turn down a passage into a field, common land where people walk their dogs. Thankfully nobody is close by. I follow a path for a couple of minutes then slip off into the foliage and settle unseen by the fence at the bottom of Gary Green's garden.

Gaps in the ivy-strewn fence provide a good view. His back door is open, bunting hanging from the trees and a sign that says: Congratulations. Susie appears, setting a table with food and drink. She calls for him to give her a hand and here he is, carrying out a crate of Stella Artois. His fiancée goes back indoors and Green remains, standing looking at his phone. Pastel shirt, half-length trousers, trainers, no socks. I can't believe the piece of filth is standing in front of me, free as you like, enjoying his new life with a bird, money in his pocket and a decent gaff after what he did. The front of the man. I have to laugh because his cap says TARGET. It's the name of his brother's building firm, but the irony is loud and clear. What a fool. I've got my Beretta nine-mill with fitted silencer pointing through a hole in the fence and I could do him right now, right where he's standing. But his missus calls down at him from a window. She tells him to finish off mowing the lawn. Get a move on lazybones. You always start a job and half finish it, go on, get lively. She's a large girl and Green is no bag of bones either, and I imagine the two of them on the job. It's not a pretty image. Then I flash back to when we were all friends, out on the piss in a club, the Ilford Island if I remember rightly, and he pointed to a big girl standing by the bar and said: A tenner from each of you if I shag fatso over there. He collected the wager, went home with her and did the deed, saying she loved it. He gave it to her every which way, banged the tart rigid and she was begging for more. He said she lived with her mother in a block of flats in Bow, another fat cunt, and next time he'd go back and give the old girl a portion too, fuck the arse off both the slags. We were laughing at the time, being lads, doing what you do, but it doesn't seem so funny now.

I remember another time, when he blacked a girl's eye. He tried chatting her up but she didn't want to know. It was in a place up Barking Road, one of the old haunts. She was a pretty blonde, pink lipstick, piled up hair. She told him he was a creep and to leave her alone, so in front of everyone he backhanded her, called her a stuck-up slag and walked away laughing as she cowered on the floor. When the girl's brother, a roofer from Dagenham, came looking for him, we gave him a hiding and put him in hospital, because Green might've been a cunt but he was one of us, one of the boys, and you didn't fuck with us because we were a team. A solid unit. The fucking top boys. It makes me sick to my stomach. If I met the man today I'd put a wad of cash in his hand and do the same to his sister. Gary Green is a fucking wrong 'un.

He laughs at his missus' nagging and turns on the mower, running it up and down the lawn, engine making a right racket.

He's edging closer, only fifteen feet from me now. The time has come. I pop off a double tap and he pauses stock still for a second, then he's clutching his chest, swaying. The motor grinds to a halt and he lands on the grass, curls up, face scrunched in pain. I fire another round, a headshot this time. The bullet gets him bang in the centre of the forehead and he's left this planet. Job done. I grab the push bike that's been strategically dumped in the bushes, emerge onto the path and cycle away. Reaching a quiet roadway I climb into the back of a waiting car. I take off my cap, shades and gloves and drop the bagged gun onto the front seat.

'All done?' asks Pete Graves, an associate I haven't seen in an age.

'Done, dusted and served on a platter mate. Let's move.'

I sit back, coming down from the high, letting the adrenaline drain. It's grey and humid and back in London the traffic is terrible, near chock-a-block, but it's a wonderful day, the sense of achievement momentous.

Back at the hotel I lie down for a restorative nap. A few hours later, batteries charged, I'm up and packing my bag. I travelled light so it doesn't take long. My flight to Malaga is at 9.55pm so I've still got some time to spare. I can't stop recalling the sight of Greeny's face as the bullets hit him. Two in the chest, then the bullseye, right in the bonce. It's a perfect memory, a scene I'll never forget. Going forward If I'm ever having a shitty day, I'll have an instant remedy now, an image to jolt me back to true happiness. I turn on the TV. Sure enough, the BBC are talking about a murder earlier today in Essex. A possible revenge hit. *Unconfirmed reports claim the son of an elderly couple brutally murdered twenty-five years ago has this afternoon been arrested and is being questioned by police.* Now that's a laugh. Don't worry old son, no evidence, you'll be home in time for *Match of the Day.*

I feel like hitting the pub, seeing some old faces, having a celebration. All my old mates, some of them no longer on this earth, dressed to the nines and smelling of beer, smoke and aftershave, out for a session, an evening with the boys, slapping my back, good old Dan, proud of me for taking action, settling the score, finally putting some lead into the cunt. I picture us in one of the pubs we'd frequent, men in the prime of life, regularly working, earning well, immersed in the magic of friendship and camaraderie. Together again, the kings of East London. I'm dreaming of a big reunion, a tour around all those old boozers, the perfect night out. But it's not going to happen. Those days are gone. I call room service and order up a few cold beers. While waiting I sit back on the bed, turning over the card in my hand. CITY GENT THAI MASSAGE. *Treat yourself to the best in olde London Town.*

Acknowledgements

Thank you to everyone who took the time to read this book. I hope you enjoyed it. If so, feel free to leave a review on Amazon, even if it's only a few lines. Feedback is much appreciated.

Thanks to my family. Also much appreciation to Joe England of *PUSH* fame, John King from *Verbal*, Mike Head from *Tangled Lines*, Roual Galloway from *Spinners*, Ian Cusack from *Glove*, Derek Steel from *Razur Cuts* and Joseph Ridgwell from *East London Press*, all inspiring wordsmiths who have featured my writing in their brilliant grass-roots publications.

A special thanks to Noel Smith, bank robber extraordinaire, who reviewed my novel in *Inside Time*.

Until next time...

More fiction from Michael Keenaghan…

LONDON IS DEAD

A NOVEL

A fierce and gripping portrait of society's criminal underbelly, LONDON IS DEAD wields a cast of flawed but colourful characters as they cross paths and swords in the streets of the capital...

Terry Hart's straight lifestyle has got him nowhere – no money and no respect from his family. When he's viciously robbed in his mini-cab by two younger men, his self-pride hits a new low. As the temptation to return to serious crime bites hard, out come the demons from a brutal and tragic past. Suddenly in East London there's a new Ripper on the loose...

Bigz is a street hustler in a world of hard knocks. He's haemorrhaging friends and inflaming enemies, which lands him at the desk of feared local don Hot Iron Mike, a man for whom an apologetic explanation is never enough. Hired as a 'pitbull on the payroll' Bigz is paired with Lil Killa, a dangerous loner with a side project: offing the men who abused him when he grew up in care. They make quite a team.

Meanwhile across town, the Kilburn Mob, a resurrected armed outfit from the 90s, have a lucrative job on the cards – and they're hiring. But all is not well between old trusted friends. As past acts of betrayal resurface, not everybody will survive...

'Excellent flow and pace. This debut novel is alive and kicking'
JOE ENGLAND, *3AM Magazine*

'Keenaghan's love for his city shines through in this driven, thumping novel'
JOHN KING

Available in paperback and Kindle.

ISBN-9798354201891

SMILER WITH KNIFE

STORIES FROM THE DARK
HEART OF LONDON

This powerful collection of stories takes you to London's drinking dens, backstreets and shadowy housing estates where coppers, criminals and the plain hard-done-by are faced with all life can throw at them. Sometimes things have to get worse before they can get better...

A teenager is disillusioned when the friend he idolises is guilty of a sick, horrific crime – when they fall out, he's forced to take part in his escapades. A moonlighting policeman is sent to blackmail a TV soap starlet; proceedings take a twist when she turns the tables and before long bullets are flying. A gangster dreaming of a world away from his domineering boss stabs a stranger in a street confrontation, an action with consequences more hellish than he could have imagined.

Brutal, uncompromising, at times blackly funny, SMILER WITH KNIFE is a gripping tour through the urban jungle and the shadier quarters of the human condition.

Available in paperback and Kindle.
ISBN 9798852186508

*

Printed in Dunstable, United Kingdom

65019499R00160